KT-153-303

DEATH STANDS ROUND THE CORNER

When Tommy Gavillan, ex-bank robber, left the old Sheldon gang and came back to England he made a good friend in Superintendent MacNeill of Central Office, and that was a lucky thing for Tommy Gavillan. This is the story of an old secret, a master criminal who had puzzled the police of two continents, and a heartbreak. Pat Gavillan, Tommy's daughter, comes into it; so does Bill Mandell who coveted her. There was Dale Hettche, Mandell's cynical American friend, Peter Spain whom nobody understood, and Mary Lou Slater who died horribly. There were other characters, too, on the broad stage. Ada Klein, the invalid; Braddock, her competent maidservant. There was mystery too, as MacNeill and his assistant, Inspector Till, were soon to find out. Who was Corporal Violet, criminal extraordinary? Tommy Gavillan knew: his familiarity with Drew Sheldon, Prince of Bank Robbers, helped him there. This is a story in which interest and speed are sustained to the very end. *A thriller which will really thrill!*

ALSO BY W. MURDOCH DUNCAN

DEATH STANDS
ROUND THE CORNER

by

W. MURDOCH DUNCAN

THE MYSTERY BOOK GUILD
178–202 GT. PORTLAND STREET
LONDON, W.1

This edition January 1956

*Printed in Great Britain
by The Anchor Press, Ltd.,
Tiptree, Essex*

To
CHERRY KEARTON
for his many kindnesses
this book is dedicated

CHAPTER I

The rehabilitation of the habitual criminal is a problem of considerable interest to the officers of law and order so that when the subject arose in discussion at Scotland Yard, certain large and cynical men would propound their rigid and unshakable belief in the old saw which concerns itself with the difficulty of teaching an old dog new tricks. Of this school was Chief Inspector Grimm, a sober-faced and voluble man who was prepared to draw on vast wells of experience to give point to his opinion.

"It never works," he would say. "Don't tell me. I know. I've seen a hundred crooks set up in good jobs—a five-pound note in their pockets, and a fortune ahead of them—but they fell down on the job. Look at Toby Moyniham, with seven convictions for fraud. He got a job with a gentleman in Bootle and held it for a month. Then he walked off with a fortune in silver and the gentleman's cheque book. Look at 'Fin' Libby. Mr. Cosgrave the bookie gave him a job in his business, and he hooked it with close on two hundred quid. I could go on telling you all day about people like that." And these gloomy facts he would emphasize with a shake of his long and serious head, or a blow of his large and forceful fist, for he was an argumentative man and applied all the normal devices of eloquence.

There was, however, a minority party and the spokesman of these sympathetic and feeling-hearted men was Superintendent MacNeill, a soft-voiced colossus from Kintyre whose philosophy had endured the full twenty-five years of his service with the Metropolitan Police Force. Thus, when the vexed and debatable question cropped up, as it invariably did when policemen foregathered, Superintendent MacNeill would shake a long, thick finger and draw the attention of the company to Tommy Gavillan.

Tommy indeed was living and walking proof of the fallacy of Chief Inspector Grimm's theory and not all the cleverly contrived arguments which that pessimistic man could devise might turn the balance by as much as one hairbreadth in the face of the evidence of Tommy's horrible career, for Gavillan had been a member of the Sheldon gang which had operated throughout the twenties and the early thirties with such devastating effect. It had been the Sheldon crowd that had looted the Manhattan Central Bank and from its vaults had taken close on three million dollars in cash. It had been Drew Sheldon who had walked into Zoraneiff's and had lifted the Khandar diamonds from under the noses of two Centre Street detectives, appointed at some considerable expense to guard them. From New York Sheldon had moved to Rome, to Berlin and to London. Wherever he went, Tommy Gavillan had been close beside him. Tommy was his right hand and his shadow.

Fate, in the person of Superintendent MacNeill, had caught up with Tommy one pleasant morning in June. Tommy had been sitting in his comfortable flat in Eton Square, pondering the inscrutabilities of Fate as manifest in the list of starters in the Derby (it was the year that that classic was won by Midnight Sun), when the policeman had walked in on him, and one glance at the Scotsman's face had been enough.

"I'll come quietly," he said.

MacNeill had nodded.

"I expect you will, Tommy."

Gavillan had sighed.

"It's the Cheal's Bank affair, Inspector?"

And MacNeill who was still an inspector had agreed.

"That's what it is. We want Sheldon. Where's Drew?"

Gavillan had chuckled.

"Never heard of him, Mac."

MacNeill had smiled philosophically. He had expected no more.

"That's a pity. You'll get seven years, Tommy."

Gavillan nodded, annoyed.

"That's probably right—and here's me with the winner of the Derby. I got it from a feller that couldn't be wrong. I was going to put my pile on it and retire from business."

MacNeill was interested.

"What was the name of this gilt-edged investment?"

Tommy Gavillan was a generous man.

"I'll give it to you, Mac. Midnight Sun. Put your pension on it. If you do you'll be able to retire and live honest."

On Inspector MacNeill's broad features there was an expression which was indicative of scorn, contempt and quiet amusement.

8

"You're daft as well as being the second biggest crook in England, Gavillan. I've had the winner of the Derby for a month. I got the information from Inspector McLean. He's got a nephew with Freemantle who trains it." He leaned over and whispered the name of the horse.

Tommy shook his head.

"You're a good copper, but a bad prophet," he observed. "All right, Mac, I'm ready to go. I'd just like to post a letter on the way. You don't mind?"

MacNeill looked thoughtful.

"Who is it to?"

"My daughter," Gavillan said and the big man was surprised.

"I didn't know you had one."

"Few people do," Gavillan told him.

Later, the accuracy of his own prognostications became apparent, for Midnight Sun did win the Derby and Mr. Justice Seebright of King's Bench sentenced Thomas O'Shea Gavillan to five years imprisonment, thus proving Inspector MacNeill wrong on two counts.

When the trial was over, the Central Office man was discussing a point of evidence with a colleague in the corridor, when an usher approached him with a request.

"The prisoner wants to see you, sir."

MacNeill was a little surprised.

"Gavillan?"

"Yes, sir. He's particularly anxious to have a word with you."

MacNeill went down to the cells below the Old Bailey where prisoners are left pending transfer and met Gavillan, a philosophical man.

"Five years isn't so bad, Inspector," the Irishman said. "I've got no kick. I've kept out of the way of the law for a long time. By the law of average I ought to have had this a good while ago."

"Yes," said MacNeill and waited.

Gavillan looked at him thoughtfully.

"That wasn't what I wanted to see you about, Mac." He ran his long fingers through greying hair. "The fact is that I'm worried. No—not about myself. I can do five years standing on my hands. It's about the girl."

MacNeill was surprised.

9

"You mean your daughter? I didn't know you were serious about that, Tommy. I thought it was a joke."

"She's no joke to me," Gavillan admitted. He looked at the large and serious man for a long time, then: "Mac—I had no great upbringing myself, and I've knocked around the world a lot. The girl doesn't know a great deal about me. Some day I'll have to tell her—but this isn't the day. She's at school—one of those girls' schools you pay through the nose for. I want her to be a lady."

"What about her mother?"

Gavillan's eyes narrowed.

"She's dead. Pat has nobody but me. One or two folk know about her. Sten and Loofer and a few of those fellers. She's an attractive kind and impulsive as hell. She's not due to leave this here school for a while, but I'll be out of circulation for a long time. I'd hate anything to happen." He fingered his long nose. "You know the kind of thing I mean. I'm not afraid of her morals—not in that way. I'm thinking she'd be a handy girl for one or two of the smart boys to know. She's got looks, style and she's got a good head. I'd like you to keep an eye on her—once in a while you could look her up."

Inspector MacNeill was aghast.

"Tommy, I don't know anything about women—especially young ones."

"That's the reason I'm asking you to keep an eye on her," Gavillan said humorously. "I'm not trying to stick you with something. I know a lot of people—people like me and people like you. You're the only one I would trust." His voice held a sudden pleading note. "Inspector, I'm going to tell you something. I didn't mention it in the box because if I had it would only have raised a laugh. When you took me that day, you were lucky. That was to be my last steal. I'm being frank with you —I was getting out of it for good. I've made enough money to last me all my days—honest money too."

Inspector MacNeill did not laugh.

"How did that come about?"

The Irishman shrugged.

"I was lucky. Clive Rendell unloaded some shares in oils on me twenty-five years ago. I've always kept them and they've been worth a fortune to me. Standard Oil bought me out only a fortnight before you picked me up. I'm well enough fixed." He grimaced. "That's the odd way the luck runs.

Anyway, that's the story. What do you think about Pat?"

There was a queer sort of appeal in the blue eyes. MacNeill saw it and was lost. He shrugged his broad shoulders.

"I'll do what I can, Gavillan. I don't say it will be much. It's a new line for me—and I can't guarantee results."

"That's good enough for me," Gavillan said. He held out his hand. "You don't mind, Mac? There's nobody here to see you."

"Damn you," said MacNeill and took his hand in a crushing grip.

Thereafter events took their course. Tommy Gavillan went to the Moor, where he was a model prisoner. MacNeill returned to Central Office, where he had promotion twice within five years, and found himself so busily employed on his legitimate business that it was difficult indeed to implement his promise to his captive. Yet there were occasions when he did drive into Hampshire to Miss Dugdale's College for Young Ladies and spend wearisome hours in the company of Miss Dugdale and her protégée, for he was in no sense of the word a lady's man.

Twice each year he visited Gavillan on the Moor, and reported progress. When Pat Gavillan was eighteen, he suggested a job, and to this Gavillan wisely agreed.

"Keep her out of mischief. I'm all for honest work. What kind of a job are you thinking about?"

MacNeill had no particular line of employment in mind.

"What about teaching?"

"I'd sooner see her on the Moor," said Gavillan frankly. "Teaching is killing work. I've seen a lot of it in my day."

"What about nursing?"

Gavillan pondered.

"That's a different proposition—just as hard in its own way—harder maybe. What does Pat think about it?"

"We'll see," said MacNeill, and three weeks later Patricia Gavillan was enrolled as a probationer on the staff of Wellwood. She was there when Tommy Gavillan came out of the big prison on the Moor. He paid her a visit, found, to his astonishment, that the long-legged, fair-haired schoolgirl he had left behind him, as a slim, capable young woman with cool grey eyes, a mouth that tilted upwards at the corners, and an air of calm assurance which rather took his breath from him.

Later, he took a house in the Hampshire village of Marks

Malden, and here she came to live with him between cases, for nursing was not only her profession, it was her life. This much she informed Tommy when he suggested that she might retire gracefully to a life of ease not to say luxury. Tommy was a little startled. Later, when he came to know her better, he was a little proud.

"She's a fine girl," he would boast. "When you think of her there with a fortune at her back and still going round the villages having to do with babies and ploughmen's wives and whatnot, it just lets you see." What it let you see he did not specify, but it was easy to suppose that the attitude of Pat Gavillan infected her father, for within a year, Tommy was a member of the County Council and talked politics with impunity.

Occasionally he came up to London. His finances were sound, his motives above reproach. When he bought a diamond necklace in Marentette's he paid for it with a cheque which was honoured on the spot. Sometimes he met Superintendent MacNeill by appointment, and they dined in Maldano's, which was Tommy's favourite restaurant: sometimes the big Scot would go into Hampshire of an evening and if work was slack would even spend a week-end in the heart of the country. On such occasions, Tommy would be the perfect host, the more perfect in that he was a knowledgeable man, and had a theory concerning the unlawful depredations of Corporal Violet, for at that particular moment, Corporal Violet was occupying the interested attention of Scotland Yard, the Berlin Police authorities, the Italian Police and the illustrious gentlemen at the Sûreté.

Superintendent MacNeill had a theory of his own, but he found Gavillan interesting. Tommy knew most of the big fellows—could see them even at this late stage in his metamorphosis. To them, his way of life may have been peculiar, but his motives were never suspect for they trusted him as he in his day had trusted them. Thus he could forgather with "Slim" Dane the confidence man, with Bertie Englehart who had taken the Tenth National Bank of New York for a cool million, could dine with Pryor the prince of forgers without the Metropolitan Constabulary looking askance, and wondering what exactly was cooking.

All this was gall and wormwood to a man of the nature of Chief Inspector Grimm, for that pessimistic man had studied crime and criminals over a long period of years, and his researches had made him dubious indeed of the designs of anyone whose integrity he had valid reasons to doubt at any time in the past.

"Mark my words," he would say ominously, "it won't last, you can't teach an old dog new tricks."

When he said this, Superintendent MacNeill would sigh.

"It all depends on the animal," he would say. "The old dog for the hard road, Grimm. Don't you forget that."

"I won't," was Grimm's invariable reply. "But you mark my words. Gavillan will let you down yet."

And in course of time this prophecy was fully justified, for there came a morning in early December when the rain drove on the window-frames and men in Central Office huddled over their desks. Superintendent MacNeill, a complacent man, smoked before a cheerful fire and considered a report from one of his most promising subordinates. He was scrutinizing this when there was a tap at the door and Chief Inspector Grimm made his appearance. There was a glint of satisfaction in his dark eyes: in his hands he carried a folded newspaper.

MacNeill watched him without favour.

"Well, Grimm, we don't usually see you at this time of the day."

Grimm smiled coldly.

"Seen the paper today?"

"Not as yet," MacNeill admitted. "Something of interest?"

Chief Inspector Grimm's smile grew wider and colder.

"Very, Mr. MacNeill." He laid the newspaper on the desk and with his own long forefinger indicated a column. "Read that." His voice was charged with triumph. "I've always said——"

MacNeill yawned.

"You're always saying something," he admitted. He lifted the paper, scanned it with an interested eye, then stiffened, for the black heavy type seemed almost to shriek out at him.

GAVILLAN ARRESTED ON COUNTERFEIT CHARGE

QUICK MOVE BY LOCAL POLICE

MacNeill looked up.

"Hell," he said thickly.

Grimm's toothy smile was in evidence.

"I warned you, Superintendent. You've heard me say it a hundred times. You can't teach an old dog new tricks."

MacNeill's eyes were far away, but in them a little devil was dancing. Of a sudden his hand came down heavily.

"Someone's slipped up," he said soberly. "It's a queer sort of move but it means something. I wonder what Tommy has to say about it."

Grimm was testy. Riddles were an offence to him.

"As I was saying, Mr. MacNeill, it's a bad business. But I've always maintained this would turn out badly. You can't teach——"

The big superintendent's eyes lit up suddenly.

"You're right, Grimm. I've heard you say it before. You can't teach an old dog new tricks. It's a God's truth, and forgery was never any ploy of Gavillan's. That means it's a frame, and I thought it would be. I wonder about that. Tommy hasn't got many enemies, but he has got one."

Inspector Grimm was rankled.

"Who is he?"

MacNeill folded the newspaper and handed it back.

"Who's the foremost criminal of the present day?" he asked gently.

Grimm pondered.

"Silas Lyne?" he said slowly.

MacNeill shook his head.

"No. Lyne is big. I'll grant you that. But the man I'm thinking of is bigger than even Silas Lyne. I mean Corporal Violet!"

CHAPTER II

"CORPORAL VIOLET!"

For a second or two Chief Inspector Grimm considered this pronouncement, and not even he was prepared to quarrel with it, for the record of Corporal Violet was black indeed.

"Perhaps you're right. But what has he got to do with Gavillan?"

Superintendent MacNeill was not prepared to say. He rose abruptly.

"I'm glad you gave me the news, Grimm. I'll look into this business. It was the Hampshire men who arrested him. I'll find out a little more about it." When the man had gone he put through a call to Winchester and was fortunate in speaking to the officer in charge of the case.

Inspector Bryde was a brisk and capable man.

"We took him last night," he said. "He came quietly enough."

"Tommy always does. Tell me this, was he surprised?"

Bryde chuckled.

"He was completely surprised."

"Didn't expect it, eh? What did he say?"

The detective pondered.

"He said something about not expecting it," he admitted, "but then these fellers never do. In a way I was sorry for him, for he's got a good reputation around the district. People like him—I liked him myself."

"You got the evidence?"

"Yes. The plates that made the Belgian franc notes were there—in his safe. I wonder at him keeping them. That sort of thing is dynamite. We found them where we expected to find them."

"It was a tip-off?" MacNeill asked.

Bryde admitted the truth of this.

"It was. We'd never have been likely to suspect a man like Gavillan otherwise. Anyway, forgery wasn't in his usual line, although we knew that the gang that had been making these notes were operating from this country. We figured they were either in Hants or Sussex. The Belgian Police had the same information. We'd known for more than a year that they were working from this side."

"It was a telephone tip?"

The inspector became confidential.

"That's correct—and I'll give you the details of it, for the call came to me at my home not to the station at all."

MacNeill was interested.

"That was unusual."

"I thought so too. It has happened once or twice before, but not often. Anyway, I was at home going over a report on an arson case when the call came through. It was a woman who was speaking."

"A woman?" MacNeill was surprised.

Bryde chuckled.

"That's correct. It puzzled me too. Anyway, she told me if I wanted to get the man who was working the Belgian franc notes, I was to go to Marks Malden right away. She said that the plates were in the house somewhere, and that Gavillan had had them there for a spell, but that he was going to get rid of them soon."

"She didn't mention the safe?"

"No. She wasn't explicit at all: just that the stuff was in the house. She hung up right away and I wasn't able to question her."

"What about the call?"

"It came from a public telephone kiosk at the station. A couple of hundred folk use that telephone every day. We didn't get anything there."

"So you went to Marks Malden?"

Bryde coughed.

"Not right away, Superintendent. I called up the Super here and he decided to speak to the Chief Constable about it. A lot of these tips aren't too reliable and we didn't want any trouble over it. In fact, if Gavillan hadn't had a record, we'd probably have ignored the call altogether. As it was, I took two men and went along. We got the plates in the safe—pretty well hidden beneath a lot of other stuff. We got a stack of Belgian currency in a big vase affair. The notes had all been struck from the plates. Gavillan didn't have a leg to stand on."

"I see," said MacNeill. He thanked the man and hung up. For a long time he sat thoughtfully over his desk. There was a problem here. Tommy Gavillan was no forger. He had the idea that even Inspector Bryde was not too happy about the success of his case. But Tommy had been most effectively put down. With his record, with so much straightforward evidence against him, Gavillan would go back to the Moor. He was still sitting there when the 'phone rang. It was Pat Gavillan, and her cool voice came to him as plainly as though she had been in the room with him.

"Uncle Mac, you've heard the news?"

"Only just," he said.

"Daddy doesn't know a thing about it," she said fiercely. "He called me up this morning to tell me." Her voice trembled a little. "Has he called you yet?"

"Not yet," MacNeill said cautiously.

16

"Will you come through to see us?" she asked.

He considered.

"I've got a slack day, I might just manage it. I'll get the afternoon train. Tell Tommy to meet me at Winchester."

In point of fact, it was Pat Gavillan who met him at Winchester, with the little brake that Tommy Gavillan used for incidental purposes, and she was grave-eyed and worried.

"How good it is to see you," she said. She took him by the arm and led him along the platform. "I've got the car out here. Daddy wanted to come, but Mr. Drake came in. He's the lawyer from London. He wanted to talk things over with Daddy."

"Drake," MacNeill said thoughtfully. "That wouldn't be Enoch Drake of Hillwood, Drake and Brabner now?"

She informed him that it was no less.

"A tall man with a bald head and very keen blue eyes."

"You describe him exactly," said the policeman, and in his voice there was a certain dryness which caused her to look round.

"You don't like him?"

MacNeill held open the door of the brake for her.

"I didn't say that."

"You didn't need to. I can tell."

He laughed pleasantly.

"You're a remarkable girl, Pat. Anyway, you're wrong. I know Drake. I neither like him nor dislike him. He's put a few questions to me in my time." He smiled reminiscently. "Not that it matters for the moment. He's with Tommy just now, is he?"

"He was when I left," the girl said. On the road to Marks Malden she discussed the outrageous conduct of the Hants Police with the amused MacNeill and made vast claims to his sympathy.

"The whole thing was put up, I'm sure of that, Uncle Mac. I wish you had seen the man who arrested Daddy. MacBryde his name was."

The superintendent rejected the imputation briskly.

"Bryde, plain Bryde."

"A horrible-looking man," Pat said. "I saw him this morning. He has a big black moustache too. It's my opinion that they put those things they found into the safe themselves. I've got a theory about that."

She developed it, and it was not flattering to the probity of Inspector Bryde and his colleagues.

MacNeill was amused.

"I don't think you should say that sort of thing, Pat. I've spoken to Bryde over the telephone and he was quite helpful."

"Was he?"

"He gave me a few things to think about," said MacNeill. He spoke no more until the village of Marks Malden had been reached. It lay in a hollow, flanked on either side with spruce woods which stretched to the slopes above. Far to the left of them as they entered the village were the grey towers of Malden Court, and he watched them disappear among the greenery.

The girl was looking up at him.

"Billy's house," she said.

He was puzzled for only a second.

"Oh—you mean Mr. Mandell."

"Yes. We had him over this morning. He read about Daddy in the newspaper. He was all for going up to London with a horsewhip and interviewing the editor of the *Monitor Dispatch*. Billy's so violent."

MacNeill had met Bill Mandell once or twice before, and remembered him vaguely as a large, fair young man who rode to hounds, attending the meet in an enormous and highly polished Rolls Royce. A cheerful and sympathetic young man, most pleasingly ugly. That he was on calling terms with the Gavillans, he well knew—that his main interest was not the genial Tommy, but the indubitably attractive Pat, he more than suspected. She eased the car gently round a curve in the road.

"Billy's a dear. I wish he were cleverer a bit. He always says and does the most unsubtle things."

The policeman chuckled.

"I didn't know you were fond of subtlety."

"I'm not, but——" She raised her hand and MacNeill, glancing to his right, saw a man sitting on the top bar of a five-barred gate. He wore a shabby tweed coat and a battered Donegal hat, and he raised a hand in greeting as the car sped past.

Pat took the next corner.

"That's Peter Spain. He's taken the Moorings. He comes over to see Daddy a lot. I wonder if he's heard the news."

Something in her voice brought a twinkle to his eyes.

"You don't like him."

She laughed aloud.

"How right you are."

"What's wrong with him?"

She considered.

"Too bossy. That's what I think. Anyway, there's something almost sinister about him. That's a word I don't like, but it describes him admirably. Daddy doesn't think so. He likes him. Personally, I don't. It's just one of those things. Perhaps it's intuition. I wouldn't care to say."

There was a little river ahead of them, its volume considerably swollen by the rains of the month. They crossed the bridge. A road opened on their left and led to the avenue. This she took. It was evident that Peter Spain was considerably in her mind.

"There's something odd about him, I always think. Anyway, he doesn't like Billy."

MacNeill was considerably interested.

"How on earth do you know that?"

"Billy told me so."

The big man laughed.

"Don't tell me they're quarrelling over you, Pat."

She was indignant.

"They quarrelled over a fox. Spain shot it. He said he would do it again. Billy swore at him and told him he would throw him into the Ede if he did. Daddy was amused. He took Spain's part."

Chyme Close came into sight as she spoke. It was a medium-sized house of cheerful red brick, had been built originally in the reign of Anne, and added to by a series of owners. Ivy and Virginia creeper covered the gables; in summer, clematis smothered the front of it, clambering over the ornate little portico. Now in the dreary drizzle of a chill December day it looked inviting, comfortable. Lights twinkled in the mullioned windows, and from the roseate glow which permeated them, it was easy to suppose that a log fire burned brightly in the long room from which they beamed forth over the rolling lawn.

Pat drew up in front of the door.

"I'll leave the brake here, Uncle Mac. We'll need it later. I wonder if Mr. Drake has gone yet?"

"His car is up here," MacNeill said.

She shook her head.

"He came by train. Flett drove him from Marks Malden. We'll go inside and find out. I don't think——"

She stopped abruptly, and MacNeill stared.

"What's wrong?"

She was looking past him towards a belt of trees. He followed the line of her pointing finger. Something dark seemed to move among the trees, then it mingled with the spruce and fir of the planting.

"Peter Spain!" she gasped.

Superintendent MacNeill rubbed at his cheek. Darkness was falling now. The light was fading, and the glance that he had had, had been brief indeed, yet he had the uncomfortable feeling that she spoke only the truth. That the interested watcher had indeed been the man who had witnessed their arrival from the top of the five-barred gate.

CHAPTER III

"SPAIN!"

For a second or two, Superintendent MacNeill stared at the girl. Then he swung round and crossed the sodden grass of the lawn at a brisk trot. He had reached the fringe of the wood when he heard her voice close at hand.

"Where is he now?"

The big man was silent. He walked up the little slope that led to the trees, parted them and sent a shower of raindrops cascading over his shoulders. There was little to be seen, for beyond the fringe, the planting was dark and uninviting. Ahead of him he could see the outline of a path, but there was no sound which might suggest anyone moving along it. He came back to the lawn.

"There's nobody there."

She looked up at him oddly.

"But you saw him. It was Spain."

He frowned.

"Was it? I wouldn't like to say." He considered for a little. "We passed him quite a distance back. How could he have got here so soon?"

"There's a footbridge over the Ede," she said, "and a path which leads up here. He could have done it if he'd wanted to. I often go that way to the village." There was a hostile glint in her grey eyes. "That's what I mean when I say he's sinister. I've seen him around before. It seems so queer. What do you think we should do?"

MacNeill laughed grimly.

"Forget it. What else is there to do? I didn't see him and you can't swear to it that you did. In any event, it's no offence to watch us from a wood." He headed back towards the house.

Pat kept pace with him.

"It's so extraordinary. I wish I could understand him. He's been here for months now. Five or six months."

They reached the four steps which led to the door. MacNeill pushed it open, holding it wide for her. They stepped into the broad, cheerful hall. A log fire burned in an old-fashioned dog grate, with a soft perfume which was pleasingly aromatic. The girl crossed the hall towards the door of the library. She opened the door, then:

"Daddy, here is Uncle Mac."

Tommy Gavillan was standing with his back to the fire. He was a man of average height, broad-shouldered, burly of build. His features were cheerful, and about him, even in this moment of stress, there was an atmosphere of geniality. He came forward with one red hand outstretched in welcome.

"Come in, Mac. I'm a glad man to meet you. Take off your coat and have a drink. You know Mr. Drake?"

Enoch Drake had been sitting in one of the big, cowhide armchairs. Now he appeared from it like some lean vulture.

"Superintendent MacNeill of course. We have met, we have met. This is the first time that we have done so—ah—as colleagues." He had a little trick of repeating the most inconsequential of phrases. Now he favoured MacNeill with a wintry smile. "Usually our exchanges are—ah—a trifle pointed; a trifle pointed. I have often attempted to shake Superintendent MacNeill's testimony, but rarely with success. Rarely with success."

"That's true," MacNeill said. He shook off his coat.

The girl had gone out. Tommy Gavillan looked around for a bell, rang it and walked over to a decanter.

"Flett will take your coat out. In the meantime, sit you

down. Drake is just leaving. Got to get the night train. Flett's driving him to the station."

The policeman sat down, stretched out his legs.

"Don't put any water in it, Gavillan. It never agrees with my stomach. Anyway, I'm no believer in it internally. Here's your good health."

Gavillan poured out a glass for himself.

"My health's good enough." He saw the policeman's inquiring glance. "Mr. Drake doesn't touch it."

MacNeill was a little startled.

"That's not like a lawyer, Mr. Drake. Maybe you're under doctor's orders?"

The older man shook his head.

"I'm a temperate man, Superintendent. Strong drink doesn't appeal to me. I've seen the effects of it too often. Crime, misery, poverty, disgrace. A bad, bad thing, a crowning evil." There was a pigskin folio on the desk top. He walked over to it now, slipped the catch and inserted a sheaf of papers.

Gavillan watched him narrowly.

"I'll hear from you then, Drake?"

"Tomorrow," the lawyer said. "I'll have a word with Braburn. He's got a very good head. It's an ugly case, an ugly, ugly case. I'm not going to buoy you up, Gavillan. That's bad policy, bad policy. The letdown is unpleasant."

Gavillan winced.

"You're a cheery sort of feller," he said humorously. "All right, Drake, I know you'll do your best." The door opened as he spoke and a small and rubicund man appeared.

"Right you are, sir. The car's waiting."

Gavillan looked round.

"Here's Flett," he said unnecessarily. "Good-bye, Drake. I'll keep in touch with you."

"Do so," said Mr. Drake grimly. With a nod which included them both, he took his departure.

Tommy watched him go.

"There's a feller for you, Mac. What a spirit. I've seen more fun at a wake, and yet he's a good lawyer. His record proves it."

MacNeill nodded. When he spoke his voice was dry.

"Yes, he's a good lawyer. One of the best. I'd rather have him with me than against me any day. He defended Keller and Rafe Enderby in that Battersea killing, and he got them

22

off. They were guilty too—I can tell you that in confidence. Where did you pick him up?"

Gavillan frowned.

"Spain put me on to him," he said thoughtfully. "He's a wide young feller. Comes up here a lot. Anyway, I'd heard of him." He poured out another drink for his guest then sat down in the chair the lawyer had vacated. For a moment or two he did not speak, then:

"You're not asking me anything, Mac."

MacNeill looked at him grimly.

"No. I'm not."

"How did you hear about it?"

"From one of our inspectors."

Gavillan's face was impassive.

"It was a frame," he said softly.

The big man nodded.

"I figured that. Who was it?"

The Irishman's eyes came up to meet his.

"I wish I could tell you that—with any certainty."

MacNeill finished his drink.

"You're thinking about Corporal Violet," he said pleasantly. "One day, Gavillan, I'm going to get that story out of you."

For a second the Irishman stared.

"Maybe you will at that," he said thoughtfully. Then his eyes lit up. "I'm puzzled about it, Mac. Bryde didn't give me any information at all. All he told me was that they were acting on information received. I knew as soon as he said that that it was a plant, but I couldn't figure out what was behind it all. They got the stuff too—right in my own safe. As though I'd keep dynamite like that in my house?" There was a little disgust in his voice. "What puzzles me is how it got there."

MacNeill pondered.

"What kind of safe is it?"

"It's a Siebler. I'll show it to you. It's an old one, and it hasn't got all the up-to-date gadgets of these modern jobs but even at that a man would have to know his business to open it in a hurry."

"Who have you had in the house recently?"

Gavillan pondered.

"Quite a few people. Mandell, Spain, Hettche and——"

The policeman frowned.

"Who is Hettche?"

"A young feller that's staying with Mandell—an American."

"What's he like?"

Tommy Gavillan was not prepared to say.

"I only saw him for a minute, and I hardly noticed him even then. Mandell is always bringing strangers over, and he brought him on the night we had a card party for the Nursing Guild. Pat can tell you. She must have spoken to him. All I remember is that he had glasses and a bit of a limp."

"So you had a card party here?" MacNeill said. "That's interesting. The house would be full, of course. Tommy, you'll kill yourself with kindness. That was when the safe was opened. When did the party occur?"

"Last Friday."

MacNeill produced his pouch and a long-stemmed pipe. He proceeded to fill this as he spoke.

"I'll see Pat about that. It may be important." He lit up and puffed in contemplative silence for a moment or two, then: "What does Drake think?"

Tommy Gavillan shrugged.

"You heard what he said. It wasn't very cheerful, but he's that kind of a feller. I don't think I've any more than a fifty-fifty chance."

MacNeill leaned forward grimly.

"You're as bad as Drake. You haven't a hundred to one chance, Tommy. I'm being brutal about it because there's no other way to be. I know it was a frame and I can think of a dozen men at Central Office who will agree with me—but it's the kind of frame-up that sticks. They got the tip. They got the evidence. You can't prove it was planned no matter what we think. I don't like the business at all." He puffed savagely. "That's that."

Gavillan sighed philosophically.

"I'm afraid you're right."

The big man nodded earnestly.

"I know I am. Somebody's put you away."

"I'll have his heart's blood," said Gavillan calmly. "How long could they put me away for?"

"You could get three years."

The Irishman pondered.

"I'll be fifty-seven when I come out. That's a hell of a jolt to a man of my years. Anyway, I'll get him even if I have to wait a century for it. When I do," he smiled unpleasantly, "you'll have another unsolved murder on your hands, Mac. I hate a squeaker. This feller——"

MacNeill's eyes hardened.

"It was a woman who put in the squeak!"

Gavillan stared. Surprise was writ large in his eyes.

"A woman!"

MacNeill gave him glance for glance.

"A woman. I'm giving you that in confidence, Tommy. Bryde gave me the information. He expected me to keep quiet about it. No policeman ever gives away the source of his information, but this is something you should know. Who was the woman?"

There was a long, long silence. That Gavillan was amazed was clear to see; that he was puzzled, equally so.

"A woman!" he said. "Well, I'm damned! No. I can't think of any woman who owes me a grudge."

"You're sure of that?"

"Certain of it!"

A log fell from the top of the fire and rolled across the stone hearth. Gavillan rose and lifted it with the tongs. His face was harder than it had been, as though some grim memory had drifted back to him out of the years. He laid down the tongs.

"No. I can't give you any help there."

The Scot watched him.

"Think it over, Tommy. You've got Pat to consider. You might be able to tell me something that could help a bit."

Gavillan shook his head deliberately.

"I'm telling you the truth. I've never done a woman a bad turn in my life—and only one man."

"Who was that?"

There was a little grin on Gavillan's face.

"Nobody you ever met. Whoever it was who did this—it wasn't that particular feller. I know that." He walked across to the decanter. "Now, a very small one. We'll talk about it after dinner, but I can't tell you any more than I've already told you. If I could—I would. The Moor is a raw place for a feller of my age."

MacNeill turned his own glass upside down.

"No more for me. I want to do a bit of thinking." He watched his companion finish his drink, shrewdly aware that

25

his revelation had shocked him out of his normal imperturb-ability. It was seldom the Irishman smoked at all, when he did, it was a sure sign that he was disturbed. He lit a cigarette now, puffed on it shortly and rapidly, then:

"There's one thing that has always puzzled me, Tommy."

"What's that?"

"We haven't heard of Drew Sheldon since you were on the Moor last."

The Irishman looked up quickly.

"Sheldon's dead."

"How do you know that?"

Gavillan tossed the butt of his cigarette away as though it had suddenly become distasteful to him.

"I was there when he died," he said, thoughtfully. He rose as he spoke. "There's the gong. That means dinner in five minutes. I'll take you upstairs, Mac. I'm fond of my meals and I like them in comfort. I may not be having them like that for a long time to come, I reckon."

With a grin he led the way from the room.

CHAPTER IV

DINNER was a more subdued meal at Chyme Close than Superintendent MacNeill had ever known it to be, for not even Tommy Gavillan's irrepressible spirits seemed proof against the threat of impending imprisonment. For the first time, the policeman saw his former prey silent and thoughtful, even a little absent-minded, and it was not until the meal was over and they had withdraw to the library that Gavillan became voluble. Then, with a glass in his hand, he looked at his ancient enemy.

"This puts me in mind of the last time I was sent up, Mac," he said. "I asked you a favour then. They say that history repeats itself. I never figured at any time that it would repeat itself like this. Here I am asking you the same sort of thing again." His blue eyes were suddenly soft. "I'm glad I had these one or two years with Pat. That girl's a wonder. She amazes me at times. The things she knows. When I was twice her age I didn't know half as much. It must have been the Dugdale woman's system of education."

Superintendent MacNeill was inclined to agree.

"Pat's all right. She'll take a lot out of this life and she'll put a lot more back into it. You don't need to worry about her."

Gavillan was suddenly serious.

"I wasn't worrying. Not until today. Now I am. I wish to heaven I knew who the woman was that you mention."

"Corporal Violet could recruit a dozen women for any job," MacNeill said almost wearily. "I don't suppose there's anything personal in it."

Gavillan was a volatile soul. His face cleared.

"Maybe you're right. Of course you are. Here am I sitting like a man at a wake when I ought to be enjoying my own whisky."

The policeman had lit his pipe. Now he blew a long cloud of smoke across the room, watched it with a critical eye.

"You wouldn't like to tell me a little more about Corporal Violet before you go up?" he asked pleasantly.

Gavillan shook his head.

"I can't tell you anything about that feller you don't know yourself," he said pleasantly. "You know that, Mac."

"I wonder," MacNeill said. "You don't like squeakers, Tommy."

Gavillan made a little grimace.

"That's true enough. I hate their guts. I wouldn't 'nose' on anybody, Mac, and I don't care who knows it. Not even you."

The big man watched him meditatively.

"You told me once you had a theory about Corporal Violet."

Gavillan's eyes twinkled.

"Did I?" he asked forgetfully. "I couldn't go over that now. It must have been a long time ago."

"It was just about a year ago."

"I forget all about it."

"I never forget things," MacNeill said. "You talked a lot that night, Tommy. You didn't say enough to give me a lead, but you told me enough to make me very interested. I'd like you to go over it again."

Gavillan shook his head.

"I can't," he said. "No. That's just the sort of thing I can't

27

do. Anyway, that must have been the night I had a lot to drink. When I get like that I'm liable to say nearly anything."

The door opened and Pat put her head into the room.

"Have you finished your talk? Do you mind if I join you?"

Gavillan welcomed her effusively.

"Come in, Pat." He drew in a chair for her. "Mac and me were just talking over old times. We're glad to see you."

The girl laughed.

"I'm not alone."

Tommy was interested.

"Who's with you out there in the corridor?"

"Billy," she said. "He's hanging up his coat."

Mandell appeared as she spoke and MacNeill found himself shaking hands with this large and ebullient young man.

"It's a long time since you've been down, Super. Hello, Tommy. I'll have a drink. I'm nearly blue with the cold. What a night! The rain's coming down in sheets and the Ede is flooded. There's a foot of water at the bridge."

Gavillan upended the heavy decanter.

"Here you are, young feller. I didn't hear you drive up."

"I walked," said Mandell succinctly. "Came through the wood. I wanted Hettche to come with me, but he's a devil for reading books. That's a thing I've no time for. It's years since I've read a book. I bought one once at Esher when I had to wait for a train—read nearly the half of it too, before I discovered it wasn't about fox-hunting at all. That was a drop. The feller that wrote it was called Hunt—Leigh Hunt. I've never forgotten the name." He raised his glass. "Cheerio."

Pat watched him impassively.

"A little reading wouldn't do you any harm, Billy," she observed dryly. "Lots of people go in for it."

"That's true," said Gavillan. "The thing's quite common."

Mandell chuckled.

"You don't get round me with a tanner's worth of soft soap like that. I'm no scholar. Never was. When I was at school they used to laugh at me—and here I am, better off than most of the brainy fellers." He shook his head, perplexed at this phenomenon, then, "What's the news, Tommy?"

Gavillan shrugged.

"Well I don't feel happy about it."

Mandell's roundish features grew doleful.

"What about Drake? He's a fearfully cunning old bird. As artful as you like. Look what he did with those murderers. You haven't done anything like that. After all, murder is a lousy sort of thing. Making banknotes is a bit different. It's clever in its own way."

It was evident that Billy Mandell's estimate of the situation was founded on friendship, not on faith.

Pat drew in her breath.

"Billy, I've told you before that Daddy had nothing to do with the forging affair." There was exasperation in her voice.

Mandell looked embarrassed.

"Naturally not," he said. "That was a slip of the tongue, Tommy. Everybody knows you never had a hand in it. What use would Belgian money be to anyone here, anyway? That's what I asked Hettche."

"Did you?" MacNeill said.

The younger man nodded.

"I did. That feller has a good head on his shoulders."

"I'll bet he has," said Tommy Gavillan. "What did he say?"

Mandell shook his head.

"I've forgotten what he said now. It couldn't have been of much importance, anyway. But what about this business? What about old Drake?"

"Drake isn't too sure at all."

Mandell blanched.

"That's a pity. I thought the feller was smart. Get another lawyer."

Gavillan looked at him grimly.

"That's no good. It's not the lawyer who's sending me up. No. I'm afraid I've had it. The superintendent here thinks so too. I'll maybe be gone for a while, Mandell. Keep an eye on things."

Billy Mandell nodded, strangely grim.

"You bet. Pat's as safe as houses with me. I'll look after her like a father. Don't you worry, Tommy." He rose as he spoke. "Now I'll have to get back. If I wait any longer the Ede won't be fordable." He looked across towards the policeman. "How about you, Super?"

MacNeill took the pipe from his lips.

"I'm staying overnight and going back in the morning."

"Good. I may see you then. There's a chance I might be

29

going up to the City myself on the morning train. Business of some sort. I've got to see my lawyers. Mendel, Caliph and Paterson. Old Caliph attends to my affairs, and I loathe seeing him. Deaf as a post, and he lives in the days of the Empire builders and all that kind of thing. He's always wanting me to go out to India and take a job. What's the sense in that. I don't need a job—and a fine-looking figure I would cut in India anyway. I loathe heat. Give me a frosty morning in dear old Hampshire with the beaters coming slowly up the middle ride and the pheasants rising from Clay Corner. That's the spot for me." There was a great deal of firmness in his voice as he looked around.

Gavillan chuckled.

"Maybe you're right. Good night, Mandell."

Mandell held out his large red hand.

"Good night."

He left the room and Pat stepped into the hall with him. Flett was coming towards them as they appeared.

"A dirty night, Mr. Mandell. Mr. Gavillan said something about driving you home."

Mandell beamed.

"You're a sport, Flett. I wouldn't have asked, mind you, but it's filthy. You've got the car handy?"

"The brake," Flett said. "This way, sir."

Pat walked to the door.

"What a horrible night, Billy. I'm glad you came over. Daddy likes to see you occasionally."

Mandell nodded.

"I enjoy a talk with the old feller—then there's you too, of course. One of these days I'll be over again—fairly soon too. Don't you worry about this business, Pat. Everything is going to turn out all right."

She shivered in spite of herself.

"I hope you're right, Billy."

The big hand patted her shoulder.

"I'm sure of it." He crossed to the opposite side of the steps for Flett had backed the brake round against them. "Good night, Pat."

He got into the car and settled himself comfortably, the rain driving on the windscreen before his eyes, pattering heavily on the roof above him. Flett settled himself down to drive. The avenue stood high, but there was one portion of it

30

which dipped down to the river level, and this, as Mandell had expected, was flooded to a depth of some inches.

Flett was a little perturbed.

"Look at the rain, sir. You can hardly believe it. Makes you think about the well-known story of Noah an' his Ark that I read about in the Bible. I've got an awful fear of water. Once I was near drowned."

Mandell rubbed at his cheek.

"Queer. I was nearly drowned once myself. I fell off a horse."

"I fell off a quay," said Flett reminiscently. "It was an 'orrible sensation. Mr. Gavillan fished me out. I'll never forget it."

They swung from the main roadway to the drive which led to Malden Court and in a moment more the lights of the house winked down towards them through the trees.

Flett drew up in front of the main doorway.

"Here you are, sir, home dry as it were. I'll get back now for I've got an early job tomorrow with the Super going away for the first train. The police are always awkward fellers—even when you're dealing with them social like."

Mandell shook a few raindrops from his coat.

"You're right there, Flett." In a burst of confidence he leaned forward. "I'll tell you the truth. I never really feel at home with them. I had a run in once with a Robert when I was at Cambridge. Punched him on the nose and took to my heels. I've never really liked to look one in the eye since then."

Flett felt his heart go out to this kindred spirit.

"I've felt like doing that myself, sir," he admitted. "Not with the Super. He's a fine feller, an' anyway, he would kill you if you did. But there has been others. Yes, Mr. Mandell, there has been others."

"I'll bet you," said Billy Mandell. "Good night."

He watched the red tail-light of the car disappear through the rain, then pushed open the door. The hall into which he stepped was long and broad, panelled and carved in a myriad presentations of scriptural forms, historical and mythological figures. There was a great fireplace with a mantel of black Italian marble and on this sat an ornate clock. It chimed gently and melodiously as he came over towards the fire. For a moment he stood there, holding his hands out towards the red embers. Then, after a moment he began to peel off his wet

31

coat. He hung this up and looked around him. There was a streak of yellow light from the bottom of the library door. He walked across to this and pushed it open.

There was a log fire burning in the big grate; the cheerful glow of it lit the room, set dancing a thousand shapes and shadows on the old walls. Two chairs were drawn up to the blaze. One of these was empty, but a slim figure occupied the other.

Mandell closed the door.

"Still reading, Dale? What you see in it puzzles me."

Dale Hettche dropped the book to his knees. He was small-featured and dark. The heavily-rimmed glasses he wore toned with the jet blackness of his hair. He spread out his long, slim fingers on his knee and inspected them meditatively.

"Every man to his own tastes, Mandell. Some of the things you do don't seem very amusing to me."

Mandell crossed to a cabinet, lifted a decanter and a glass. "Will you have one?"

"A very small one—with a spot of soda."

The syphon hissed pleasantly.

"It's a swine of a night," Mandell said. He listened to the sob of the wind in the tall trees outside and shivered pleasurably. "Makes a feller damned pleased to be indoors."

Hettche had picked up his book.

"What about Gavillan?"

Mandell carried across the glasses. He laid one beside the smaller man, sat down and stared into the heart of the fire.

"Gavillan is in good spirits. That feller always is."

"That's the Irish in him," Hettche said. He yawned as he spoke. "I had a visitor tonight."

"Who was that?"

"Spain. He came in shortly after you went out."

Mandell blinked.

"That's like his gall. That feller has a hide like an elephant. You just can't snub him. One of these days I'm going to lose my temper with him."

Hettche smiled faintly.

"I don't know that that would be wise. Never make an enemy where you can make a friend. You're too impulsive, Mandell. Anyway, I don't know that I'd care to say much about the outcome of a scrap between you. Spain looks to me

32

as though he'd be a pretty hardy sort of chap." He closed his book suddenly. "Gavillan wasn't upset then?"

"Not visibly."

"Who else was there?"

"Just the policeman. I've met him before. MacNeill his name is. I can't figure out a Scotland Yard johnny taking up with old Gavillan, but it takes all kinds to make a world."

"What about the girl?"

"Pat? She was there, of course. Worried too. There's something about that girl that appeals to me, Dale." Mandell's pleasant features were creased into a frown. "Pretty as a picture she is. You ought to see her."

"I have seen her," Hettche said wearily. "You've pointed her out fifty times to me—and all on the one night."

Mandell agreed.

"I'd forgotten about that. Anyway, she's my type. Very much my type. And one of these days I'm going to——!"

Hettche laughed gently

"Don't start to tell me about it again, Bill. I don't think she'll marry you and that's my honest opinion."

Mandell looked at him scowlingly.

"And why not?"

The smaller man sighed.

"I could give you a lot of reasons, but I'll give you just one. She doesn't strike me as the sort of girl who'll marry to please anyone but herself, and I wouldn't say that you cut the most romantic figure, Bill. Take my advice, I've been watching you for a while, and the onlooker sees most of the game." There was an air of quiet amusement in his voice. "My advice to you is to forget it—and forget it quickly."

Mandell scowled more heavily.

"What's wrong with me?"

Hettche rose.

"A lot of things. Anyway, matrimony interferes with business. When I tell you that, I'm speaking from experience. My own experience. Good night!" He left the room, walking very quickly.

CHAPTER V

IT WAS dry next morning when Superintendent MacNeill entrained for London. The drive to Winchester had been made along flooded roads, partly sodden fields and bleak, grey woods. Rain still dripped from every surface, and Tommy Gavillan accepted these unfavourable manifestations as grim portents of the future. He was driving himself, and MacNeill sat beside him at the front of the brake, his grey eyes fixed pensively on the road. He listened to Gavillan for a moment, then sighed.

"I certainly don't like it, Tommy. You've had my opinion and you've had Drake's. The man is only speaking the truth. Whoever worked this did it to put you away. I hope it will collapse. Anyway, I'll do what I can."

"You're a good feller," Gavillan said.

He waited with the policeman until the long train was drawing out of the station, and even then he stood watching the guard's van disappear from sight. MacNeill was a square policeman. He had met a few of them in his time, but this mountain of a man from the grey north was the one person who had managed to penetrate to the core of his being. He went back to the brake and drove towards the shopping centre. There were one or two purchases that had to be made: regarding these, he had explicit instructions, and he had just completed his task and was carrying his purchases out to the brake when he was aware of an interested audience. He looked round and saw a broad-shouldered young man in brown tweeds, watching him from the pavement, and in his eyes there was a glint of amusement.

Tommy Gavillan dropped the contents of his arms into the brake.

"Spain! Where the devil did you come from? It's early for a feller like you to be afoot."

Peter Spain nodded. He was bronzed and dark, his brown eyes were insolent, hard-looking. About him there was a sense of capability, an odd alertness and that indefinable character-istic which Pat considered sinister. Now he came across the pavement.

"Hullo, Gavillan. I was up at the station. I saw you there."

"I was seeing a friend off," Gavillan said.

"I know. I spotted him. A pretty big fellow."

"He's a policeman," Gavillan said shortly.

Spain took a short, heavy-bowled pipe from his pocket, filled it and puffed a cloud of smoke.

"I brought the car into Porter's. The clutch is slipping and causing me a bit of trouble. Anyway, it's time it was overhauled. I was going home by bus. I'm glad I saw you."

Gavillan opened the door.

"Get in," he said. He walked round the front of the car, started her up, then, when they were on the road, "I suppose you'll have heard the news?"

Spain smoked meditatively for a moment.

"About you? Yes—I read about it. I was over at Mandell's last night. I thought I might pick up some information there. I didn't like to come to the Close when I knew you had a visitor."

Gavillan looked round.

"How did you know that?"

"I saw him arrive. Pat drove him," Spain said. "I didn't want to butt in—but I knew Mandell would have no hesitation. That fellow has a hide like an elephant."

Gavillan was a little surprised at this display of consideration.

"Holy Smoke, but you're changing your tactics, Spain. You don't usually worry about etiquette and the like of that. Anyway, we did have Mandell over. He didn't wait very long though."

"I know that," Spain said. "I didn't see him, but I spoke to his friend for a while. A queer fellow Hettche."

Tommy was interested.

"What's queer about him?"

Spain considered.

"I can't exactly put my finger on it," he admitted. "But he's queer for all that. Anyway, I don't like men that wear rings."

Gavillan, a much-travelled man, brought the voice of experience to bear on this peculiar problem.

"It's a foreign custom. Americans do it a lot. I'll tell you the truth, I've worn a ring myself. Not a big one, mind you. Nothing ikey—nothing flash. Just a nice, neat, wee one." He

35

negotiated a curve. "Look at the water lying there. If it freezes there's going to be a lot of fun. I've never seen the Ede so high before. I wonder what that's a sign of?"

Spain took the pipe from his mouth.

"Never heed the Ede, Gavillan. What about this trouble of yours?"

The bluntness of the question did not shock Tommy Gavillan who was used to a certain amount of publicity in the matter of his misfortunes.

"Oh, that! You've read the paper. You know as much as I do about it. I've had legal advice. It may be pretty nasty. It was a frame-up, of course. I'm not being virtuous about it. I'm enough of a philosopher to accept the bad with the good."

Spain's eyes were unfathomable.

"Who did it?"

Gavillan shook his head.

"I wish I knew. I mean that, Spain. Whoever it was, was fairly clever. I certainly never expected to be attacked from that angle."

Spain looked round sardonically.

"But you did expect to be attacked? Why was that?"

Gavillan shrugged his broad shoulders.

"I've had a little trouble in my day," he said softly. "It's a thing that happens to most of us, Spain. I've made my enemies. You know the sort of life I've led. You can't do that without rubbing off the corners at some time. A few folk don't like me."

"So you expected trouble?"

Gavillan was irritated.

"Ain't I telling you I did? Lots of folk have long memories."

Spain chuckled.

"I'll bet they have. It's a pity you haven't, Gavillan. Anyway, I'll give you a piece of advice. Don't make any new ones." His voice was gentle, but there was an undercurrent of steel in it.

Gavillan scowled.

"At my age you don't start to do that sort of thing, Spain. I thought a feller that had travelled as much around the world as you would know that."

Spain knocked out his pipe. They were turning on to the

little road which led to his house, and he stared up through the trees at it.

"Look at that. Twelve rooms, and only half of them furnished. One or two would be enough for me. I'm not a fussy sort of fellow at all. I don't like big houses, especially when they're empty like this."

Gavillan regarded the grey outline of the Moorings.

"Used to be a naval feller that lived here. An admiral or something like that, he was. Name of Cyre. He had only one eye."

"I've heard of him," said Spain.

"I met him once or twice," Gavillan said profoundly. "A bit of a comedian, he was. I was surprised when he gave the place up. Why did you take it over?"

Spain brooded darkly.

"I often wonder that myself. In a way I like it. I'm fond of the country, but there isn't any company. You—Mandell—Mrs. Klein and the Fosters. I don't know what I'll do when you go away, Gavillan."

Tommy drove up to the front door and stopped. As he did so, something moved by the mullioned window and he looked up instinctively. For a brief second he saw the outline of a woman's face there, then, in an instant, she had stepped back into the room. He had a glimpse of long, green ear-rings, of a wealth of black hair.

Spain was climbing out.

"Come in and have a drink," he said.

Gavillan glanced at his watch. It was close on eleven o'clock and he shook his head regretfully.

"Sorry, Spain. It can't be today. Pat's waiting for some of these things I've got here. I should have been back half an hour ago."

Spain did not look unduly annoyed at the refusal. For a second, something that might have been relief flickered in his eyes, then:

"All right, I'll take a walk over sometime today, Gavillan. I want to have a little talk with you."

"Sure," said Tommy. "Come any time. I won't be going anywhere—not for a week or so." He laughed drily. "After that I may not have a chance to see visitors very often."

"You'll see me," said Spain. He raised his hand as the car shot away, watched it speed down the driveway. For a long

37

moment he stood there, his eyes coldly humorous. Then he turned and went into the house. The hallway was deserted, but to the left of it was the morning-room. He pushed open the door and stepped inside.

The woman who was sitting by the fire looked up. She was in her late thirties, was dark and oddly attractive. Her elegantly coiffured hair was piled high on her forehead, and her long, slim fingers touched at it delicately. She smiled at him as he approached.

"Hullo, Peter. I wondered where you'd got to this morning."

He tossed aside his hat and sat down.

"Did you now?"

She nodded.

"I even went out to look for you in the woods."

His eyes hardened.

"That was dangerous, Mary Lou. I told you I didn't want you to be seen around this part. I meant that. If any of these hicks set an eye on you there would be trouble."

She watched him with some irritation.

"I don't see that it matters. I could be your——"

He shook his head.

"You can't start that sort of stuff in this part of the world. What goes down in the Bronx or in Chi or even in Golders Green doesn't impress country folks very much. I didn't want you here. You complicate things too much. We've got too much at stake. I've put a fortune into this affair."

"Ten thousand dollars?"

He nodded evenly.

"Just ten thousand dollars, honey. That's a fortune to me. I had to work long enough to get it. Now I want it back." He walked moodily over to the window, stared down over the tree tops which fell away below him to the river.

Mary Lou Slatter watched him for a moment. Her green eyes were almost sulky. Then she went across slowly and put her arms round him so that he turned quickly. He pulled her hands down.

"Don't get amorous."

She looked at him then laughed.

"All right, Peter. I didn't mean it just that way. An agreement is an agreement, but I'm getting tired of all this. I've been cooped up here for a month now and I hate it."

38

"I told you not to come."

"I wanted to," she said. "Why shouldn't I? It's my business more than it is yours. I wanted to be on the job. Instead of doing anything worth while I've been stuck here with Silk until I could scream."

"Silk won't mind you screaming," he said pensively.

She went back towards the fire.

"That's the way of things. A deaf mute for company. I want to go up to London!" Her voice was rebellious.

Spain considered this calmly.

"No dice. You came here against advice. Now that you are here you'll have to stick it out. I can't take a chance. I don't want anyone to know I've got a woman staying here. Suppose someone saw you!"

She laughed harshly.

"Someone did."

He stiffened, then came towards her.

"Who was that?"

"Gavillan. I was at the window when he drew up. I didn't see the car until it was right on top of me, then I jumped back."

The brown eyes were inscrutable.

"And you say he saw you?"

"I think so. I seemed to catch his eye." She saw the anger on his face. "What's the odds? Gavillan may soon be away. You told me that yourself. This time next week he may be on the Moor and——"

He nodded.

"That's correct. But he could do a lot of talking between now and then—and a lot of talking could mean a lot of trouble. Gavillan was the last person I would have had see you!" He walked irritably the length of the room, then: "I've half a mind to let you clear out. London's a pretty big place. You could keep out of the way there!"

Her eyes were excited.

"You're a darling, Peter!"

"Don't get kittenish," he said. "The trouble is that the car has gone. I might have driven you into Winchester tonight, but I won't have it back before the end of the week." He was watching her closely. "That means you'll have to content yourself here."

Disappointment showed in her eyes.

"Couldn't you get a hire?"

"And have everyone in the district know there was a woman here?" He shook his head emphatically. "We're not having that."

"Then couldn't I walk to the station?"

"There's no station at Marks Malden."

"Where is the nearest one?"

He considered.

"Meredale. That's almost seven miles away."

She laughed contemptuously.

"What's seven miles. I've done three times that in a day." She crossed to a book-case, produced an ordnance survey map and spread it on the table top. For a moment she studied it, then, "Where are we?"

Spain laid his finger on the spot.

"That's Marks Malden. Meredale is over here. It's a fair seven miles. There's a train at ten-twenty-seven from there. I know that because I've caught it." He stared at her thoughtfully. "If you're really keen on it, you can do it. I'm not in favour of it. You know that—but on the other hand there's probably more danger in your being here."

She laughed aloud.

"Not for me, there isn't. I had certain romantic ideas. I'll admit that, Peter. Don't blush. I thought you might forget one or two things."

He looked at her coolly.

"I don't forget much, Mary Lou. Anyway, women aren't my weakness. You ought to know that by this time."

She laughed wryly.

"I think I do."

There was a footstep in the hall and she heard the door open.

"Silk," she said.

It was indeed Peter Spain's mute servant. The man looked across and nodded. She watched his fingers, fascinated, as he communicated his message to his master. Then, when he had gone out:

"What's he saying, Peter?"

"He told me that he saw someone on the avenue an hour ago."

She was barely interested.

"Why should anyone be on the avenue?"

"I can think of reasons," Spain said slowly. "He could be watching the house. You're a responsibility, Mary Lou."

She changed the subject abruptly.

"I don't know how you can bear Silk. I think he's horrible."

"He's been with me for years," Spain said.

"I know that. I can't stand him. Those horrible fingers of his! When he's telling you something, I want to shiver. I hate his hands. There's something about them that frightens me. I was in a play once in Delaware, and one of the actors had hands like Silk. In the play he strangled his wife. I used to shiver when I saw him come on the stage. I was his wife."

He looked at her in genuine surprise.

"Were you? How odd! Silk used to be an actor."

She stared at him.

"Silk? But I thought he'd been born like that."

"He was in an accident of some sort," Spain said. "It was in the Eastern States. I don't know when it was, but he lost his voice. He was paralysed for a couple of years. Then he regained his power of movement." He laughed coldly. "Perhaps you may be old friends. Silk hasn't drawn my attention to the fact. I must ask him one of these days." He went across to the door. "All right, you can make your plans. I won't be here tonight. I've got another little job in hand. Leave around eight o'clock. It's a straight road. I've shown it to you on the map. You can't go wrong."

"What about clothing?"

He considered.

"Leave that to me. You don't want to carry anything—no matter how small it is. A woman carrying a case is always noticeable. I'll have a couple of cases sent on to you. I'll send them to Silver's Hotel in Kensington. You'd better put up there."

"Yes," she said.

Spain opened the door.

"All this is against my better judgment," he said slowly. "I don't like it at all. You're a problem, Mary Lou, and when a person is a problem to me, I usually get rid of him."

There was a little glint of amusement in her green eyes.

"You won't get rid of me so easily, Peter."

"You think not?"

She shook her head provocatively.

"I'm thick-skinned. I didn't used to be. There was a spell

when I was very sensitive. You'd hardly believe that, but it's true."

Peter Spain sighed.

"After what I've heard in the last week or two I'd believe anything," he said, and the door closed on his broad shoulders.

CHAPTER VI

PAT was waiting on the doorstep when Gavillan got back, and she hailed him as soon as he got out of the brake.

"Mr. Drake called up half an hour ago. He wanted to speak to you, and he said it was very important."

Gavillan followed her inside.

"I'll call him now," he said. He put through a call to the lawyer's office, but Drake was at the Law Courts. A polite assistant was able to give him no information at all, was unable to suggest when the lawyer might return.

"Mr. Drake doesn't keep regular office hours," the man said. "Some days he doesn't come in at all."

"I see," said Gavillan. He hung up and went through to where the girl was waiting for him, and told her of his failure to locate Enoch Drake.

"Probably he'll ring again," he said. He lit one of his cigarettes, took a couple of puffs and tossed it away.

Pat watched him with worried eyes.

"You're upset, Daddy!"

Gavillan chuckled.

"I've got reason to be, kid." He sat down and stretched out his legs. "I'm not going to talk about this affair. You know what it means. I'd give a fortune to know what's behind it."

"You don't know?"

He shook his head.

"The funny thing is that I thought I did. Now, I figure I was wrong. All wrong or at least part wrong. Anyway, I'm taking care of things right now. You'll be well enough attended to. I want you to keep on the house, if they send me up. MacNeill knows it's a frame, but there's not a half-dozen men in England who would believe that. They don't understand me." He laughed gently.

42

The girl leaned forward.

"You said a moment ago you'd give a fortune to know what was behind it. Have you got a fortune?"

He looked up sharply.

"You've never asked me that sort of question before, Pat."

"No. I've often wondered though. We seem to be very well off."

"We are," Gavillan said complacently. "I've got a business head on my shoulders. I'll bet you never thought of that before. Anyway, I've got enough put away to look after your needs and mine. A quarter of a million is a right tidy sum."

She drew in her breath.

"Quarter of a million, Daddy?"

"Made it out of oil," Gavillan said. "It's all on the level. One of the big companies bought me out. I might have stood out for more, but I never was greedy. Anyway, I'm having the bank pay two thousand a year into your account. That ought to keep you comfortably until I come out. No! Don't interrupt me, Pat. This is business. It's got to be talked about some time." He looked at her kindly. "You're getting to be a regular young woman. I can never remember that you aren't a kid any longer. You'll have ideas of your own before very long now."

"What do you mean?"

He coughed.

"Mandell's hanging around a lot."

She smiled faintly.

"He's nice in his own way. Very obliging too."

"He's a fine boy," Gavillan said heartily. "A grand lad. I don't say he's the smartest, but a slick brain isn't always a good thing to have."

Pat smiled more faintly still.

"Billy's not exactly a boy. He can't be far short of forty."

Gavillan was astounded.

"Well I'm damned! Do you think not? Look at the head of hair he's got! You'd never expect that he was a day over thirty. Anyway, it isn't a man's age that counts. It's his—his man-of the-worldness, if you know what I mean. Mandell won't be old at sixty."

She turned the discussion abruptly into a channel which was of a great deal more interest to her at the moment.

"I've always wanted to ask you something, Dad."

43

Gavillan's brows contracted.

"Ask away then," he said cautiously.

"It's about mother."

There was a little silence.

Gavillan's face had hardened. An odd little glint crept into his eyes. She had seen it before on just such an occasion as this. Now she saw him grow old beneath her gaze.

"She's dead."

"I know that. She died when I was a baby."

"That's right. I was in Denver at the time. She was in a little place well to the West of that. I forget the name of it now—one of those Indian sounding places." He spoke slowly, as though he were turning the dusty pages of an old volume, and the printing he read was blurred and faded. "It's not a thing I want to talk about—much. You're old enough to understand that." His blue eyes came up to meet her grey ones. "That's one of the things a man like me just can't bear to think about—let alone talk about."

She saw the pain in his eyes.

"I'm sorry. You loved her very much?"

Gavillan nodded.

"We'd only been married three years. That isn't very long. Maya was young, and very beautiful."

"I wish you'd kept a picture of her," she said unsteadily.

"I only had one," the man said. There was a little touch of bitterness in his voice. "I didn't want to look at it again. I tore it into a million pieces. After all, I had you."

"Am I like her?"

He shook his head.

"Not in the slightest. You're more like me." He chuckled suddenly. "I'm not trying to flatter you. Your mother was fair too, but it was a different sort of fairness. Her father was a Swede. I guess that's where she took her colour from." He jumped up. "I'm going through to the study. I've got to sign some cheques and things. Don't talk about her, Pat. I find it hard to get her out of my mind. Maybe some day you'll understand how a feller feels when a thing like that happens. I hope not—but the world's a cruel, cruel place."

He made his way to the study, opened the big safe which had so much interested Inspector Bryde. There was a panel at the back of it and when he pushed on this, it tilted back to disclose a small cavity. He slid his hand into this, took out a

44

large, flat envelope and carried it to the light. From it, he removed a photograph, and stared at it for a long, long time. It was the photograph of a girl, ash blonde and delicately featured. She wore a quaintly patterned Hungarian blouse. He remembered the blues, the greens, the reds of it now. Across the bottom right-hand corner, and in large, almost childish characters was written:

> *To Tommy*
> *With all my Love*
> *Maya.*

Very deliberately he tore it into shreds, then crossed to the fireplace and tossed the fragments into the red embers. When the blaze had consumed them he came back. There was a small envelope within the larger one, and it was addressed to himself.

> *Mr. Thomas Gavillan*
> *279½ Apt. D.*
> *Westenfeldt Mansions,*
> *Detroit, Mich.*

He remembered the moment that it had arrived. He had been drinking ice-water and sweltering in a July heat wave. From the window of his apartment he could watch the crowds milling on the white, baked concrete of the street below. Heat had been rising from the oven that was Woodward Avenue, but it had not been the heat that had made him sick.

He drew out the single sheet of paper the envelope contained. The handwriting was that of Steve Rose, and Rose was a dead man these seven years. He wrote:

> *Mortensen Hotel,*
> *Melver Street,*
> *Peel City.*
> *July 8th.*

Dear Tommy,
> *I've had some luck at last. Pitt put me on to it too. They're here in Peel City, living at a hotel in Kister Avenue, the Van Diemen Hotel. It's a swell place. Sheldon has grown a moustache. Maya looks quite pleased with things. I followed her into Purser's—that's the biggest store in Town. She bought some stuff there and paid for it by cheque.*

*Sheldon calls himself "Wilbur D. Manson". Maya is reg-
istered as "Lottie Manson". Drew has a car—a big Chrysler
roadster. If you want me to keep with them—wire me here.*

                                                    Yours
                                                      Steve.

Gavillan smiled queerly. It was not easy to forget the
sequel to the letter he held in his big, red hand—not that he ever
wanted to forget it. He had been an angry man, but his anger
had never been of the red-hot, violent type. That day he had
been cool, icy. He remembered the look in Drew Sheldon's eyes,
when he had walked into the suite at the Van Diemen Hotel.
That was something which he would never forget. Maya, he had
not looked at, at all.

Now, after all these years, he was able to think back on
those moments with a cool dispassion. The white fires of rage
had burned themselves out. He sighed and tore the letter into
shreds. These too, he consigned to the fire. So much for the
past! Those grim reminders were better gone. What Pat did
not know, could harm her but little. He had always tried to
maintain a certain illusion—that much was his duty to his
daughter. Then, with a shrug, he went back to the safe.

MacNeill's news had been disquieting. The information had
been given by a woman. There was no woman whom he knew
who might have been in a position to leave behind her the
incriminating evidence that Bryde had found. Of the few
women he had ever known, only Maya had cause to hate him,
and that hatred had grown out of his own contempt for her,
of his magnaminity. He examined the safe again. It was old,
but was still a formidable object to anyone who was not an
authority on the subject of safes. It was easy to decide how the
attempt had been made. Opportunities for entering Chyme
Close existed, without a doubt, for there were occasions when
both he and Flett were absent together. He chuckled suddenly,
and slammed the heavy door shut. For a long moment he stood
in front of it, and in his eyes there was something akin to
amusement.

Tommy Gavillan was a menace and a reproach to someone
in high places. That much was very evident. He wondered how
long hatred might last in a man's heart, for he was a mag-
nanimous man himself. A gong was ringing now. It signified
that lunch was ready and he went down to the dining-room

46

below. On the stairway he met Flett, a bottle of beer in one hand, and a table napkin in the other. The little man raised a hand in deference.

"There you are, Mr. Gavillan. I was along for a bottle of beer for you. The case is near empty, I'll order another one."

"You're an optimist," said Gavillan, and went inside.

CHAPTER VII

IT WAS late afternoon when Superintendent MacNeill called Chyme Close, and it was Flett who answered the telephone.

"Mr. Gavillan's in the study," the servant said. "He's been there all day burning papers. What a smell there is in the house an' the fireside is full of burnt paper. It'll take me a week to clear up the mess. Wait a minute and I'll get hold of him." He laid down the receiver and walked through to the little room in which his employer was engaged.

"That's the Super," he said.

Gavillan appeared in a second.

"Funny, I had the idea he would call. Light the hall, Flett. The place is as dark as a tomb." He went along to the telephone, sat down on the old farm chair which stood beside it. "Hullo, Mac!"

MacNeill's voice was grim.

"I've been doing a bit of research, Gavillan. I've gone with my story to the Public Prosecutor. I don't know whether he believes me or not. I've also had a word with Chief Inspector Tarr. Tarr was working on that forgery business. He thought that Delacroix and Stehfer were on that job. He swears that Delacroix did the penwork for the note. I told him the whole story, and he's inclined to believe me. I'm telling you that to keep your spirit up—not to——"

"They never were higher," Tommy said.

"What about Drake?"

"He rung up, but I was out. I haven't heard from him since."

MacNeill was silent for a moment or so.

"Well, we'll have a word with him later. I think he should

47

know what Inspector Tarr thinks." He spoke for a moment longer then hung up. Tommy Gavillan went back to the study.

MacNeill was a tower of strength at a moment like this. No matter what the crisis, the Scot was the sort of man who might be relied on to rise to the occasion. He heard Pat's light footsteps in the hall. In a moment more she pushed open the door.

"Was it Mr. Drake?"

Gavillan shook his head.

"It was Mac."

"What did he have to say?"

She listened silently while he told her, then:

"Daddy. Why should anyone want to send you to prison?"

Gavillan grinned.

"I can't tell you that. I wish I knew."

"It must have been someone around the district," she said, "and there are so few people who come here."

He ticked them off on his fingers.

"Mandell, his friend Hettche, the Dysarts, the people from Belfort, old Mrs. Klein from Blandfort, one or two folks from the village."

"And Peter Spain!"

He looked up quickly.

"Spain of course. I hadn't thought of him. You can rule him out. Him and Mandell and Hettche."

She sighed.

"If you start ruling everyone out, you'll be left with nobody at all but old Mrs. Klein, and it certainly wasn't her. She's old and crippled with rheumatism and everything else."

"That's a fact," said Tommy Gavillan.

The telephone broke the silence that followed. Pat went through to it. It was Spain who was calling, and that unpleasant young man was in a questioning mood. She had met him like this before.

"Is there any news?" he wanted to know.

"None that I know of."

"What about the lawyer from London?"

Pat sighed.

"So far he hasn't been able to tell us anything."

"Have you heard from the Scotland Yard fellow?"

She was a little exasperated.

"I can't talk about these sort of things over the 'phone,

Mr. Spain. You can't expect me to. In any event they don't concern you."

Tommy Gavillan came through to the hall.

"Who is it? Spain? I'll talk to him."

She relinquished the receiver, heard her father say:

"I thought you were coming over?"

Spain had every intention of doing so.

"It won't be for long, for I've got some business to attend to tonight. You dine early? I'll come across for coffee. I've got to go up to the City tomorrow, and I may be there for a day or two. If there's anything I can do—any inquiry I can make, all you have to do is tell me."

"We'll talk about that when you come over," Gavillan said.

Spain was agreeable.

"I won't be late." He hung up, sat on the edge of the table and looked across to where Mary Lou Slatter sat. "That's that. I'm going to pin Gavillan down tonight. The chances are I won't have another opportunity."

She sat on the arm of a chair, an orange stick in her hand. With this she poked at an offending cuticle.

"I hope you get something."

Spain shrugged.

"I'm not hopeful. That guy may never have met Cutten. Even if he did, it must have been a long time ago. The probability is he doesn't know a thing. But he's deep. Just how deep I can't tell. He had a Scotland Yard man at the house yesterday."

"How do you know that?"

"I saw him," Spain said coolly. "Pat brought him from Winchester in the brake. He was big enough to have filled a lorry."

There was a little rattle of raindrops on the mullioned windows. He rose and crossed to them, parted the heavy drapes so that he could see out over the lawn. The clouds were scudding across the sky; a watery moon cast a cold brilliance over the tree tops and he nodded approvingly at the sight of it.

"There won't be much rain. Clouds are too high for it, and there's a good moon. That will let you see the road. You branch left at Malden Mere. There's a clump of spruce trees at the fork in the road. You can't go wrong there. Don't leave before eight. I don't want you to get to Meredale Station too much ahead of the train."

"I won't," she said. "I can kill time on the way."

Spain nodded his satisfaction at this suggestion.

"You're wise. It would be just like your luck for someone to notice you, and after the job we've had, that would be a pity."

"Wouldn't it?" she said gently. "Especially if it was Lee."

He was not amused.

"Forget Lee for the moment, and listen to me. You've got the address of the hotel. Go there when you get to the City. I sent a wire in your name this afternoon. They'll be expecting you. Your cases will arrive tomorrow. If you want to get in touch with me—use the telephone. Don't do it unless you have to. You never know who might be listening in to you in these country exchanges. I don't believe in taking chances."

"You're afraid?"

His dark eyes met hers.

"Me? I'm panic stricken. How are you for money?"

She pondered.

"I've got a hundred pounds in small notes. I won't need any more than that. When shall I see you?"

"I'm going up to the City tomorrow," Spain said. "But I won't come along to the hotel. I may give you a call tomorrow night. That's not a promise." He looked up at the clock. "Now I've got to go. Time yourself on the road. If you leave here at eight o'clock you ought to be at Meredale by ten. If you like I'll send Silk along with you for part of the way."

She looked up quickly.

"Why?"

"It's a lonely road," he said slowly.

"I'm not afraid."

He frowned at her.

"That doesn't cut much ice. You've had a lot of your own way, Mary Lou. One of these days all that stops." He went across to the door. "Good night." With a nod he was gone. She heard his footsteps in the hall, then they died away and the house was silent.

It was close on seven o'clock now. She had already made a light meal in preparation for the walk which was ahead of her. She went up to her room, tidied it up, and sat down on the edge of the bed to consider her plans for the next hour or so. Spain was correct. It would not do to leave the Moorings too early. If she reached the station at Meredale any time after ten o'clock, she would be early enough. She had studied the ordnance survey map, and knew the route that she must follow. She kicked off her shoes, lay back on the bed and for almost an hour lay on top of the covers. When the hands of the clock were creeping round towards eight, she rose and prepared herself for the road.

Eight o'clock was chiming when she stepped into the hall. It was oddly silent. Of Silk there was no sign at all. Presumably that enigmatic man had retired to the fastness of his own room in the upper portion of the house. She went quietly down the hall and she had all but reached the door when the telephone rang.

She stiffened where she stood, felt her heart pounding oddly. It rang several times, then there was silence. She stood for a moment or two and wondered who had been the caller. Spain had few telephone calls. Was it possible that it had been he, himself, calling her? It was too late now to test that theory. She went out into the night.

The rain had ceased, but heavy clouds hung low in the sky. The full, watery moon silvered the tree tops, and the avenue was a strip of lemon in its light. She moved towards it, stepped on to the verge of the sodden grass and walked to the main road in the shadow of the trees. When she reached the road, she halted for a moment to listen for any sound which might suggest some movement close at hand. There was none. The night air was still and calm.

She stepped out and walked quietly along in the direction of Malden Mere. It lay some two miles along the road, a stretch of sluggish oily water, fringed with bulrushes and verged with willow scrub. For a mile or more she walked. The road swung away from Marks Malden, climbed the gentle slope behind the village, so that when she stood on the crest of the little rise, she could see the lights of Chyme Close beneath her.

For a moment she paused to rest, and as she stood there, something seemed to move on the white ribbon of road behind her. She thought a shadow edged to the side of the road, and she was instantly alert. She listened for a moment, but there was no sound of footsteps.

Again, she took the road, but by now her senses were alert. Once or twice she heard a footstep in the distance, then for a matter of moments there was silence again. She halted again under a towering oak to consider her position. It was foolish to imagine that she was being followed. Her imagination was playing her tricks. On a country road of this sort, there were bound to be occasional wanderers, each of them on an errand no more culpable than that on which she herself was employed.

When she started off again, the road seemed deserted, and although she halted once or twice to listen, no sound could be heard at all. Whoever had been on the road behind her had gone. Unaccountably, she felt a little surge of relief. She was not nervous by nature, and for the moment she was almost annoyed at her own vague fear.

Malden Mere was ahead of her now. She could see the silver sheen of the water in the moonlight. There was a little copse at the fork of the road and she approached it now. As she did so, the clouds swept over the moon so that the light of night faded eerily. She increased her stride. Once, many years before, she had watched an eclipse of the sun. She had stood on a bleak hillside in Nevada and had watched the ominous shape of the moon appear against the ball of fire. It had been a summer's day, the heat had been stinging, the rocks blistering to the touch. Then, in a moment or so it had changed. There had been a wan eerieness about it which she had never forgotten. The crickets which had filled the air with their chirruping were silent, the birds stilled, the rocks had grown bleak and cold, so that for a moment she stood alone in a dead world.

She felt like that now. There was the same eerie stillness in the air, the same silence. It was broken suddenly by a whirring sound which came upon her so suddenly that she caught her breath. Then she heard a familiar bird call, and knew that she had heard flighting duck. A second or two later and they descended on the oily surface of the Mere, and the sound of their turbulent wings on the water caught her ears. She walked onwards, a little more relaxed.

Then, as suddenly, there was a break in the clouds. The moon came through in a splash of silver. It shone across the Mere, fell aslant the road, and in the light of it, she saw someone standing on the side of the copse ahead of her!

She caught her breath. Then, as she stood there the moonlight fell across his features and she felt a finger of ice touch at her heart.

Silk!

Mary Lou Slatter stood in petrified amazement.

Silk here!

She felt a cold and horrible dread seize her: a fear that she had never known in all her life. The man had reached the shelter of the copse now. When she looked again, he was gone!

It had been Silk that she had heard behind her then. This cold and terrifying figure had followed her from the Moorings! There could be little doubt about that! Less doubt still about his motives. She began to run, and as she did so she was aware that she had left the road: that she was making for the open, moorland which lay beyond the Mere. She felt her feet sink in the wet, slimy ooze; knew that one of her shoes had dropped off. For moments she ran, then of a sudden she could run no longer. Her heart was pounding like a trip hammer, her chest was contracted so that the very act of breathing was torture for her.

She collapsed on a cold, wet heather hag. How long she lay there, she did not know. The moon had come out again; the night was calm and still, and the white, silvery road was deserted.

She drew herself together. This was folly! She was behaving like some terror-stricken girl. Her imagination had taken possession of her, had made captive her faculties. She rose shakily to her feet. When she listened there was no sound to disturb the peace of the night.

Mary Lou Slatter sighed.

"I'm a fool," she said half aloud. The very sound of her own voice was encouraging to her. "How could Silk get here! That's mad. I'm imagining things!"

She walked steadily back towards the road. For a second or two she considered. She was wet to the skin, and the one shoe that she did possess had lost its heel. Very obviously she could not proceed towards the City in such a condition. She would return to the Moorings. Tomorrow she would make another bid.

She kicked off her shoe so that she could walk with some measure of comfort on the hard flints of the road. The moon was fading again. This time there was rain in the clouds above. She felt the first cold drops of it on her face. She stepped out more quickly and as she did so she heard a footstep on the hard road behind her. In a second she swung round. The same tall, dark figure was reaching out towards her, and in that second she knew that she was already dead.

"You!" she gasped.

She saw the hard face very close to her own, then two hands with the strength of steel gripped her by the throat. The night went black and the light of the moon faded and died with her!

CHAPTER VIII

THERE came a day a week later when Tommy Gavillan rose, shaved and breakfasted with his daughter and then gave her implicit instructions before he went out to the waiting car.

"I'm glad you've got this nursing job of yours to attend to, Pat. That kind of thing makes life much easier. It keeps your mind off a lot of other things, and that's the beauty of it."

She watched him, grave-eyed. She had wanted to go up to London with him on this day, but Tommy was obdurate.

"Courts aren't pleasant places. Not for young ladies. I hope you never see the inside of one, Pat. Anyway, you're not coming to see me in the dock. I would hate that."

She made one last attempt.

"You won't change your mind, Daddy?"

He shook his head.

"Not me. A regiment of foot soldiers wouldn't make a Gavillan change his mind if he didn't want to."

She accepted this dictum.

"You'll telephone me after the—the trial?"

He chuckled gently.

"I'm not certain of that—but someone will." He rose abruptly and went out to the hall. When he came into the morning-room, he wore a light tweed overcoat and had a little case in his hand.

"That's my razor," he said humorously. "I wish they let you grow a beard. I was always fond of the Navy for that." He put his head on one side like a listening bird. "That's Flett bringing the car up. I won't keep you any longer, Pat. I'll write to you."

"Yes," she said.

He came over towards her and kissed her.

54

"That's that. It's not nearly such an ordeal as I'd figured it would be. Mac will be along to see you one of these days. If you need any help about anything you go to him. He'll see you right. He promised me that." With a nod, he turned and walked out through the corridor.

She stood very still. His footsteps sounded on the stone flags of the hall, then on the steps and on the gravel. She heard the door of the car close sharply. It started up and pulled away. The house was suddenly quiet and dead. Very slowly she walked up to her own room. There she threw herself on the bed. There were hot, blinding tears in her eyes, and a dull, dead emptiness clawed at her heart.

For a long time she lay there, then a shaft of pale, gusty sunlight fell aslant her cheek. She opened her eyes, lay for a moment or so longer, then rose. She bathed her face, powdered and went across to the window. She stood there for a long time, her eyes staring over the green lawn below. The spruce wood stretched down to the river; she saw sunlight dapple the water and her heart gave a little throb of pain.

Tommy had loved Chyme Close. Here, he had been happy, happier than he had ever been in his life. He had told her that often. Here, he had hoped to live out his days, and in those peaceful moments he had not reckoned on such a climax as this.

She went downstairs. The maid had begun to clear away the things from the table. Now she looked at the girl.

"I'll have another cup of coffee, Lena."

"Yes, Miss Pat."

The girl poured it out for her, added sugar and cream.

Pat watched her for a second or two.

"I won't be wanting lunch today, Lena. I'm going into Winchester. There are one or two things I have to do there."

When the girl had gone, she finished her coffee and went through to the study. Without the presence of Tommy, it seemed barren and bleak. His cigarette-case lay on the desk top. She lifted it, opened it and counted the cigarettes. There were seven of them left. Tommy was no smoker. He had bought that twenty a week before. She laid it down again and as she did so the telephone rang.

For one moment she wondered if this might be Superintendent MacNeill, but it was a much more ebullient individual.

Billy Mandell was excited.

"You haven't left yet, Pat? That's good, I'll come over and——"

"I'm not going up to London."

He was considerably astonished.

"Eh? How's that? I thought you wouldn't want to miss it and——"

She sighed.

"Daddy didn't want me to go."

"Oh!" He was silent for a second. "Has Tommy left?"

"Yes. He's going up by train."

He was a little offended.

"I could have taken him. He should have known I'd do that. Least a feller could do for a friend. I'll get along. I'll come in tonight and give you all the grisly details."

She hung up. Billy Mandell was no diplomat. She went through to the study and was putting the little room in order when she heard the sound of a car in the driveway. A moment later came the maid, drying her hands on her apron.

"It's Mr. Spain to see you, Miss Pat."

Spain followed her into the room.

"Good morning, Pat," he said.

The girl had gone out.

Pat looked at him gravely.

"Good morning. Was it Daddy you wanted to see?"

He shook his head.

"No, I knew Tommy had gone. I saw him at Winchester. I drove in to have a word with him." He sat down and lay back a little wearily. "I thought I'd drop in for a moment or two—just to say 'good morning', and things like that."

She smiled faintly.

"That was nice of you."

He nodded. His dark eyes seemed to have lost a lot of their insolence.

"I figured you'd be a little lonely." He groped for his pipe, filled it and looked up. "You don't mind if I smoke? Anyway, I had a little message from old Mrs. Klein over at Meredale."

Mrs. Klein was a recent friend of hers.

"Oh! What was that?"

"She wants you to come over this morning."

She hesitated.

"She didn't telephone."

Spain's dark eyes were amused.

"Her telephone is out of order. The line is down there. I came round that way from Winchester. I had occasion to call on her and she asked me to bring the message. Her arthritis is bad again. She can't move very much. The maid was carrying her downstairs when I arrived."

"Of course I'll go round."

"I could drive you over," he suggested.

She considered this.

"No. I'll take the brake. Flett has the car just now. Anyway, I'd have to come back. I meant to go into Winchester in any case."

He sighed his satisfaction.

"I'm glad you're going." His eyes met hers for a second and in them she saw something a little softer than she had ever seen there before. Then, in a second it was gone. "You'll probably be a little lonely. Tommy asked me to call." He tapped on his pipe stem with a lean, brown finger. "I want to say how sorry I am about all this, Pat. It shouldn't have happened."

There was something so measured and deliberate in his voice that she looked up.

"What do you mean?"

He took the pipe from his mouth.

"Did Gavillan tell you anything?"

"No. Only that he knew nothing about the things the police found here. Only that someone had left them there deliberately."

He nodded.

"That's true. Gavillan's a queer stick. Tommy knows more about it than he pretends." His voice was ruminative. "I'd like to get to the bottom of it myself."

She felt the colour come to her cheeks.

"Then you think he does know something about it?"

"Good heavens, no! Not in that sense. Tommy is as innocent as you are. But that's no answer to it." He took the pipe from his lips and leaned forward towards her. "I tried to get him to talk about it, but he wouldn't rise at all. I'd like to know the reason for that. I'd like to know why anybody wanted to put him away."

"There can't be a reason," she said dully.

Spain scowled.

"There's got to be. The man who did this was clever. He knew what he was doing, and he took a chance. If he'd been caught with that stuff on him he'd have got what he planned for Gavillan. That's obvious enough. A man doesn't take a chance like that unless he stands to gain a lot. This fellow must have figured it was worth the risk. I wonder why."

Pat brushed her fair hair back from her forehead.

"I hadn't thought of it like that."

He looked at her irritably.

"What other way was there in which you could think of it?"

She did not answer for a moment, then:

"Did you tell Daddy that?"

"No. I didn't need to. He knows." His eyes were puzzled. "I wonder what MacNeill thinks about it?" He looked at her as though he expected an answer. "His point of view would be valuable."

She shook her head.

"I haven't heard."

"Didn't he discuss it with you when you brought him here?"

"No. Not that." She was watching him as she spoke, noted the eagerness which underlay his apparent diffidence, then of a sudden: "Why were you watching us that day?"

He looked surprised.

"I happened to be there when you passed."

"But you crossed the Ede and came up to the house here."

His eyes were expressionless.

"Did I? What makes you think that?"

She told him bluntly.

"Someone was there. I was positive it was you. I saw that brown tweed jacket. It looked like you." Her voice was defensive.

"Mandell wears brown tweeds."

"This wasn't Billy. It was a smaller man."

He scowled.

"What about his lady-like friend?"

"Mr. Hettche? I don't think so." She looked puzzled. "I'm sorry if I was wrong. I only got a brief glimpse of the man. I'm very sorry."

He jumped up.

"Don't apologize," he said handsomely. "Anyone is liable to make a mistake. I'll have to get away now. If you hear from Tommy tonight, you'll give me a call."

58

She promised to do so, and followed him into the hall.

"I'll go over and see Mrs. Klein. It was very good of you to come over with the message."

"I'd have come anyway," he said cryptically. She watched him go out to the car, then went upstairs to dress. The brake was in the garage at the rear of the house. She went round to it and drew it out on to the driveway.

Flett came into sight as she backed out. The little man stopped the car on the avenue as they came abreast.

"Well, Miss Pat, that's that."

"Daddy got away all right?"

"As chirpy as you like," said Flett. "Joking there like he was going to a ball. What a feller Mr. Gavillan is. He sent his love to you." He shook his sober head. "A fine, fine man. Is there anything you want me to do, Miss Pat?"

"No, I don't think so. I'm going over to see Mrs. Klein." She raised her hand in salute, and drove away. In a moment more she had reached the main road, had swung on to the road which led to Meredale.

The sun was higher in the sky now, and for all the time of year there was heat in it. The spruce and pine of the woods around were blue-green in its golden balm, and the frosty air was cool and fresh on her face. She trod down on the accelerator so that the little brake found speed on the slopes and roared over the inclines.

Malden Mere lay on her left. She watched the sun glisten on its oily waters as she sped past. Above it, she met two men on the road. One of them wore tweeds, and carried a gun in the crook of his arm, while a labrador lurked at his heels.

It was Haydock, Mandell's gamekeeper. He raised a hand in salute as she drove past. In a moment more she had left the Mere behind, for the road swung high over the hill. From the crest of it she could see the red-tiled roof of Blandfort and soon she was in the short avenue which led to the house.

Blandfort was of red brick, was shambling and comfortable. The window shutters were painted white, and on the lawn that surrounded the house sheep were grazing contentedly.

Mrs. Klein was sitting by the window of the morning-room. She saw the woman as soon as she approached the house, and waved a hand in greeting, caught the older woman's smile of welcome.

In a moment more she was in the hall.

"Don't move, Mrs. Klein. I'll come through just as soon as I shake off my coat."

She came through as she spoke, tossing her fair hair about her.

Ada Klein held up her cheek to be kissed.

"So glad to see you, dear. Do sit down. Peter was a pet. I asked him to go round to see you. I knew you'd be upset today, and of course the telephone isn't working. It never is. We've had a perfectly filthy time with it recently. You'll wait for lunch?"

Pat laughed.

"Yes, I'll even do that. Afterwards I must get back."

Mrs. Klein nodded.

"Of course, of course you must." She was a thin-featured woman in her late fifties, a pleasant and voluble soul. At one time she must have been beautiful, but the crippling arthritis which bound her to the chair on which she spent her days, had left its ravaging mark on the features. Her hair was white and beautifully dressed; she tried to raise her hand to it now and failed miserably.

"This is one of my bad days. It must be all the rain that we've had. England is a bad place for my complaint, but there we can't have everything we want. Morton used to say there was no climate like the Californian climate. That was where we lived when he was alive. But I don't know. Heat is as bad for me as cold." She looked down at her fingers in exasperation. "What would you make of that. I couldn't even hold my teaspoon this morning. Braddock had to feed me. She's a treasure. I don't know what I should do without her."

Pat had met Braddock, her maid, a large and prepossessing woman. She nodded and sat down.

"Yes. She's very devoted."

Ada Klein's eyes lit up.

"She is indeed. A perfect gem. She's been with me for years. I picked her up by accident in a little place out in Arkansas." She sighed as she leaned back in her chair. "I don't suppose I'll ever see Arkansas again. Not that it matters much. Tell me about your father, Pat. I know you must be worried."

Pat Gavillan frowned.

"There isn't much to tell."

"Of course not." The older woman was indignant. "But it has all been a mistake. You'll see that I'm correct. The police are always making mistakes of some sort. This is just another of their blunders."

Pat had been staring out of the window as she spoke. Of a sudden she leaned forward.

"Who is that man, Mrs. Klein? I—I thought he was watching the house." She flushed a little. "That sounds silly."

Mrs. Klein followed her pointing finger.

To the left of the house, the ground rose swiftly to a tree-covered knoll. A pathway skirted this, and there was indeed someone moving about. A tall, thin man, who carried in his hand a pair of field glasses. She saw him raise them to his eyes. Then, of a sudden he disappeared from view and there was only the green of the pine wood.

"How peculiar!" Mrs. Klein said.

The door of the room opened as she spoke.

Braddock came in. She was a tall, flat-featured woman, of forty. Her frame was large and awkward, the hands which held a small silver tray might have been the hands of a workman.

"Your medicine, ma'am."

Ada Klein took the two tiny capsules slowly, lifted them to her mouth and swallowed them without effort.

"Thank you, Braddock." She looked at the big woman. "We saw a man on the path in front of the house just now, Braddock."

The big woman nodded.

"Yes. He's been there off and on all week. There and in the wood. I saw him up at the Bailiff's Gate, and at the wood. An oldish man with glasses. He's looking for something, I guess." She was silent for a second, then added, "Or for someone."

Mrs. Klein frowned.

"Most extraordinary. You've seen him before?"

"A dozen times," Braddock said patiently. "He's harmless enough, although it surprised me to see him here."

The older woman looked up at her with some interest.

"Then you know him?"

Braddock nodded impassively.

"Yes, I know him. He's Mr. Spain's manservant. They say he's deaf and dumb. I don't know about that—his name is Silk!"

CHAPTER IX

"Silk!"

Mrs. Klein's voice was interested. "How extraordinary. And a deaf mute too. I wasn't aware of that. You say he is Mr. Spain's servant."

Braddock indicated that this was the case.

"They say he's a very quiet man."

"Naturally," said Mrs. Klein. "Poor fellow. And poor Peter. So awkward in every way for him. I wonder what he wants around here."

Braddock was not prepared to offer a suggestion. She made her way to the door, the tray still held in her large hand.

"Lunch will be ready in five minutes, ma'am."

It was a little longer than that before they sat down for Ada Klein had insisted that the dining-room should be used in honour of her guest.

"Usually I have a tray lunch," she said. "It's such a bore, but it makes things easier for Braddock. You have to consider your help nowadays, and of course Braddock deserves consideration."

They sat in the large and comfortable dining-room under the stern and admonishing gaze of a man in armour who gazed down upon them from an oil painting above. Mrs. Klein was not enamoured of it and said so.

"It was there when I took the house from the Humbles," she explained. "I wanted to take it down, but Mrs. Hughes Humble was very upset at the thought. I think it was her great grandfather or someone like that. Someone very dear to her."

Pat was a little amused.

"I doubt it, unless she was a very old lady indeed. I don't think that men wore that sort of thing even in Mrs. Humble's great-grandfather's time."

"Probably not," Ada Klein said. She brought the conversation round to something that was apparently of more interest to her.

"I wonder what poor Silk was looking for?"

Pat could offer no suggestion at all.

"It's a remarkable thing," said Ada Klein, "but I knew a

deaf mute once. It was in the States too. He was a doctor and a very clever one too. Morton thought a great deal of him indeed."

Pat looked up interested.

"You've spent a lot of your life in the States, Mrs. Klein?"

The older woman nodded. She was silent for a little, then:

"Yes, I was born there—and married there too."

Pat was intrigued.

"I'm almost surprised to hear that. I could have believed that you were English."

Mrs. Klein smiled. It was evident that she was pleased.

"Quite a lot of people have made that remark. No, I was born there. But of course you are not interested in the life of an old woman."

When lunch was over, Braddock made her appearance, and Mrs. Klein permitted herself to be carried back to her chair.

"I could walk," she said, "but it's so painful and takes so long. Braddock doesn't mind. She's strong, tremendously strong."

There seemed every reason to believe that this was indeed the case. The big woman bore her through with effortless ease. Then, when they were seated again, Mrs. Klein sighed.

"I suppose you'll be going back to your nursing, Pat?"

The girl nodded.

"Yes, I—I may wait for a day or so. I've got a job in hand at the moment. Anyway, if Daddy goes away I don't want to be here."

"You wouldn't like to stay at Chyme Close?"

"Not by myself."

Mrs. Klein gave a little laugh.

"Your father will come back again. Bless me, I wouldn't even worry about that. The police are always making mistakes. They sent Morton a summons once for parking by a fire-hydrant and it transpired it wasn't even his car at all. There's no end of the silly mistakes they make. You take my word for that."

The girl smiled.

"That would be in America, Mrs. Klein."

"Police are police the world over," the woman said, then: "Have you seen Mr. Mandell recently?"

"Billy? I spoke to him on the telephone this morning."

"A pleasant young man," said Ada Klein. "He has a friend living with him just now. Hetty his name is."

63

" Hettche," Pat said. "I've met him twice. A nice, quiet sort of man. He doesn't have much to say."

Ada Klein was prepared to agree.

"That was my opinion. I said as much to Mr. Mandell. You can always speak quite freely to him. He's so understanding. Anyway, he only laughed. He said that Mr. Hettche was a woman-hater and that he kept clear of female company, but that he had always plenty to say at home."

Pat was amused.

"That may be true. He came to Dad's card party, but I think Billy bullied him into it. I remember that he sat by himself most of the night and read a book."

The old grandfather clock began to chime. Ada Klein looked up.

"Two-thirty! I had no idea that the day was so far advanced. Now I have to get more pills. Horrible. Take care of your health while you have it, my dear."

Braddock came in as she spoke. There was a tray in her hand, with a small bottle, a teaspoon and a glass of water. She measured out a dose, administered it and held the glass to the older woman's lips, then: "Will you be wanting tea to be served here, Mrs. Klein?"

Pat sighed.

"I'll have to be going now. I hate to run, but it's most necessary. You have your tea here on your tray as usual." She jumped up, kissed the older woman's cheek.

Braddock had retreated as far as the door. There was an odd little glint of amusement in her dark eyes. It faded in a second, but the girl felt a sensation of uneasiness touch her.

Ada Klein was smiling.

"I won't try to detain you, Pat. It was so good of you to come over to see me. Anyway, you won't forget to come back. I'm a very lonely old woman—but of course you know that."

"Yes, I'll come back," Pat said, "and soon. Good afternoon, Mrs. Klein." She went out into the hall to where Braddock was standing.

"Mrs. Klein doesn't seem quite so well today, but I suppose it's the weather."

The big woman agreed. She had a deep but pleasing voice.

"Yes, it's the weather. With all the rain we've had you couldn't expect anything else." She went across to the door and as she did so the 'phone rang so suddenly that the girl started.

For a second she looked up at the servant in surprise.

"I thought the telephone was out of order."

Braddock nodded placidly.

"They've been working on the line this last day or so. It must be fixed now. Pardon me, miss. It may be a call."

Pat went out to the car thoughtfully. She was still puzzling the incident as she drove down the avenue towards the main road. The afternoon was changing now. The sun was sliding down into the West and long, grey shadows stretched already over the moorland. The woods were hushed and still and the whisper of night was in the air. To the left of her was a ploughed field, the long rows of pitted potatoes nearly flanking the roadway. She watched half a dozen brownish shapes pick their way from the base of them, and realized that Billy Mandell's pheasants were feeding before making for their roosting quarters in Malden Court.

She had travelled for more than a mile when ahead of her on the road she saw a tall, stooped figure, walking along in the direction of Marks Malden. The man did not look round as she approached, then, when she was close to him, she recognized the figure she had seen on the path above Blandfort. This was Silk, Peter Spain's peculiar manservant. She was about to swing clear of him, when of a sudden she was seized with an odd impulse. Instead, she drew up and pointed to the road ahead.

Silk stood rigid, then she saw recognition in his eyes. He removed his hat and nodded courteously. She saw that he was an older man than she had imagined him to be, that his features were sere and lined. She indicated the seat at her side and it was evident that the man understood what was in her mind. For a second he hesitated, then she saw him smile.

She leaned across, opened the door and waited until he had taken the seat behind her. Then she started up again.

"Can you understand me, Silk?"

He was aware that she was speaking, but she saw him shake his head. He laid one finger on his lips and shook his head.

She took the hill that led to Malden Mere. From the summit, it lay a stretch of water copper-coloured in the sun glow. Behind it the woods of Malden were green and blue black, and the grey mists of evening rose like smoke in the night air.

She was little more than half-way down the long incline that led to the water when she saw someone crossing the soft, mud-filled marsh at a lumbering trot. The man was coming towards the road, his arms signalling as he came.

Silk had noticed him too. She felt the man touch at her sleeve, saw that there was some interest in his lean features. She nodded to him, and turned her eyes back to the road. Where it touched the fringe to the marsh, the man had halted, and she recognized him now as Haydock, the gamekeeper. His companion was still at the water's edge. He was standing ankle deep among the reeds, his eyes turned towards the road.

Pat applied the brake and drew up beside the gamekeeper. The man was breathless from his exertion, and she saw perspiration on his forehead. He put up his hand and wiped it away.

"Miss Gavillan"—his voice was a thick gasp—"it's a good job you came along!" He licked his lips. "Derry and me were——"

"What's wrong?" she asked quickly.

He pointed back towards the water.

"There's a body there . . . a woman! She's been drowned." He swallowed as he looked at her. "It was the dog that found her. I wondered what was troubling him for——"

She stared at him.

"A woman?"

"Yes, she's dead. I was hoping someone would come along. I'm sorry it had to be you, miss. It's very upsetting, but if you would drive into the village and tell Pitman——"

She got out of the car.

"Of course. But is there anything I can do?"

The man shook his head.

"No, miss. She's been dead for days by the look of her."

"Is she a local?"

He rubbed at his unshaven cheek.

"I don't think so. Never saw her before in my life!"

Pat walked across the stretch of rough, rank grass. She was vaguely conscious that Silk was following at her heels.

Haydock caught up with her.

"It isn't a nice thing to look at, Miss Gavillan."

"I've seen death often enough before," she said quietly. "Anyway, I'd better have a look before I fetch Pitman. The police will want all sorts of details."

Haydock protested the requirements of the police strongly. "That don't need to trouble a lady like you, miss. Anyway, it's all bog an' marsh an' water. You'll get soaked getting there. It's up to your——" He coughed awkwardly. "Deep enough, anyway."

She ploughed through a morass of water weed and moss. The footing was rough and uncertain, and the icy touch of the bog water reached the calves of her legs, climbed to her knees. Then, of a sudden they were on a strip of dry land, studded with stones and heather hags.

Derry was standing in front of her. He was the local carpenter, a ruddy little man, who had lost much of his colour in the presence of hideous death. He had already removed his cap. Now he looked up at her with grave eyes.

"Well, miss. A bad, bad job. Poor lady, she's been drowned, though how it happened, heaven only knows."

The woman was lying at the edge of the water. They had drawn her on to dry land, and she lay there, wan and white in the fading light of day. Her hair was long and lank. The black tresses straggled across the dry, cold stones of the banking.

Derry coughed.

"She's a stranger to me, miss. I don't suppose you know her."

Pat Gavillan shook her head.

"I don't. I've never seen her before. She certainly isn't a local person. She looks like someone from the City. Her clothing is well cut and expensive. That dress was——" She stopped abruptly.

Silk had reached the group now. She saw him stare down at the dead woman with anxious eyes. For one brief second recognition fired in them. Then it was gone and his lean features were blank and impassive. She did not speak, but in that second she knew that unknown though she might be to Marks Malden, the woman who lay dead was no stranger to Peter Spain's manservant.

CHAPTER X

FOR a moment Silk stood still, his eyes searching the white, drawn face. Then he stepped backwards almost deferentially.

Haydock had noticed nothing.

"You don't know her?"

The servant may not have heard the question, but he most certainly understood its import. He shook his head slowly.

Pat looked at the gamekeeper.

"I'll drive you back to the village, Haydock. Derry can wait. We won't be any more than ten minutes."

The gamekeeper agreed and they returned to the car. They drove into Marks Malden and drew up in front of the police station. Police-Constable Pitman occupied a comfortable little modern bungalow, to which a small garage was attached. In this was his motor-cycle and he was engaged in polishing it up when they arrived. He came out to the gate to meet them, a large and genial man, big-shouldered and bald from forehead to occiput. He raised his hand to his head as he came forward.

"Well, Miss Gavillan, nothing wrong, I hope?"

"There's been an accident," the girl said. "It's Haydock's story. I'll let him tell it."

The constable held open the gate.

"You'd better come inside then. What is it?"

Haydock cleared his throat.

"It's a woman—drowned in the Mere."

Pitman was astounded.

"That's a bad affair. When did it happen? Did you see her go in?"

Pat shook her head.

"She's been in the water for several days. I was coming back from Blandfort and Haydock stopped me."

The policeman took them into the small charge-room.

"Sit down here, miss." He brought in a chair for her. "Now, Haydock."

The man's story was plain enough. He and Derry had been in the Low Wood behind Malden Court for a shot at pigeons, but they had had little luck. They had decided to return by way of the Mere to have a shot at the duck.

68

"They come in from five o'clock on," the keeper said. "We thought we'd get there early and pick out a dry corner for ourselves. It's a cold job at the best of times. Anyway, we just got to the Low corner when old Balty started acting funny. He's a wise old feller and as quiet as a mouse usually, but he kept on whimpering and growling and he wouldn't sit at peace. He got up and made off for the water and when he got there, he started to bark. I went after him and there she was —lying in to the edge." He mopped his forehead. "We better be getting back. Derry won't enjoy his job and it's getting pretty dark. If you've got a pair of gum boots you'd better bring them for there's a lot of water lying about."

Pitman asked no more questions.

"I'll 'phone through to Sergeant Tooke. Like as not he'll come over at once." He crossed to the telephone and put through a call. When he was finished, he looked round. "We'll go over on my bike. You'll want to get home as quickly as you can, Miss Gavillan. Anyway, there's no reason why you should wait."

The girl agreed.

"I'd like to change. I'm pretty wet. I've got Silk out in the brake."

Pitman blinked.

"Mr. Spain's man. The deaf and dumb gentleman. I've seen him around a bit. He's a great walker. Where does he come in?"

She told him where she had picked up Silk.

"Of course. He probably was out for a walk. He's on the road a lot in all sorts of weather." He accompanied her out to the car. "Thank you for driving over with Haydock, miss. It was very good of you. We'll just manage over now before darkness."

She got into the car and drove off. Silk was watching her, on his thin features a glance of inquiry. She pointed in the direction of the Moorings and he nodded his understanding. In a matter of moments she was approaching the house. The avenue was ill-kept and dilapidated, the gutters choked with rank and poisonous beech leaves.

She drew up at the front door, and Silk opened the door of the car and stepped out. As he did so she heard a voice from the opposite side of the car.

"Hullo, Pat. I didn't expect company."

Spain came round the gable of the house and approached them. He was bare-headed, a pipe clenched firmly between his teeth. His dark eyes were puzzled, almost inquiring. She saw him look at Silk and the servant's hands came up.

Spain took the pipe from his mouth.

"Silk wants me to thank you for your kindness," he said. He nodded to the man and Silk withdrew. Spain was still watching her. "Where did you pick him up?"

"This side of Blandfort." She hesitated for a second, then: "He was there this afternoon. We saw him close to the house."

Spain nodded and unconsciously plagiarized Police-Constable Pitman.

"He's a great walker."

"He seems to be," she said drily. "They've seen him around quite a lot recently. Braddock was telling me that."

"Probably so. He hasn't any company, and I'm not much trouble to him. He has a lot of time off and most of it he spends wandering around the countryside. He's a most polite old fellow, but the very fact that he isn't able to talk to people makes them suspect him. I hope Mrs. Klein wasn't annoyed though."

"No, I don't think so. She seemed more surprised than annoyed."

"I'll explain things to her on the first occasion I have to go over."

She looked at him thoughtfully.

"You could 'phone her." She saw his eyes narrow. "Yes, I mean that. Her telephone is in order now."

He nodded calmly.

"They get around to fixing these things. I'll do that, Pat." He looked back towards the house. "I won't ask you to come inside. You'll probably be most anxious to get home."

"I am," she said, then: "We had a most unpleasant happening on the way back."

"What was that?"

She was watching him closely as she spoke.

"Haydock stopped us by Malden Mere. He was very upset. He and Derry had just found the body of a woman."

She heard him draw in his breath.

"The body of a woman! Good heavens, Pat! Where was——"

"She had been drowned," the girl said. "In the Mere. I saw

70

her—a young woman. I think she must have been beautiful in life."

He stood rigid, but for the moment he had averted his face. When he spoke his voice was level enough.

"That was horrible. Did you know her?"

"No. She was a stranger to me. Indeed, nobody knew her unless it was Silk."

She knew that his hard eyes were fixed steadily on her own.

"Silk? Surely not. Why do you say that?"

She smiled calmly.

"I mean that all of us were able to deny that we knew her except Silk. It wasn't possible to get his opinion."

For a second he did not speak. When he did she sensed the relief that was in his voice.

"Of course. I see what you mean. I'll see him at once." With a nod he swung round on his heel and made for the house. He heard the car start up. It was on the bend of the drive when he went into the library.

Silk was standing by the fire, and his thin features were alert. He raised his fingers, manipulated them for a moment, and the younger man stood still. When the servant had completed his information, Spain nodded, and the man went out of the room.

There was a decanter at hand. From it Peter Spain poured out a glass. He sat down with it in his hand, drank it over and stared into the dull, red heart of the fire. Then he sighed and rose to go.

Mary Lou Slatter was as much an embarrassment in death as she had been a problem in life!

His own car was in the garage at the rear of the house. He went out to it and drove to Malden Mere. It was dark by the time he arrived there, but two cars had been drawn up by the roadside and from the road he could see lights moving about on the marsh. He concluded that a stretcher party was returning with the body, and he was correct in his surmise, for they were approaching the road as he drew up. He got out of the car and watched them traverse the last few yards.

Pitman and a uniformed man unknown to him were in the lead. In the rear he saw the raw-boned figure of Haydock, and it was to the gamekeeper that he spoke.

"Well, Haydock, you've had an unpleasant experience."

The man peered through the darkness.

"Mr. Spain? Yes, sir, we have indeed."

Pitman had stepped on to the road. Now they laid down their burden for a moment, and the constable wiped the perspiration from his forehead.

"It's warm work, sir—even on a cold night. Your man would tell you about the—the accident?"

"Miss Gavillan told me about it first. I questioned Silk. It's not easy to get a great deal out of him. He is naturally upset."

The policeman nodded.

"I don't wonder at it, poor feller. Still, it isn't likely your man would be able to give us much information about her. She isn't a local at all. I've never seen her in my life before."

Spain looked down at the dark bundle at his feet.

"Do you mind if I have a look at her?"

"Certainly not, sir. She's not marked badly." The constable bent over and drew back the rubber sheeting which covered Mary Lou Slatter. He held a light in one hand as he did so.

Spain looked down at her steadily for the space of a full minute. His cold eyes took in the discolouration around the dead woman's throat. Long immersion in the water had probably obliterated some of the signs of violent death which she must have borne. He turned away, knew the policeman's inquiring gaze was upon him.

"No. She's a stranger to me. Poor woman."

He watched them lift her into the waiting van. Then:

"There's nothing I can do to help, Pitman?"

The constable coughed.

"If you would be good enough to drive Derry into the village, Mr. Spain, I would be very much obliged. The van and the car are going through Meredale and I can only manage Haydock."

"Certainly," Spain said. "Good night, then." He walked across to his car, Derry at his heels. The little man was a silent passenger and it was easy to suppose that the events of the evening had been an ordeal for him. He said as much as he got out of the car and proffered voluble thanks for transport.

"I'm very pleased to have the obligement, sir. It was very good of you. I had about enough of it out there. I'm past the age for these kind of capers an' I'm wet to the 'ips."

"Take a good stiff glass of rum and get to bed," said Spain, and the carpenter agreed that this was the line of action he had been intending to follow in any case.

Spain drove through the village slowly. There was an oddly

speculative glint in his dark eyes, as he considered this new predicament which had arisen. There would be trouble now—and trouble of a sort which he did not wish to encounter. The police would institute an inquiry which could only lead to embarrassment so far as he was concerned. He was nearing Chyme Close now, and of a sudden he swung to the driveway and bore down upon the house.

There were lights in the library. He saw the cheerful glow of a log fire as he crossed towards the door. He touched the bell, pushed the door open and met Flett coming towards him. The servant was pleased to welcome him.

"Well, Mr. Spain, come right in. Miss Pat's in the library. I figure she's pretty upset about things."

"There's been no word from London yet?"

Flett scowled.

"Not a word. You'd think Mr. Gavillan would have got a call through by this time. Him or Super." He scratched at his head. "It fair beats me. The last thing he said was he'd call." He nodded towards the door. "You know your way, Mr. Spain. I'll take your coat."

For a second Spain hesitated, then shook it off.

"Thanks, Flett." He pushed open the library door and stepped into the room, his eyes circling it. At first he thought it was empty, then he sensed a movement from the opposite side of a high-backed chair. He coughed.

"Who's that?"

Pat Gavillan's voice sounded a little husky.

Spain walked across towards her.

"It's me. I thought I'd come in for a moment. You've had no word, Flett says."

She looked up at him. In that second she was a very little girl, her eyes red-rimmed with weeping.

"No, not yet. It's almost seven o'clock. I can't understand it. It isn't like Daddy. He promised me he would 'phone." She changed the subject abruptly. "What about Silk?"

Spain dropped into a chair.

"I questioned him. Of course he knows nothing about the woman. He never saw her before in his life."

She looked up at him silently. He was smiling, but there was no mirth in his smile.

"I went along myself to see if I could be of any help. I had a look at her too."

"Did you recognize her?" Her voice sounded hard in her own ears.

Spain shook his head.

"No, I've never seen her before. A person couldn't forget a woman like that. Quite young, I'd say she was—pretty too. No. She was a stranger to me—and to everyone else. That's rather queer. How did a stranger happen to be in the vicinity of Malden Mere—and why should she find her way into it?"

Pat looked into the heart of the fire.

"That's difficult to say. I suppose the police will make inquiries. They're quite good at that routine sort of work."

He nodded without enthusiasm.

The telephone rang out abruptly and he saw the girl go white. She came to her feet very slowly.

"That will be—for me!"

She went out of the room. And Peter Spain walked to the fire and stood with his back towards it, his eyes on the door. Then, after a long, long time he heard her returning. She walked very slowly, her footsteps, lingering, dragging almost. The door opened and she stood framed in it, her features white as alabaster.

Spain said very softly:

"Well?"

She shook her head.

"I—I can't believe it."

"Was it Gavillan?"

Her eyes came up to meet his and in them was triumph.

"No. It was Superintendent MacNeill. Daddy appeared in court this afternoon . . . before Mr. Justice Beaufort. There was a flaw in the indictment. The case was dismissed on a technicality!"

CHAPTER XI

IT WAS close on noon next day when Tommy Gavillan arrived at Chyme Court, a highly amused man. He met his daughter on the doorstep, kissed her and grinned.

"I told you I'd be back, Pat. Did I or did I not?"

"You did."

He nodded complacently.

"There you go. The luck of the Irish. That proves it. I'm going to drink to my own success, lassie." He led the way into the library, poured out a drink and sat down to consider it.

She leaned against her chair and he drew her down on to his knee and held her there for a long moment.

"Don't tell me you were worried, Pat."

She shivered.

"I was. An awful lot."

He chuckled.

"Not me. I never worry. Not nowadays. Why should I? It's bad for the blood pressure. A doctor feller I met in York told me once he'd known a patient's blood pressure to jump sixty inches or notches or points or whatever they call it, just because he got mad at a feller. That was enough for me." He patted her hand. "Cool as a cucumber, that's me. The only other feller who was as cool was Mac."

She laughed.

"Was he glad?"

Gavillan winked at her.

"You never can tell. Mac never shows his feelings. That's with being a Scotsman." He scratched at his ear. "I wonder if he had a hand in it. Him and Drake between them. The judge too. I wouldn't put it past them to work a fiddle in the interests of justice. The Prosecutor didn't look at all upset." He sighed deeply. "There you go. I'm a suspicious old goat. Mandell was in the court. He was beaming all over his face and made more noise than an end man in a Minstrel show. It's a wonder they didn't run him in for contempt. You've got to be careful in these here courts. They're liable to pinch you for anything to get the money off you. The government's that hard up."

She slid to her feet.

"I'll go through and see about lunch. Lena's so excited."

He watched her go. When he was alone, he poured another drink. Then made his way through to the study. He had brought his little case back with him. Now he opened it and took out an envelope. For a second or two he stared at it then went to work on the door of the safe. When it swung open, he dropped the envelope inside. He was about to close the door when something took his eye, and of a sudden he stiffened.

In front of him was a small metal cash box. The lock had been forced years ago, for he had a habit of mislaying keys, and he had secured it since that date with a length of white tape, held by a reefer knot. There was no reefer knot now!

He unwound the tape, opened the box and examined its contents. They were, so far as he knew, intact. He closed the box and turned his attention to the interior of the safe. For ten minutes he went through its contents and at the end of that time he was satisfied that it had been opened in his absence.

He made his way back to the library and was sitting there, his eyes half closed when Pat returned.

"That's that. It was a blessing I went through, Lena forgot the stuffing for the fowl."

He was shocked.

"Imagine that! On this day of all days." He looked at her pensively. "By the way, Pat, I didn't leave you the key of the safe, did I?"

"No." She looked surprised. "Have you lost it?"

He scratched his head.

"Not exactly. But you know what I'm like with keys. I'll find it in one of my other suits." He lay back comfortably. "Had any company while I was away?"

"Only Peter Spain."

He was interested.

"When was this?"

"He came over just after you had gone yesterday. He came back again at night. He didn't wait very long either time."

"I see. What did you do with yourself?"

She laughed.

"I wasn't even lonely. Peter came in to tell me that Mrs. Klein wanted me to go over to Blandfort in the afternoon. Her telephone was out of order and she couldn't 'phone. He'd been there for a moment in the morning."

"And you went?"

"Yes. And stayed for lunch. I didn't get back until late. Something horrible happened."

"What was that?"

"A woman was found drowned in the Mere. Haydock found her when he was out shooting. He stopped me on the road." She told him of the incident, and he listened with interest.

"A stranger, eh? That's queer. You don't get many strangers around these parts. Especially strange women. I wonder how she got up there?"

She could give no answer to this at all.

"It was horrible. Poor soul, she must have gone off the road, she wore a coat, but her shoes were gone. They must have dropped off in the water."

Gavillan frowned.

"Maybe so. You say she was young?"

Pat reflected.

"It wasn't easy to tell. She might have been thirty-five or so. Dark and rather striking. She wore ear-rings—green pendant ear-rings. At least, she wore one. The other was missing."

Tommy Gavillan stiffened.

"Green pendant ear-rings!" He shook his head. "A bad, bad business. Well, the police will attend to the affair and they're welcome to it. Is that the lunch gong I hear?"

It was indeed the lunch gong. They went through to it and enjoyed the excellent meal which had been prepared for them. When it was over they retired to the library for coffee and here they had a visitor.

Billy Mandell had arrived a few moments earlier, was in an ecstatic frame of mind, insisted on shaking hands with Gavillan again and thumped him on his broad shoulders.

"What a feller! Tommy, you've got all the luck in the world! I could have shouted for joy when the feller next to me told me what the judge was talking about!"

"You did!" Gavillan said.

Mandell denied the imputation.

"Not me. I reckon I know how to behave myself in a court of law. I've been before the Beaks twice. Doing seventy in a built-up area." He swore in a fury of recollection. "I can mind my Ps and Qs when I have to. I could have hugged old Drake. What a feller! Imagine him thinking all that up off his own bat, an' proving the law was wrong. It just goes to show a feller doesn't know where he stands in this country."

Tommy Gavillan laughed.

"Something like that. Have a drink?"

Mandell was agreeable.

"Anything but coffee. If it's whisky just give me a spot you could put in your eye. I'll tell you when to stop."

He was singularly lax in his doing so and Gavillan filled the glass with professional dexterity.

"There you are."

"We'll drink to your luck," said Mandell. He raised the glass. "Here's hoping you don't get caught again, Gavillan." He drained it dry, wiped his lips on a white linen handkerchief. "That's that. All the papers are full of it. There's a screed in the *Eastern Monitor* and another in the *Tribune-Examiner*."

Gavillan looked at his watch. "I'm going to leave you now. I've got a little business to attend to in Winchester. I won't be any longer than I can help."

Pat was dismayed.

"You're not rushing away, Daddy?"

He patted her head.

"I am—but I'll be back. If it wasn't important I wouldn't go away like this—but business is business."

"That's true," Mandell said earnestly. "My lawyer is always telling me that. Come over one of these days, Tommy. We'll have to arrange a spree of some sort. This calls for a celebration."

Gavillan pondered.

"I'll think about it. I like to do my celebrating at home." With a laugh he left them and made his way to the hall. When Flett appeared:

"Get the car out, Flett. I'm going into Winchester."

He went up to his room. When he came down again, Flett had brought the car round and was standing by it, wiping the windscreen with a chamois duster. He looked round.

"There you are, sir. As clean as a new pin. Look at the polish. You could see your face in her, she's that clean."

Gavillan nodded.

"You weren't using the car yesterday then, Flett?"

The little man reflected.

"Well, sir, I was. I had to go into Winchester in the afternoon and Miss Pat had the brake. It was an emergency, if you know what I mean. A feller rung up an' said I was wanted at the Hants County Hospital; said my brother was in there."

Gavillan was interested.

"You've got a brother? And was he there?"

Flett shook his head in disgust.

"Not a hair of him. It was a joke. Some fellers have got a funny idea of a joke. Anyway, they never even heard of Sid. I came back right away, but I was annoyed, for it was Lena's half-day an' the fires was out. I had to light the three of them when I came back."

"Tough luck," said Gavillan. He climbed into the car and on

the road to town, pondered on the implications of this new set of circumstances. Flett's call to town had been arranged to coincide with Pat's visit to Mrs. Klein. That had meant the house was empty. It was a purely fortuitous circumstance that the maid's day off should fall on the same afternoon. That had meant there was no danger of discovery at all. Flett must have been gone for at least two hours—had probably been longer than that. In two hours, a capable man could have opened a much more formidable safe than his own.

It was late afternoon when he reached the County town, and once there he drove to the Police Mortuary, parked his car in front of the building and went inside.

When an attendant appeared, he nodded to the man.

"Name of Gavillan. I live out at Marks Malden. You had a body brought in from Malden Mere yesterday."

The man pushed open a door.

"Come in here, sir. That's correct. What did you say your name was now? Havilland?"

"Gavillan," said Tommy. He spelled it for him.

The attendant went out. In a moment he returned with a tall, lean individual in blue serge, and about this stranger with his scrupulously clean collar, his clipped moustache, and his recent haircut, there was everything that went to suggest a sergeant in the Brigade of Guards.

Tommy looked at him humorously.

"Police?"

The man agreed.

"Yes, sir. Detective-Sergeant Tight." He pondered for a moment. "You're Mr. Gavillan? The one who's been in the papers lately. I wondered about that."

"I'm the lucky one," said Tommy. There was a certain weariness in his voice. "I hope this don't mean it's going to start all over again, Tight!"

The policeman coughed.

"You wanted to see the woman who'd been brought in from Malden Mere, Jenks said."

"That's correct. My daughter was there when they found her. She gave them a little bit of help, for she had the car there at the time."

Tight nodded.

"That's correct, sir. I heard there was a young lady." He led the way through a narrow door. "This way, Mr. Gavillan.

79

It isn't a nice place this, but it serves its purpose. There you are. That's the lady."

Gavillan stared down into the dead face. For a long, long moment he stood there, then he averted his gaze, and the attendant covered the woman's features. He was conscious that Tight was watching him closely, then:

"Do you know her?"

Gavillon shook his head.

"No, I don't."

"You've never seen her before?"

"She's a stranger," Gavillan said with decision. "I told my daughter I'd come in and have a look at her. A young woman too. Queer how she should get up to the Mere like that!"

Detective-Sergeant Tight agreed.

"It's queer indeed. I wish you had known her, sir. We haven't found out anything about her at all. Her picture will be in the papers tonight. You'll see it there for a week. Murder's a bad business."

Gavillan stared.

"Murder!"

Tight nodded. His hard eyes were on those of the Irishman.

"Murder, sir. You didn't know that? She was dead before she was put into the water. They did a p.m. this morning. There was no water in her lungs. She was murdered all right. Dr. Blake says she was strangled. You didn't see the bruises on her throat. I didn't pull the sheet down far enough."

Gavillan stood very still.

"Murder! That's a horrible thing. I didn't suspect that. Well, you'll have your work cut out to do anything with that!"

"That's my opinion too," said Tight wearily.

Gavillan smiled grimly.

"I wish you luck in your job." He went out to his car, a thoughtful man. He had driven as far as the old Guildhall when he saw a paper boy. Of a sudden he stopped the car and tossed out a sixpence.

He took the newspaper, opened it out. Sure enough, in the centre of the front page was a photograph of the woman at whom he had been looking. Tight's prediction had been true. Under the crude harsh photograph was the blunt sentence:

DO YOU KNOW THIS WOMAN?

He read a little more, then:

> *Information which may lead to identification should be communicated to the Chief Constable at Police Headquarters.*

He frowned grimly, and was about to toss the sheet into the back of the car when something in the adjacent column caught his eye. He looked at it and read:

DAYLIGHT ROBBERY IN HATTON GARDEN

DIAMONDS VALUED AT £80,000 STOLEN

Then, a little farther down:

AGAIN CORPORAL VIOLET

For a second or two Tommy Gavillan stared.
Again Corporal Violet!
He smiled grimly. Corporal Violet was clever. They called him the cleverest criminal since Coleman Streeter—the Napoleon of Crime. Perhaps they were correct. He drove away, his blue eyes narrowed in thought. Matters were coming to a head here. One of these days there was going to be a shock for someone, and the blow could not fail to strike close to Marks Malden, for that the woman who lay in the bleak, grey mortuary, was the woman who had stood behind the mullioned windows of the Moorings and watched him drive up with Peter Spain, he was very, very certain.

CHAPTER XII

THERE was a conference at Scotland Yard that morning, and the Commissioner was in the chair. Colonel Cameron was a large and formidable man, and he filled it excellently in every sense of the word. With him sat Superintendent Gale, who had broken the Riek gang and hanged Peter Riek for his sins; Superintendent Telfer who had taken Otto Liebler, prince of bank robbers; Chief Inspector Kyle, terror of race-track gangs and the strong-arm boys, and certain other outstanding and notable officers of the Metropolitan Police Force, who in their aggregate would have been a nightmare of hideous proportions to that element among the citizenry, who had cause to love them least.

Superintendent MacNeill had not appeared when the meeting began, for the conference was an emergency one, and he was engaged in an investigation of his own on the premises of Zaron and Boaz, of Hatton Garden. It was late when he appeared; most of the conversation was over, but Colonel Cameron eyed him grimly.

"Well, Superintendent, what do you think of it?"

MacNeill finished lighting his pipe. He glanced round the long table at his colleagues, then nodded.

"The Divisional man was right. It was Corporal Violet. I'd stake my pension on that. The technique was perfect. There were six men involved. Zaron was the only member of the firm who had a key to the vault. They waited for him to arrive, and forced him to open up. There was a lot of stuff there, but they didn't take it all. Zaron says that the fellow who did the selecting knew as much about diamonds as he did. He didn't waste a second and the stuff he rejected was all poor."

"What about identification?"

MacNeill shrugged.

"These fellows wore nylon stockings over their faces. Zaron couldn't tell you what any of them looked like at all. Neither could any of the staff. The whole thing was over in a matter of fifteen minutes."

Superintendent Gale nodded.

"That's Corporal Violet without a doubt. They're slick workers. The slickest known. They always use these silk stockings to cover their faces. I tried one on myself and it's ideal for the job. It doesn't impair your vision at all, and nobody can recognize you. A long way better than a mask that could be knocked off in a struggle."

"That's true," agreed Kyle. "Anyway, Corporal Violet works according to the book. They worked just like that on the Jefferson steal, and on the Simla Bank job."

The Commissioner tapped out his pipe.

"Well, we'll meet again in three days' time. We've got to get Corporal Violet—and we've got to get him soon. The
82

Home Secretary yarned me for an hour about him this morning. He's in a hell of a mood, for they gave him a roasting in the House not ten days ago, and he knows what's going to come his way soon. Gale, I'm leaving you to bring in the Finney boys. You're certain they were in that Wellborough silk steal?"

"As sure as I'm sitting here," Gale said. "I've gone over all the territory a score of times. Ed Finney leaves his mark on everything he touches—he's that neat. Besides I've got a 'friend' who knows a thing or two. He tipped me off. I'll take the Finney crowd when I want them. Mind you, I don't say that we'll get any farther ahead by doing that. I'll be frank with you there. Corporal Violet is too smart to let the Finneys and the Driscolls and the Jake Avery sort of folk know anything about him. They don't call him Corporal Violet for nothing."

"That's true," the Commissioner admitted.

Here he was correct, for Corporal Violet was indeed the problem of the decade. Grey-headed detectives with many years of experience of crime and criminals, debated among themselves as to whether Central Office had ever had to cope with a more talented and versatile antagonist, and the consensus of opinion was that if his equal had appeared on the horizon of the Metropolitan Police, it had been in the comfortable old days of gas light and hansom cabs, when reputations had been made easily.

There was some truth in this point of view. In the three years that Corporal Violet was known to have operated in the Metropolis, he had established a reputation for himself that no criminal in the past ten years had equalled. He was catholic in his operations, sufficiently enterprising to move from silk robberies to stock swindling, from larceny to murder.

It had been Corporal Violet who had taken the Madras Specie Bank for a cool hundred thousand: who had lifted the Marchioness of Zanda's jewels from the safe in the Hotel Lasson. It had been Corporal Violet who had held up Paymaster Major Howe on the Aldershot Road and had lifted close on twenty-seven thousand pounds in cash from the military vehicle that had provided his transport.

Such enterprise had not gone unnoticed. The newspapers had been quick to elaborate on the successes of this extraordinary individual and it had been a historically minded crime reporter on the staff of the *Eastern Dispatch and*

Recorder who had christened this new bandit the "Napoleon of Crime". In a later article he had altered his designation somewhat, and had called him "Corporal Violet", adding in parenthesis that Corporal Violet had been the name by which the little Corsican general had been known to most of his troops.

The name had stuck as such epithets will. At Scotland Yard, the file on his depredations was headed:

CORPORAL VIOLET

and the grim, hard-eyed men whom he recruited to his ranks were similarly tabulated by worried detective officers who had no more accurate appellation which they might apply to them. That much of his success depended on the nature of the men he employed was a recognized fact at Central Office. Of them, several of them had been taken by a vigilant Constabulary, and all of them had been hard, bitter army deserters, several of them of foreign birth and extraction. There were places where such suitable material might be recruited and trained along unconventional lines, and the men were dangerous, for they would use firearms if trouble threatened and men who shoot at the drop of a hat are never popular.

Superintendent Telfer, a large, raw-boned man from the North, had a contribution to make.

"Solus is in town again. One of my boys saw him in Piccadilly the other day. He'd have pinched him, but the crowd was too thick."

Kyle was interested.

"Harry Solus?"

Telfer nodded grimly.

"Harry Solus. He was with the crowd that held up Marny's. He got a crack on the head from a brick somebody threw. Two or three people identified him. He had to take his left hand out of his pocket, for he was pushed to make the car."

Harry Solus was remarkable in that only one finger remained on his left hand as a result of an interesting experiment with a bottle of nitro-glycerine with which he had been entrusted.

MacNeill looked up.

"Solus works for Corporal Violet. Pick him up if you can. The sooner the better. My idea is that we should bear down on them heavily from now on. Crack down on all the heavy

84

muscle boys, the toughs and touts. Sooner or later we'll cripple Corporal Violet. If we use enough force we can smash the men he works with quicker than he can recruit new material. Make his wastage too hard for him to handle. If you do that, you'll put him out of business. It may be the slow way, but it certainly is the sure way."

There was a general murmur of approval, and on that note the meeting broke up. MacNeill remained, for the Commissioner had a word for him in private.

"I'm worried about this business, Superintendent," he said. "I didn't mention it in the room there, but the newspapers have been playing up those questions in the House. The Home Secretary was quite blunt. He wants a shift. Someone suggested bringing in Brigadier Platt. I'm against that. Our own men should be good enough to handle this."

MacNeill rubbed at his rather large nose.

"Brigadier Platt did a good job in the Army," he said thoughtfully. "But Provost work is different from the Civil Police. No, we don't want Platt. Not yet."

Cameron filled his pipe.

"You haven't any fresh ideas?"

MacNeill's eyes were inscrutable.

"I don't talk about my ideas, sir. Not while they're still ideas. This is a pretty big thing and the man we're after is as clever as any half-dozen of us. I'm not under any illusion about that. I know my own limitation. He's a born organizer—one of the coolest brains I've ever come across. That fellow should have been a general. No wonder they call him Napoleon!" He shook his head in patent admiration. "He's too smart. There's nothing he won't touch. That's what makes him so difficult to deal with. He's not like the usual run of criminals. Most of these men are specialists. Johnny Zare touches nothing but banks. Connor wouldn't look at anything but furs and silks: the Haringa crowd operate only in the diamond line. That means that sooner or later you can get them, for their field is limited."

The Commissioner sighed.

"I know. In the end you can pick them up for you know where to look for them and where to bait the trap. Corporal Violet is no specialist, and yet he has all the skill of the best of them."

Here he spoke only the truth as the record of this extraordinary criminal went to prove. Corporal Violet might remain very much in the background, but the results of his planning were worked out brilliantly by the men he employed and bespoke a thoroughness which might well have been utilized on a worthier project.

So much, the Commissioner suggested in the slightly savage and cynical tones of a man who has commanded a regiment of infantry, then:

"Do what you can, MacNeill. I'd like to take this beggar." He did not say "beggar", but his feelings were aroused and he had had a vigorous morning.

Superintendent MacNeill was grave.

"I hope we're lucky, sir. We'll have to be." He smiled very faintly. "Luck plays a big part in these jobs. So does hard work. I've found out that." He rose as he spoke. "I've put in a lot of hard work in the case for all I've got. Maybe it's been worth it, however."

The older man looked up.

"What are you thinking about?"

MacNeill had reached the door. He stood there and looked back, his grey eyes cool and thoughtful.

"I'm thinking about Tommy Gavillan," he said.

Cameron considered.

"He got off yesterday. I was glad of that. It had all the ear-marks of a frame, and his record has been clean enough for the past year or two. Why do you think of him now?" There was curiosity in his voice.

MacNeill looked at him thoughtfully.

"Gavillan is a man of strange loyalties," he said slowly. "I've known him for a long time now. That is one thing I've noticed about him."

The Commissioner was puzzled.

"Loyalties are all very well, but what have they got to do with the problem of Corporal Violet?"

"That's what I'm wondering," said MacNeill slowly. "Gavillan was the right-hand man of Drew Sheldon and Drew Sheldon was one of the smartest men who ever puzzled Whitehall or Centre Street. He disappeared ten or twelve years ago. Gavillan says he's dead." A cold smile came into his eyes. "I'm wondering now if Tommy is sure of his facts."

"You mean that Sheldon is Corporal Violet?"

"Just that," MacNeill said. "I'm not suggesting he is—but

I've got an idea he could be. If he is, Gavillan would be the first to know it. Tommy's smart. Don't think he isn't. He knows every trick in the book—and a few that aren't. But if he is—he won't tell. I know him of old. That puzzles me. To-morrow I'm going down to Winchester to have a word with him."

"Winchester?" the Commissioner said. "That was where they found the woman who was murdered. A nasty job."

Superintendent MacNeill stared.

"What woman was this?"

"Nobody knows as yet." Cameron groped among the documents on his desk, found a sheet of paper and glanced at it. "This is the business. Matterson wants us to send a couple of men down. I was going to send Inspector Judd and Inspector Wrenn." He glanced up over the top of his glasses. "She was found in some lake—Malden Mere was the name of it. Here it is. The police surgeon says she was strangled." He handed across the sheet of paper.

MacNeill read it through. When he was finished he looked up.

"You haven't spoken to Judd as yet, sir?"

"No. The information was only brought in a few moments ago."

Superintendent MacNeill sighed.

"That's fine," he said. "I can't think of anything better. I'll go along myself. There's no use sending a boy on a man's errand." With a nod, he went out.

CHAPTER XIII

AN AFTERNOON train took Superintendent MacNeill to Winchester and in his company Inspector Till, a polite and polished young man who had descended on Central Office from the Police College at Hendon, whence he had arrived at a still earlier date from that rival institution on the banks of the Isis. At Winchester they were met by a sergeant of police who escorted them to headquarters and here the Chief Constable had a word with them.

Major Matterson was a quiet-voiced man with calm eyes and an air of tranquillity which accorded strangely with his military rank, yet he was a sound administrator and a good policeman. He took MacNeill into his own office and waved him to a chair.

"Glad to have you here, Superintendent. I've heard a lot about you though we've never met." He smiled faintly. "I asked the Commissioner to send a good man. I didn't think he'd send just such a good one."

MacNeill was a little amused.

"I hope we don't disappoint you, sir. I'm glad that you called us in. You were pretty quick on the job."

Matterson nodded.

"If the woman had been a local person, we shouldn't have troubled. As it is she's a stranger. So far nobody knows who she is. Nobody can suggest where she came from. More extraordinary still, we have no record of any missing woman who answers her description, even vaguely. Under the circumstances, I thought it best to have outside assistance. The probability is that investigations will have to be conducted much farther afield, and Scotland Yard has the organization for that sort of thing." He touched a bell on his desk. When a constable appeared: "Ask Inspector Cleaver to come here."

Inspector Cleaver was of average height, a weather-beaten man with a pleasant smile and a steady eye. He greeted MacNeill with some warmth.

"I've met you twice before, Superintendent. I was a sergeant at the time. I don't suppose you'll remember me but it was at——"

"Southampton," said MacNeill. "The day we took Joe Oates. You jumped him after he pulled a gun. I remember it."

The Chief Constable rose.

"I'll leave you to talk things over, gentlemen. I've got a meeting in twenty minutes." He went out and Inspector Cleaver produced his pipe.

"I'll run over the case with you," he said, "and give you what we've got on it so far. It isn't a great deal. We haven't been able to locate anyone who knew the woman as yet."

For five minutes he spoke while the Central Office man listened attentively, then:

"That's about all. There's no doubt about it being murder. The p.m. report is there for you to see. You can have a word with the pathologist whenever you like. She was dead before she went into the water. There was no water in her lungs at all."

"Strangled?"

"Yes. So the doctor says. There were bruises and discolouration around her throat. She had been in the water for at least a week. We found one of her shoes. I'll show it to you in a minute or so. It had been purchased in New York."

MacNeill's interest quickened.

"In New York?"

"Yes. Her clothing had been purchased there too—at least, some of it had, for there was an American address on the tags. I called in at one of the big shops in the town and asked the manager if that sort of thing could be got in England. He was quite definite that it couldn't be at the present time and that those particular shops had no agencies here. We'll go through now and have a look at them."

They went into the inspector's room where Till was already making an examination of the shoe, a blouse and a white silk slip. He looked round as they appeared.

"Hedwig, Untersohn and Kelly," he said conversationally. "That's the New York outfitters. They're a good firm—not cheap stuff at all. I got a suit there once."

"What about the shoe?"

"Made by the Anfield Company," Till said. "I don't know them, but the stamp says Seattle."

They made a brief examination of the remainder of the clothing, but there was nothing which was of further interest. In a moment or so MacNeill nodded.

"I don't think we'll find anything fresh here. We'll go across to the mortuary."

Cleaver was agreeable.

"I'll have Sergeant Tight take you over. He's been there most of the day."

Tight appeared a moment later and escorted them on the grim errand which they had to perform. He stood beside them in silence as they stared at the woman who lay before them, then, when they had stepped out to the car again:

"You don't know her, sir?"

"I'm afraid not," MacNeill said.

Sergeant Tight shook his head.

"I've got an idea we're going to have trouble there. I was

at the mortuary all day waiting to interview anyone who turned up to get a look at her. It wasn't very nice."

"Did anybody appear?"

"A woman from Reading—a Mrs. Kay. She only took one look and cleared out. She was looking for her daughter, but this wasn't anything like her. The only other person was a gentleman from Marks Malden. It was his daughter who—well, she didn't find her—but she was there pretty soon after they did."

"From Marks Malden?"

"Mr. Gavillan," Tight said. "You know him?"

MacNeill's eyes hardened.

"Yes, I know him. So he was interested? Queer." He pondered this morbid curiosity of Tommy Gavillan for a moment, then: "Very good, Tight. We'll get along to Marks Malden now. Tomorrow I'll have a look at the Mere and the ground around it, though I can't see that it can tell us anything that it hasn't told you."

A car had been provided for them and they drove Sergeant Tight to police headquarters then took the road for Marks Malden. It was dark when they arrived at the village and the cheerful lights of the cottages came to them through a smear of rain. They stopped in front of the Malden Arms. Accommodation had been secured for them here, and the landlord was on the doorstep to welcome them when they arrived.

"Glad to see you, gents," he said. "I'm Bolton. We've got your rooms ready and a fire an' all. Come this way."

He then led them to two comfortable rooms in which a fire blazed cheerfully, patted the bed and commented on the excellency of the mattress which was provided.

"The very best, gents. Bought it at the big sale at Malden Chase a year back. That's the very beds the gentry used themselves. Not the like of them to be got in the country nowadays. I'll leave you to get yourselves ready. When you are, just come down. There's a meal waiting for you."

There was indeed a meal of gargantuan proportions awaiting them, and its size was only equalled by its excellency. Bolton waited on their requirements, and when they were finished cleared away the dishes from the table.

"You can use this room, gents, while you're here. There's another sitting-room for the commercials and there's nobody else here at the moment."

When he had gone MacNeill lit his pipe.

"You don't know this part, Till?"

Till did not.

"I was stationed here for a week or two during the war, but I never got out of the guard-room," he admitted frankly.

The superintendent produced a map. He spread it out on the table top and leaned over it.

"That's Malden Mere, where they found the woman."

Till looked at the map.

"Queer how she should find herself in a place like that, Super. It isn't near to any place."

"Not very," said MacNeill. "Unless you count Meredale or Marks Malden. Even Low Oxley is twelve miles distant."

"But if she'd come from any of those places, they'd have missed her," Till said vexedly. "It's very queer. She couldn't have been brought there by car from some place, eh?"

MacNeill pondered.

"I wondered about that myself. She might have been but for one fact."

The younger man frowned.

"What was that, Super?"

"They found her footprints in the bog," MacNeill said quietly. "Tight thinks she had been running. She lost a shoe. There were several footprints. If she was brought in a car, she got out of the car and ran for it. That may have been the way of it. I wouldn't pass judgment on it yet." He took out his pipe and filled it. "We'll go over that problem tomorrow. There's another angle to it and one the locals haven't mentioned yet."

"What's that?"

"She may have been living here," the big man said.

Till was puzzled.

"But why wasn't she missed? Why hasn't her absence been notified to the local police?"

"I can think of reasons." The superintendent struck a match. His grey eyes were thoughtful. "Cleaver had taken her fingerprints. He sent them up to Central Office today. I'm carrying that a step farther and wiring them to New York."

"You think she may have a police record there?"

The big man chuckled.

"Probably not. But they use fingerprints a lot more in the States than we do here. Banks use them—factories use them—and there's always the police to fall back on. Anyway, if she's an American that's the logical place to begin. I like to be thorough and the Government pays the charges." There was a ghost of a smile on his face as he left the room. He was gone for no longer than a moment. When he returned he said: "I was taking a look at the weather. Do you feel like walking across to Chyme Close?"

Inspector Till was of an age which finds walking tedious.

"I'll get the car out, sir. It's a dirty night."

"I think we'll walk," MacNeill said. "I may want to go one or two places where a car wouldn't be exactly handy. Get your coat."

They went down to the road. The mild smear of rain was a steady drizzle now and they turned up their collars against it as they walked through the village. In a moment or two, the lights of Marks Malden had fallen behind them and they were on the slight incline which led to the higher ground, then, where a road forked to the right, the big man indicated it.

"That takes you to Malden Court."

Till was interested.

"Who lives there?"

"The local bigwig; name of Mandell. He's one of the hunting and shooting type—a big fair fellow. He took this place over a couple of years back. Got a five-year lease of it."

Till was amused.

"How do you know all this, sir?"

"I made inquiries," MacNeill said. "I like to know my locality and it helps to know the people. Beyond the Court there's another house—the Moorings they call it. The occupant is a chap by the name of Spain. I saw him for the first time quite recently. He has a lease on the Moorings for a year only. What does that indicate to you, Inspector?"

Inspector Till considered this problem for a long moment.

"That he doesn't intend to stay here," he said finally.

MacNeill nodded in the darkness.

"Anything else?"

"Nothing that I can think of," said his subordinate. He felt a little touch of curiosity. "What does it mean to you, sir?"

"It means that he came to Marks Malden for a purpose," said Superintendent MacNeill, "and that purpose had to be fulfilled within a year. He's got five or six months left. I wonder what's going to happen in them?"

They had swung off the main road now. As they did so, they saw the headlights of a car coming along from the village. It passed them and disappeared from sight. Then, in a moment more they heard it pull up. As it did so, they heard the sound of a bird flying towards them in the darkness.

Inspector Till looked round.

"That fellow is turning."

Sure enough, in a moment more they heard the sound of the car approaching. The headlamps appeared on the road behind them and of a sudden MacNeil's big hand gripped the shoulder of his colleague. He drew him towards the shelter of the beach hedge, pressed him back in the shadow as the car slid past.

Inspector Till was a little mystified.

"What's wrong, sir?"

The Scotsman was silent for a moment, then:

"Nothing that I know of—only somebody got out of the car back there. That's a queer, queer place to drop a man. There's only the wood and a field."

Till coughed.

"Did you hear him, Super? I have to confess I didn't."

"I heard the pheasant," the Scot said drily. "It came this way. Those fellows don't frighten easily. They roost near the road and they're used to cars."

He stepped back into the road and they walked up the avenue towards Chyme Close in silence. Then, when the lights of the library twinkled through the darkness, MacNeill sighed.

"When you've been a policeman for thirty years, you get suspicious of everything. That's one of the heartbreaks of the job. I wonder who was in the car."

"One of the locals," Till suggested.

"A local wouldn't have missed the road," the Scot said shortly. "Whoever it was drove past and got out of the car. Either that or he let out a passenger. That doesn't make sense and I hate a mystery." He walked on, silent in his irritation. In a moment more they had reached the house.

MacNeill put his finger on the bell. From within they heard the sound of footsteps. The door was opened and Flett appeared, his head twisted to one side inquiringly.

"Well, if it isn't the Super himself!" He shook his head in an ecstasy of welcome. "Come right in, sir. Imagine that, and at this time of night too. Miss Pat's just gone to bed. She's got a cold on account of her getting her feet wet."

MacNeill stepped inside.

"Where's Gavillan?"

"Across at the Court," said Flett. "He went over there tonight to see Mr. Mandell. It isn't often that he goes out, but they asked him to come." He pondered for a second. "Mr. Spain was going too. They were talking about this here lady that got herself drowned." He rubbed his hands together. "I'll give him a call, sir, and tell him you're here."

MacNeill hesitated.

"No. I wouldn't do that. We'll just walk back. We're at the Malden Arms. Tell him I'll come back in the morning."

Flett was disturbed.

"Mr. Gavillan won't like it if you don't have a drink, sir! He might not be late. If you want to wait——"

"We won't," MacNeill said shortly. "Anyway, we may meet him on the road. Is he driving?"

Flett smiled at the fatuous nature of the question.

"When did you ever know Mr. Gavillan to walk, Super?" he demanded. "He took the brake." He considered for a moment. "Anyway, you may meet him on the road. It all depends the way he comes. If he comes out of the north gate he'll come beyond the Malden Road, and if he comes by the south gate he'll come in at the back and you won't see him at all. I think——"

He broke off suddenly, for on the still air of night came a thin, sharp crack!

Flett had stiffened. Now he swung round.

"What was that, sir?"

Crack!

Again they heard the staccato report.

"Rifle!" snarled MacNeill, and made for the door.

CHAPTER XIV

FOR the space of five seconds the big man stood on the bottom step, his eyes peering into the darkness. There was no light of any kind to be seen, but from the road came the sound of a car slipping into high gear.

MacNeill looked behind him.

"There he goes! Till, get on the telephone. 'Phone Winchester and tell them to block the roads. Tell them there's been a shooting. That car may make for the coast. London would be hopeless for them." He gripped the servant by the arm. "Get out the car—and double to it, Flett."

The little man streaked for the rear of the house. In a moment more, the headlights of the car lit up the avenue as he swung out of the garage and approached the house.

"Where to, Super?"

"The cross roads," MacNeill said. He scrambled into the front of the car, and it gathered speed on the drive. A moment more and they had reached the road, and as they did so they heard the sound of a car approaching at high speed.

Flett was staring out into the darkness.

"He's running without lights!" he gasped.

MacNeill saw the black silhouette no more than fifty yards from them, heard the roar of a powerful motor.

"Ram him!" he snarled. He felt the car spin round as Flett bore on the wheel, heard the screeching of brakes as the speeding car swerved to avoid them. That it did so was no more than good fortune for Flett had taken the centre of the road. Now he applied his own brakes, they saw the fugitive car going into a skid on the wet surface, saw the driver's vain attempt to drag her round. The off wheels took the verge of the road and sank on the soft shoulders. The car careered across the road and side-swiped the stone pillar of the gates. It rolled over twice and then the motor was silent.

Flett wiped the perspiration from his forehead.

"That's that!" he said thickly.

MacNeill was already on the wet slippery road and sprinting across towards the wreck. As he reached it a man scrambled out, took a step or two forward and sagged to the road.

The policeman looked over his shoulder.

"Keep your eye on this fellow, Flett."

The little man came up as he spoke.

"Trust me." He went down on his knees. "Got a gun, feller?" He fanned the man with calm efficiency, but he was unarmed.

MacNeill had wrenched open the door of the car. The driver was twisted horribly, but he was still conscious. He looked up at the big man, and when he spoke his voice was a whisper.

"All right, chum. I've had it."

MacNeill got his big arms round him and lifted him out. He carried him across to the side of the road, and as he did so he felt the man's body go limp in his arms.

Flett was looking round.

"There's a car coming up the road, Super, I'll stop him."

Twin headlights had appeared round the bend of the road, and as the car drew nearer they heard the beat of the engine slacken. It pulled up and someone got out.

Flett was waving his arms.

"Hullo there! There's been a smash!"

Tommy Gavillan walked towards them in the glare of the headlights.

"Hello there, Flett. Who's that? MacNeill?"

The superintendent looked at him impassively.

"I didn't expect to see you again!"

Gavillan chuckled.

"The luck of the Irish. I came out of the south gate. They had a rope across the road—a wire rope anchored to two trees. It threw me round to the ditch. When I got out somebody let loose with a rifle."

MacNeill nodded.

"He's over there. You were lucky, Tommy."

"I got out on the blind side," Gavillan said. "The first bullet cut the coat off my shoulder. I dropped then." He laughed gently. "Where did you come from, Mac?"

MacNeill sighed.

"Business takes me to a few places, Tommy." He walked across to where the driver lay, went down on his knees beside him.

Gavillan followed him over.

"Is he bad?"

"He's dead."

The Irishman stared.

"Damnable. The car piled up, I suppose. Poor devil. What about this other feller?"

He walked across to where Flett was standing guard over a sick and dizzy prisoner. The little man looked up at his approach.

"He's all right, Mr. Gavillan. Knocked silly a bit, but there's no bones broken. He was in the back of the car. That saved him. Sit up, feller, and smile at the gentleman." He prodded him with the toe of his boot and the man drew himself into a sitting position.

"All right," he said. "I know when I'm licked."

MacNeill had come across. For a second he looked down at him, then lifted the crippled left hand in his own.

"Hello, Harry. I learned you were around." There was an odd elation in his voice. "I never heard you were fond of the country!"

Harry Solus stared up and in the light of the headlamps was able to detect and recognize an ancient enemy.

"Mr. MacNeill!"

The Scot chuckled.

"The world is a small place, Harry. I heard a man talking about you only this morning. I didn't think I'd see you so soon." He bent down and jerked the man to his feet, slid his hands over him.

Flett watched with professional interest.

"He's clean, Super. I searched him."

"I'm all for being thorough," the policeman said, but on this occasion his thoroughness found no reward, for Harry Solus carried no weapon of any sort.

MacNeill went back to the car and made a brief search but there was no sign of the rifle. He returned to the little group.

"They ditched it," he said. "And that was the wise thing to do. A rifle is easily spotted and it's a hard, hard thing to explain away."

Gavillan was looking towards the car.

"What about getting back to the house?"

MacNeill nodded.

"We'll do that. Flett, wait here and keep your lights on the road. I'll send Till down to join you. All right, Solus, this way." He assisted the man across to the car, got into the rear with him.

Gavillan got in and drove them to the house. At the door they were met by Pat Gavillan, a dressing-gown round her, and Inspector Till a little awed in the presence of so much feminine loveliness.

Pat ran down the steps to greet them.

"Daddy! You're all right!"

Tommy chuckled.

"This is my lucky day, Pat. Never was righter Look at

you out in all the rain. You'll be in bed for a week. Go back to bed."

Till joined them, a curious man.

"What happened, Super? I heard a crash!"

Gavillan grinned.

"You certainly know a crash when you hear one, young feller."

"They wrecked the car," MacNeill said. "Flett drew out in front of them and they swerved to avoid us. They must have been travelling at sixty. The driver is dead. This is the man who did the shooting. I don't think you've met him, Till. Name of Solus—Harry Solus."

Inspector Till knew Solus by name and repute. He was as startled to find this *habitué* of the big city in Marks Malden as an Arctic explorer might have been to discover a king cobra at the North Pole.

"Well, I never! What's the world coming to?"

MacNeill pushed his captive forward.

"Take him into the library. I'm going to telephone the local police station. We'll have to get an ambulance out here and a break-down van to lift the car off the road."

He went through to use the telephone. When he made his way to the big room he found Tommy Gavillan drinking to celebrate his fortuitous escape from violent death.

He laid down his glass and sighed.

"I needed that. How about you, Mac?"

"A very wee one," said MacNeill. He watched him pour it out. "No—not as wee as all that. That'll do for Solus. Till's a temperance man. He belongs to a lodge of some sort. The Good Templars or something like that. I'm all for it. No man should touch strong drink until he's over fifty." He carried a glass over to Solus. "Drink that, Harry."

Solus took it. He was lean of build, hard-eyed. Now his hand trembled and MacNeill noted it.

"That's shock. You'll be getting a bigger one directly. Find your tongue, man, for you've got a lot of talking to do."

Till had drawn on his top coat.

"What do you want me to do?"

"Wait with Flett till the police get here from Winchester. They're sending out a doctor right away. Have him come up here for a look at this fellow."

Till went out and MacNeill beamed his satisfaction.

98

"Now, Harry, a little co-operation."

The man scowled.

"Look, MacNeill, I'm not talking." He had regained much of his composure now and his small dark eyes were hard. "I know my rights. I don't know what you're getting at!"

The big man eyed him thoughtfully.

"Where did you ditch the rifle?"

"What rifle?"

"Tell him what rifle, Tommy," said the obliging policeman.

Tommy Gavillan told him what rifle in violent and expressive language.

Solus shook his head.

"I know nothing about it. I never heard of it. All I know is we were driving along an' the car skidded an'——"

MacNeill's big hand gripped him by the hair of his head. He felt a pull which all but lifted the top off his skull and he was on his feet. The big man pushed him with the flat of his hand so that his shoulders struck the panelling of the wall.

"Talk, Harry."

Solus licked his lips.

"Damn you, MacNeill, you can't handle me like this!"

"What makes you think I can't?"

The man's face was livid.

"I know the law. You daren't lay a finger on me before witnesses! I'll have the coat off your back for this."

Gavillan shook his head wearily.

"Where's the witnesses?"

Solus pulled at his collar which had suddenly grown tight.

"You daren't lay a hand on me. If you put as much as a mark on me, I'll have you on the carpet!"

The Scotsman drew him closer with one heavy hand. He held the other back and looked at it.

"How'd you like to try this for size, Harry? The Winchester police were told there was a car crash, and that one man was killed. Naturally they'll expect the other one to be knocked about a bit. What do you think, Tommy?"

Gavillan was eloquent in his agreement.

"What else could they expect? If we slap the hell out of this feller, Mac, who's to know the difference?"

MacNeill tightened his grip.

"That's correct. What do you think, Solus? Talk or I'll go

to work on you. If I do, you'll look as bad as anybody could look and as Gavillan says, who's to know the difference?"

There was a little silence, then Solus licked his lips.

"O.K., MacNeill." He felt himself pushed into a chair. For a moment he sat there, then: "What do you want to know?"

"All you can tell me."

"That isn't much," Solus said. "Lavery was driving. We were told to come down here and get Gavillan. Lavery did the fixing. I don't know who put him up to it, an' that's the truth. We were to get a hundred apiece for the attempt—and another hundred each if it came off. We were given the rifle and a length of wire and Lavery was told where to fix it across the road."

"How could he tell in the darkness?"

"He'd been here before—earlier in the day. I came down by train to Winchester. He picked me up there. I was to do the shooting."

"You're good with a gun?"

Solus sniffed.

"Fairly. I was an instructor for a while during the war." He looked up. "That's all I know. It was a Lee Enfield, Mark IV, but it had seen a lot of use. It fired high. I couldn't get enough light and I made a mess of it."

"You don't know who put Lavery on to it?"

"No. That's the truth. I don't."

"Was it Corporal Violet?"

There was a little silence. The man's lips thinned out.

"I tell you I don't know. Lavery handled that end of it. He had a lot of contacts, that feller."

"He's lost them all now," MacNeill said with grim humour. For a moment or two longer he questioned the man, but Solus could give him no more information. He searched him again, went over his clothing more thoroughly, but neither his pockets nor his cheap leather wallet yielded anything which might even remotely have been taken to suggest a clue.

In the end, MacNeill sighed.

"All right, Solus. I'm holding you for the Hampshire Police. This is outside my bailiwick, but I think we'll have you back to London one of these days. The charge will be attempted murder. You know what that means?"

Harry Solus knew full well what it meant.

"What will they give me, MacNeill?"

The policeman shrugged.

"Maybe a five; maybe a seven. In any case, you'll get a long spell, Harry. This has been a bad night's work for you."

There was the sound of a car on the gravel of the driveway. Gavillan left the room. When he came back a moment later Inspector Cleaver was with him, and behind them an elderly man who carried the black bag which was the badge of his calling.

Cleaver was a serious man.

"Well, Superintendent, you seem to have run into trouble right away. We saw the car. The man is dead. He has a driving licence made out in the name of Cannavan."

"His name is Lavery," MacNeill said. "This is the fellow who did the shooting. Name of Solus—Harry Solus. We've been keeping our eye on him for a while."

The doctor made a brief examination.

"A little shock. That seems to be all. You've been very lucky, my man."

Superintendent MacNeill smiled in sympathy.

"Very lucky, Doctor. I think he realizes that now." He looked across at Gavillan. "I've had enough for one night, Tommy. I'll come up and talk to you tomorrow. One thing only I want to tell you, Tommy, and if you're a wise man you'll listen to it."

Gavillan looked up interested.

"What's that?"

The Scotsman looked into his blue eyes.

"Don't play your luck too long, Gavillan. The time to stop is when you're ahead of the game."

There was silence for the space of half a minute.

Tommy Gavillan laughed jerkily.

"Maybe you're right, Mac. Anyway, I'll sleep on it."

"Good," said Superintendent MacNeill and led the way out.

CHAPTER XV

SERGEANT TIGHT appeared next morning shortly after daylight had set in and together they drove in the direction of Malden Mere. When the water appeared before them, he drew the car into the side of the road. They donned the gum-boots which had been provided and the sergeant took them as far as the water's edge.

"This was where she was found," he said. "You can see how the ground is scuffed up."

MacNeill was staring across the Mere.

"There's a boat-house along there—and a slip."

"That belongs to the Court," Tight said. "They come up here to fish in the summer-time and the like of that." He was a little interested. "You don't think a boat was used? I had a look at the boat-house yesterday, but the lock was intact. I didn't ask to see the boat."

They made their way towards it. It was close on a hundred yards away, but the ground here was harder and firmer. MacNeill kept his eyes on the surface, but there were no tracks of any description. The boat-house, when they reached it, was of solid construction and comparatively new. The door was stout and firm, and was secured by a large padlock.

Tight tapped it with his finger.

"You wouldn't get into that very easily."

The superintendent raised his eyes an inch or two.

"It wouldn't be very difficult," he said drily.

Tight, following his gaze, saw the key hanging above the door from a rusty nail. He coughed apologetically.

"Well, I'll be damned! I'll have to keep my wits about me. If the killer had known about that, he could have taken the boat. Perhaps that's what happened."

They went inside and examined both the rowing-boats which the house held, but there was no indication that either of these had been used recently. They left in a moment or so, and Tight took them down to the end of the Mere at which the body had been found.

"The shoe was lying over there. I'll show you the spot. You'll be able to see the one or two footprints. They're not very clear, but we photographed them and took casts. I covered them with a sheet of glass in case someone would want to see them."

There were indeed one or two heelprints in the soft ground. Till, who was an authority on footprints, examined them closely.

"You're probably correct, Sergeant. She ran through here —and she had lost a shoe by the time she had got this length." He frowned. "Who was she running from?"

"The man who murdered her," Tight said.

Superintendent MacNeill looked at his young colleague. Till was puzzled.

"If she was running and he was chasing her, where are his footprints?" he asked, not unreasonably.

Tight was silent, then:

"I hadn't thought of that. It's very queer."

The superintendent's eyes were twinkling.

"I wondered when somebody was going to ask that," he said. He was almost jovial now as he led the way back to the car. "It's a queer affair. The woman is a stranger—an American, presumably. No one has ever seen her before. She was walking along this road and since no one saw her on it, it must have been at night."

"That's right," Tight agreed.

MacNeill splashed through a pool of water.

"She was afraid—terrified. We know that because she ran through here. She didn't keep to the road. That means that whoever she was frightened of, was on the road."

"Someone in a car?" Till said.

MacNeill considered.

"Perhaps so. I'm not sure. It could have been. But the man didn't follow her, for we haven't found his tracks. He waited on the roadway. If there was a car—there were at least two people in it. The car drove away, but one of them waited—and the woman came back."

Till drew in his breath.

"That sounds likely."

They had reached the police car now, and they began to change into their shoes. MacNeill spoke no more until he had completed this necessary task then:

"It's a puzzle for the moment, but we'll leave it at that."

They got into the car and drove to the village. There they left Tight to return to Winchester. There was a telephone message awaiting them, and this Bolton delivered. Inspector Fennell had called from Scotland Yard to say that the fingerprints he had received from the Winchester Police were not in C.R.O.

MacNeill accepted this information philosophically.

"We can't expect too much," he said. "I've a job for you, Till."

"What's that, sir?"

"Get hold of the local constable and go round the village, from door to door. I want to find out if anyone has ever seen anyone who answered to the description of this woman in the district."

Till considered this assignment.

"The local policeman will be a big help there. You want me to concentrate on the village?"

"Yes, I'll go to the Court and the Moorings. I'll call on Gavillan just now, and for that reason I'm taking the car."

He left the inn and went out to it. He was almost a mile out of the village when he heard the horn of a car behind him. In the rear view mirror, he saw the bonnet of a large Rolls creeping up on him with effortless ease. It slid past and as it did so he recognized the cheerful features of Mandell.

The younger man had seen him. Now he raised his hand in a gesture of recognition, and applied the foot-brake so that the big car came to a stop. He was out of it quickly for a man of his bulk, and he came back to where the policeman had stopped.

"Hullo, MacNeill, I got the surprise of my life when I saw you there. Couldn't believe my eyes. Where did you come from?"

"The village," MacNeill said. "I'm investigating this business at Malden Mere."

"Oh, that?" Billy Mandell was a little disappointed. "You've heard about Gavillan? But you haven't had much time to learn about anything yet. Somebody tried to shoot him last night." His voice was trembling with suppressed excitement. "Just you think of that, Super. Right here, in Marks Malden. What's the world coming to? It's all these damned Socialists that's in the Country. Nothing else. I was saying that to Hettche only yesterday." He stopped for breath. "Poor old Tommy."

"Who told you about it?"

"Pitman—the local Robert. I went over to see Gavillan at once to get the story. He wasn't at home."

MacNeill frowned.

"I was going to Chyme Close myself."

"Then you can save yourself the trouble," Mandell said firmly. "Gavillan's out and Pat has gone with him. Flett doesn't know when they'll be back. You'd think a feller like Tommy would have enough sense to know his friends would be worried until they had seen him. He's a queer, queer feller."

He had commenced a little diatribe which went to prove just how queer a fellow Tommy Gavillan really was when the policeman cut him short.

"I was coming over to Malden Court for a word with you, Mandell, however, we can discuss the matter here."

Mandell was intrigued.

"Come up to the Court by all means. We don't get many visitors. I'll drive on ahead. Nothing like comfort when you want to talk about things." With a wave he went back to the car, started it up and drove off at a speed which Superintendent MacNeill had no desire to emulate.

In a few moments more he drew up behind the Rolls in front of Malden Court. Mandell was waiting for him in the doorway and was prepared to accord to him the honours of an Admiral of the Fleet paying a formal visit to a ship of the line.

"Come in, Super, and make yourself at home. I don't have many folks here at all and I like company better than anything else." He ushered the big man into a long, oak-panelled room. There was a broad fireplace of red brick and an enormous fire was blazing in it, and Billy Mandell ushered his guest into a chair which was so positioned that when he dropped into it, the soles of his feet were a scant few inches from the blaze.

"Have a drink, Super. Nothing like comfort in the house. I'm all for it—and there's nothing more comfortable than a fire and a glass in your hand. Smoke?" He produced a heavily carved cigar-box and held it under MacNeill's nose.

MacNeill waved them away.

"I'm a pipe smoker. I'll have a dram though. I haven't had one since yesterday." He watched his host pour it out. "Thank you, Mr. Mandell. I can do with this. It's a fine, fine thing a drop of whisky, especially when you're under the weather a bit." He raised his glass. "Here's your good health."

Mandell sat down. In the sharp light of the winter's sun he looked a little older than he usually did, a little more serious. There was a streak of grey hair at his temples which the policeman had not noticed before. He lit a cigarette, then:

"What's on your mind, Super?"

MacNeill set down his glass.

"That was grand whisky. I'll tell you what brought me down here then." He told the younger man of the case on which he was working and Mandell listened attentively. When he had finished the tenant of Malden Court nodded.

"And you want to find out if anyone in the district knows anything about this woman?"

"That's correct. The Winchester Police are checking up on this end of it. I can't see that we'll get much satisfaction out of the job, but that's just the normal routine work we've always to go through with. Now, I've got a photograph of her here." From his pocket he took an envelope and ultimately a photograph. It was a harsh crude positive, the handiwork of an unromantic police photographer, and he handed it across to the younger man.

"There she is. About five feet six, she must have been. Her hair was dark."

Mandell looked at it curiously.

"This is the picture that was in the paper!"

"That's correct. Do you know her?"

Mandell shook his head.

"Not me. Never laid my eyes on the lady."

"Do you mind if I have a word with your staff?"

Billy Mandell jumped up.

"I'll get 'em in for you. One at a time, eh?"

"One at a time."

"There's Sykes the butler, Mrs. Cash the cook and two maids." He went over to the door, rang a bell and when the butler appeared:

"Sykes, this is Superintendent MacNeill from Scotland Yard. He's here to ask a lot of questions about this woman who was drowned. You tell him all you can."

Sykes was old, a little deaf and an unpromising candidate for questioning. He rarely went out, for he suffered from rheumatism and this was bad weather for him. He examined the photograph, was certain that he had never met the woman in his life before, although he thought she resembled a parlour-maid who had been in the house with him when he was butler to Sir Willoughby Dayus.

"That was forty years ago," he admitted, "but I've got a great memory for faces. I never forget a face."

MacNeill gently waved him away.

Billy Mandell motioned the old man out of the room. When he had been dispatched to prepare his underlings for a similar ordeal, Mandell sighed.

"Not much there," he said commiseratingly. "Here comes the cook. I don't think she'll be much better."

His prophecy was fulfilled in detail. Mrs. Cash had never seen the woman of the photograph before, and said so regretfully.

"It was an 'orrible crime. I read all about it in the paper. Poor lady. There's no saying the kind of men that's going about."

Within ten minutes, Mandell had finished his task and the entire staff of Malden Court had returned to the comparative privacy of their quarters to discuss this new and startling invasion of their rights and privileges as citizens.

Mandell was a little disappointed at the result.

"I hoped maybe you would pick up something," he said. "I didn't think you would, mind you, but you never know what the servants can find to talk about and they sometimes see a lot more than you think. Anyway, that's everybody except Haydock the gamekeeper, and the Winchester Police have talked to him until he hasn't got a whisper left."

MacNeill pondered, then:

"What about your friend?" he suggested.

Mandell frowned.

"My friend? Oh, Hettche!" He ran his fingers through his hair. "Hettche is in London. He went down by car yesterday. Anyway, he wouldn't know. He's rarely over the doorstep. Spends his time reading books when he's here. No, he certainly wouldn't know her!" He laughed at the absurdity of the suggestion. "Hettche's a woman hater. Never speaks to them or about them. He wouldn't even pass the time of day with the maids."

"Queer," said Superintendent MacNeill.

Mandell shrugged his broad shoulders.

"That's my opinion too—but you can't change him."

"You've tried, have you?"

"I've tried and better tried," Mandell said. "I've asked him out here, there and everywhere, but you won't get him to stir in company. It's a—a mania with the feller."

"A phobia?" the policeman asked thoughtfully.

Mandell agreed.

"A phobia. That's the word I was looking for."

"You got him out to Gavillan's party!"

Mandell nodded grimly.

"With a struggle—and that finished me. He sat in a corner by himself all night and read a book. Never spoke to a damned soul. That's no way for a gentleman to behave at a party." He laughed as he looked up. "It's a good job we're not all alike. I'll tell him you called. When he comes back I'll give you a ring."

MacNeill rose.

"It may not be necessary, but you know what these routine jobs are like. If you don't see everyone, you might miss the man who does know something. If you do that, you might as well not see anyone."

Mandell followed him out to the door.

"Come back again, Super. One of these nights I'll have you and Tommy over! Maybe we can arrange it. I'll call round on him and see. I want to get the gen on all this business, anyway."

"Fine," said MacNeill. He got into the car. As he did so something moved at a window high up in the front of the house. He saw a white, thin face, heavy dark horn-rimmed spectacles. For a second only he saw the curious eyes staring down at him. Then the face was withdrawn.

He switched on the motor, let it run for a moment and pressed his foot down on the clutch. The big car moved forward slowly and as it went Superintendent MacNeill's grey eyes were alive with interest. The mysterious Mr. Hettche might have his peculiarities of conduct, but he was not alone in that. So far as his avoidance of feminine society was concerned, Superintendent MacNeill was prepared to be tolerant indeed. What did interest him was his equally remarkable intention of avoiding the company of the police.

He drove back to Marks Malden a very curious man.

CHAPTER XVI

WHEN the police car had disappeared among the trees of the driveway, Dale Hettche turned away from the window at which he had been standing. His dark eyes were thoughtful as he made his way down to where Mandell sat in the library.

"What was he wanting?"

Mandell lit a cigarette.

"Information," he said slowly.

Hettche sat down.

"About whom?"

"He's investigating the murder of that woman who was found in the Mere."

The smaller man frowned.

"Queer to find a policeman with the reputation of MacNeill on a case like that."

Mandell was not perturbed.

"They'd ask for a good man, Dale, and the Yard would oblige. MacNeill would be at a loose end." He shrugged the matter away. "I told him you were in London."

Hettche frowned.

"Was that wise?"

"I think it was. You don't want to see him unless you have to. He may come back, of course, in which case you'd better have a word with him. If he doesn't, I'll be just as well pleased."

The smaller man walked across to the window.

"He questioned the staff. I heard you call them up."

Mandell chuckled.

"And a damned good laugh it was too. Old Sykes would have yarned to him all day. He once knew a woman who looked like the woman in MacNeill's photograph. It was about forty years ago."

"Then she was young?"

Mandell was cautious.

"The girl in the photograph? Not particularly."

"Who was she?"

Mandell lit a cigarette.

"How the devil should I know? Or where she came from either." He was silent for a moment. "I don't like these kind of things happening, Dale. We don't want the police in the district if we can help it."

Hettche's smile was cold.

"That's true enough." From where he sat, he could see a broad-shouldered figure in tweeds approaching the house. "You're going to have another visitor."

Peter Spain was on the steps when Mandell went into the hall. He looked at the man from the Moorings curiously.

"Hullo, Spain. What brings you here?" There was no warmth in his greeting, but if Spain noticed it, he gave no sign of having done so.

"You had MacNeill here?"

Mandell nodded.

"Were you speaking to him?"

"No. I saw him arriving. I was on the way over." He walked through the hall towards the library. "Mind if I sit down."

"Sit down," Mandell said, with a curious lack of enthusiasm. When the man had done so, he found a seat for himself. "What interest have you in MacNeill?"

Spain took out his pipe, rubbed the bowl of it along his nose.

"Not a great deal. I wondered why he was here."

"You'll have an opportunity to ask him," Mandell said pleasantly, "for he'll be across to see you."

"What's his business?"

"He's in charge of this murder case."

"Which murder case?" Spain asked pointedly.

"This business at Malden Mere."

Spain's eyes were inscrutable.

"I see. I suppose I'll have a call from him then?"

"You will," Mandell said with conviction, "and soon too."

Spain puffed thoughtfully.

"I can't tell him anything," he said thoughtfully. "I could guess a few things perhaps, but the law isn't interested in guesswork. Where is Hettche?"

"In London."

Spain was surprised.

"So soon? He's a damned fast worker. He was here when I came across the lawn. I could see him from the slope." There was a sardonic twist to his lips. "That's what you told MacNeill, I take it?"

Mandell laughed aloud.

"You're a cool devil, Spain. I don't know whether I like you or not." There was an edge of steel in his voice. "Yes, I'll be frank with you. That's what I told MacNeill. Hettche hates meeting people and obviously he couldn't know anything about this damned woman."

Spain was prepared to concede as much.

"That's probably true. I don't object to stringing the law along." He puffed for a moment or so. "I wonder why they sent MacNeill out on a job like this?" There was a note of amusement in his voice, of a sudden he leaned forward. "Did he say anything about the attack on Gavillan?"

110

"Not a damned word." Mandell was a little incensed. "You'd have thought he'd have been full of it. I went over to see Tommy to get the story. He was out and Pat was with him."

Spain's eyes were amused.

"That's what Flett told me too." He shrugged the matter away as he rose. "All right. I'll get away. I wanted to find out about MacNeill. He couldn't tell you anything? Couldn't give you any information?"

"He was looking for it," Mandell said.

Spain pushed his Donegal hat to the back of his head.

"This is getting to be a very mysterious part of the world. I'm beginning to think I've had enough of it."

Mandell smiled pleasantly.

"You're lucky that you can go when you want," he said thoughtfully. "Very lucky." He walked through to the hall. "If MacNeill drops in, I'd be obliged if you'd keep quiet about Dale. It would look damned funny if he heard he was still here. I should have let him speak to him, but you know how it is when you've got a guest."

"I know full well," Spain said. He raised his hand in salute and went out of the house. He crossed the lawn towards the spruce wood and as he went he was whistling softly. When he reached the fringe of trees he looked round. Mandell was still standing where he had left him.

There was a pathway here which led to the rear of the wood. A footbridge led across the Ede, and ten minutes walking brought him to the sparse acres of woodland which surrounded the Moorings. He made his way disconsolately along the pathway and as he went he turned over in his mind the problem which had puzzled him for more than a year. He was still pondering it when the rambling, untidy outline of the house loomed up ahead of him, through the trees.

Silk was on the lawn, a walking-stick in his hand, and the man was approaching in his direction. Of a sudden he caught sight of his employer and bore down upon him. He stood with him for a moment then pointed to the house.

Spain nodded and went up to the house. He made his way into the long, low-roofed morning-room and the woman who stood by the fire swung round at his entrance.

"Hello, Braddock," he said.

Ada Klein's tall maidservant was dressed in a suit of rough

tweeds which did nothing to dispel the illusion of masculinity. She was smoking a cigarette. Now she tossed the end of it into the fire and sat down.

"I was afraid I was going to miss you, Peter."

He shrugged.

"I was across at Mandell's."

Her eyes narrowed.

"I wouldn't do that too often. Ada wouldn't like it. Anyway, it's dangerous. Mandell must know now what he suspected before. That fellow could be dangerous."

Spain patted his hip.

"I can take care of myself pretty well."

She shook her head.

"I don't know about that. A lot of smart people have made that mistake. I think it's risky. You know what happened to Gavillan last night?"

"I know what nearly happened to him," he said, then: "How is Ada?"

"She's fine. She could actually move around a little today. Sometimes I think this place really does agree with her. Only she's worried. You've been away so much."

"I know!" he said. His face was suddenly hard. "I was in London—trying to trace her. I had a hell of a time. I was at every little hotel in the West End. It wasn't easy at all. I booked rooms for her at Mellanby's Hotel in Kensington. It's one of the best private hotels in the city. I sent her bags there. She was booked in the name of Mary Dane."

Braddock lit another cigarette.

"When did she leave here?"

He made a rapid mental calculation.

"On the night of the twelfth."

"Then she's been dead for ten days."

Spain nodded.

"As far as I can figure. I sent her off by way of Meredale. I wanted her to have Silk along with her for company. She wouldn't have him." He laughed grimly. "Mary Lou Slatter would have her own way in everything. I sent him off to follow her just because I was afraid. Not of that—I didn't think Cutten suspected—but I wanted to be on the safe side."

"And Silk saw nothing?"

"Not a damned thing. He got ahead of her on the road. He thinks she saw him when the moon came up, for she started to run away from him. Silk was afraid to go after her in case she would start to scream. He nipped back into the wood. That was all so far as he was concerned. He has only his eyes to rely on —no hearing at all. The moon went away and the rain came on. It stayed on for the rest of the night."

"And Mary Lou was lying in the Mere," she said slowly. Her heavy brows were drawn into a frown. "I'll tell Ada. She's been terribly worried. It wouldn't have been so bad if you had come across."

Spain shook his head.

"Too dangerous. And I was away most of the time. For the last week I've been walking round London looking around for her. What a grim joke. I didn't know about it till I saw the newspaper. Poor Mary Lou Slatter!"

Braddock's expression was grim.

"Poor Mary Lou Cutten! She was a fool not to divorce him. That would have saved her a lot of trouble."

"It would have saved her life," Spain said harshly. He reached for his pipe, lit it, then: "You took a chance on coming over here by daylight."

"I brought over a basket of eggs," Braddock said, "and I came the back road. I left the car at the Spinney Road. Nobody ever goes round there. Anyway, eggs are always a good alibi. Everybody uses them—even the Gavillans."

"You've been round there?"

"I'm going," she said. "Ada wants to see the girl. She's very fond of her. I like her myself. Old Gavillan may be what he is—he's got a very sweet daughter."

Something moved by the doorway and in a flash Spain was on his feet. He took two strides across the room and as he did so he heard someone laugh gently.

"Who's there?" he said.

The door was pushed wide to the wall.

"Old Gavillan himself," said a familiar voice.

Tommy Gavillan stepped into the room. He was smiling but the smile was cold and deadly.

CHAPTER XVII

FOR the space of two seconds no one spoke!

Peter Spain stared at the Irishman with an odd dismay in his dark eyes. How long had Gavillan been there? How much had he heard?

Gavillan was looking round him with an air that contained a certain grim amusement, then:

"I didn't know you had company, Spain."

Spain looked at the woman.

"This is Mrs. Braddock. She is Mrs. Klein's nurse."

"I've heard of you," said Tommy. He looked at her for a moment. "I've met Mrs. Klein once or twice. Pat talks a lot about her."

Spain had regained his composure.

"Have a seat, Gavillan—and a drink. Mrs. Braddock is just about to go."

"You've got to pay me yet, Mr. Spain," the big woman said and Spain had the grace to blush.

"Of course. I'd forgotten that. How much?" He groped in his pocket and she laughed a deep, rumbling laugh.

"I'll get it next time. You can leave it with Silk." She lifted her handbag from the chair on which it was lying. "One pound, seven and sixpence," she said. "Good day. Good day, Mr. Gavillan. Give my regards to Miss Pat."

Gavillan came up to his feet.

"Good day, Mrs. Braddock."

Spain escorted her out to the door. His eyes were hard and when he spoke his voice was cold.

"I warned you not to come here, Braddock. That's the sort of move that could ruin everything we've worked for."

The big woman frowned.

"He won't suspect anything—but it was bad luck. Do you think he was outside the door long enough to hear anything?"

"Heaven knows!" said Spain piously. He let her out and returned to the room.

Gavillan was sitting where he had left him, his blue eyes staring meditatively into the fire. He looked up as the younger man came into the room.

"That's a pretty big woman."

Spain nodded curtly.

"She tops me by two inches and I'm five feet ten."

"Where did Mrs. Klein pick her up?"

"I can't tell you that. I think she's been with her for years. Are you interested in Mrs. Braddock?" There was a challenging note in his voice which Gavillan did not miss.

"I'm interested in a lot of people, Spain."

Spain's features were impassive.

"I'll bet you are—and not without reason." He relaxed so suddenly that he seemed a different man. He walked over to the decanter. "Have a drink, Gavillan. I was coming over to see you today anyway." He poured out a drink and brought it over.

Gavillan accepted it.

"Thanks." He pushed it to one side.

Spain watched him carefully.

"What's on your mind?"

The Irishman sat back in his chair.

"A lot of things, Spain. I've had a pretty full time recently."

"That's true," Spain said.

Gavillan lifted the glass to his lips, tasted it thoughtfully. Spain watched him with some amusement.

"Go on. We don't dope our whisky."

"Some folk do," Gavillan said. "I knew a feller in the States who did that. Name of Camello. He ran a 'speak' and he'd dose a customer's drink with arsenic for a suitable fee." He smiled as at some ancient recollection then became practical, and when Tommy was practical he was brisk.

"You heard what happened to me last night?"

"I did. The village was full of it. Pitman told me about it this morning. So did Mandell. Somebody tried to shoot you."

"That's correct," Tommy said.

"They got the man?"

"Name of Solus—Harry Solus. Did you know him?"

Spain shook his head.

"Not me, Gavillan. I don't know many of those kind of people."

"I wondered about that," Tommy said. "That's what brought me over here. I came to find out."

The younger man's eyes were expressionless.

"What do you want to find out, Gavillan. Don't beat about the bush. I like straight questions and answers."

Gavillan pushed aside the glass which he had only tasted.

"Right. I'll put it to you straight, Spain. You've been here for six months now—and in that time a few odd things have happened in this vicinity."

"Such as what?"

Gavillan eyed him steadily.

"Such as you coming about the house a lot. Such as someone breaking in last October while I was in Ireland and Flett was in London. I never mentioned that to the police because I wasn't sure about it. A window was forced at the back of the house. Nothing was taken—nothing at all."

Spain gave him glance for glance.

"And you think it was me."

"I think it could have been."

The younger man shook his head decidedly.

"It wasn't. That's my answer to you there. Why should I do that, Gavillan?" His voice was curious.

Gavillan said slowly:

"I couldn't figure out. Someone got in. A tramp or a burglar would have taken something. There's plenty of silver and stuff around. This feller didn't, but he did look around. I figured afterwards it was a reconnaissance effort."

"I see. When did you think of that?"

Gavillan's face hardened.

"After the police found those plates in my safe," he said. "The break-in puzzled me. When the other thing happened I put two and two together. The first time he was casing the place. He had a chance to examine the safe, look for burglar alarms and check up on the house. Two months later, the big job was carried through."

Spain's eyes showed a measure of approval.

'I think you're right. I didn't know there had been an earlier attempt." He puffed meditatively. "Yes—I think you're right."

"I know I am," Gavillan said. "That little trick nearly put me away for keeps. It was only a fluke that let me get by—the sort of thing that crops up once in a lifetime. The feller who worked that fiddle could never have anticipated a legal technicality knocking the bottom out of the case."

Spain made no answer and the Irishman leaned over.

"That didn't work, so they thought out another trick—only this time they didn't trouble about being subtle. They just used the old-fashioned strong-arm method."

"And it didn't work!"

There was a little grin in Tommy Gavillan's blue eyes.

"It didn't. I'm a lucky, lucky feller. But that kind of luck can't last for ever, Spain. Anyway, I'm not the kind of feller that lets somebody take a poke at him, without poking back again."

Spain blew a little cloud of smoke.

"I think I know what you mean. The best form of defence is attack."

"I couldn't have put it better myself," said Tommy Gavillan calmly. "Anyway, I'm no sitting rabbit. I've been a lot of things in my life but I've always been able to handle my own difficulties." He leaned forward and his voice hardened. "What brought you to Marks Malden, Spain? I want an answer to that!"

Spain's insolent eyes met his.

"I guess I liked the place."

"Why?"

"For the usual reasons. A fellow has to anchor somewhere."

Tommy Gavillan nodded.

"I figured you'd say something like that. I've been keeping my eye on you for a little, Spain—and I've learned a lot, I've learned an awful lot."

"Such as?" Spain asked gently.

Gavillan held up a big hand and ticked off the points on his stumpy fingers.

"Such as the fact that these things I've spoken about have happened to me since you came to live here. Such as the fact that on the day of the trial, you carried an invitation to Pat to visit Mrs. Klein. You said her 'phone was out of order, but it rang while Pat was there. You didn't want the old lady to telephone in case Pat refused to go over. Anyway, the invitation gave you an excuse for calling."

Spain removed the pipe from his mouth.

"Go on," he said gently.

Gavillan nodded.

"I'm going to. While Pat was away somebody called Flett to the Hants County Hospital in Winchester. It was a fake call—but Flett fell for it and went away. That left the house

117

empty. While it was empty somebody paid a visit to it and went through the safe. That isn't easily done, Spain. It isn't everyone who can open a safe. I reckon the man who did that was the same man who had been there before—and I reckon you were that man!"

"You're doing a lot of reckoning," Spain suggested. There was a little sneer in his voice which Gavillan didn't fail to note.

He leaned forward.

"Maybe I am—but I came over here today to let you know just how much I know."

"And it's quite a lot," Spain said. His voice was serious. "I didn't know you suspected just as much. What makes you think I was as interested in you as all this would suggest?"

Gavillan sat back and dug his hands into the loose pockets of his tweed jacket.

"Ever hear of a man called Sheldon? Drew Sheldon?"

A little spot of colour crept into the younger man's sallow face.

"I've heard of Sheldon," he said softly. "He was an old friend of yours, Gavillan."

"He was," Gavillan said pleasantly. "He isn't now."

"What happened to him?"

The Irishman looked into the dark eyes.

"It's a pretty small world," he said slowly. "I've an idea you maybe know that, Spain. I've an idea you know a lot of things that no ordinary feller could know. I've had that idea for a week or two now. No—don't stop me. I came over to have this out with you. There's something going on that I don't understand—but I understand enough about it to know that you're playing a damned deep game."

The younger man was very still.

"So you've come for a reckoning, Gavillan!"

"That's right."

"When anybody comes to me in that sort of mood," Spain said softly, "I'm prepared to listen to them. I'll work along with a man who's reasonable—but he's got to have something to give himself. I'm not buying any pig in a poke. All you've told me means nothing to me. I'm not greatly interested in the sort of things you figure out for yourself. What I am interested in is facts."

Gavillan showed his white teeth in a smile.

"You want facts? Right—I'll give you one or two. There

was a woman murdered here a few days ago! That's the first of them!"

Spain drew in his breath.

"Well?" he said harshly.

"The second of them is that you knew her! She had been living in this house! Don't lie to me. I saw her last time I was here. She was standing by the window when we arrived!"

Spain did not move at all for he saw the small, squat automatic in Tommy Gavillan's hand. How long it had been there he did not know, but there was menace in the black muzzle which pointed at him.

Gavillan raised it a very little.

"Who was she?"

"Her name," Spain said softly, "was Mary Lou Slatter. Her maiden name, I mean. She married a man called Cutten. Lee Cutten."

Gavillan stiffened.

"Lee Cutten? There was a Lee Cutten in the old Sheldon crowd. I never met him, but Sheldon spoke of him a lot. He was in the East. He handled things for Sheldon out in California!"

"That's right," Spain said. "She didn't get along with her husband. A lot of women don't. Lee left her flat. She was foolish enough to follow him to England! Now she's dead!"

The Irishman stared.

"You're Cutten! You kept her here and——"

Spain shook his head.

"No, I'm not Cutten. I think you and I had better have a talk, Gavillan. There's a lot to explain." He watched the Irishman rise.

Gavillan looked down at him.

"Don't move," he said. "We're going to have a talk—but it isn't going to be here. You're coming over to Chyme Close, Spain. And you're not going to talk to me alone. MacNeill is——"

He felt something knock his arm and he swung round with the speed of light.

Fast as he was, Braddock was faster! The big woman's hand engulfed his own, gun and all. She swung it round with incredible strength and applied a professional grip.

The automatic dropped to the floor. In a second Spain had retrieved it.

"Now you'll maybe be sensible!" he growled. "Stand still, Gavillan, or——"

As he spoke there came the sound of a car in the driveway. It passed the window before his startled eyes and at the wheel of it he saw the large and formidable figure of Superintendent MacNeill.

"Hell!" he said. His hand went to his pocket and when it appeared there was something like a tiny silver cylinder in it.

Gavillan lurched forward.

"Damn you!" he roared.

Spain squeezed the rubber bulb which was in his palm. There was a little puff of bluish vapour and it took the Irishman between the eyes. He staggered back. The world began to whirl around within the confines of his brain. There was a blinding, absorbing light within him, then of a sudden it changed to blackness. He slid forward and only the strong arms of the woman sustained him. Very gently she held him, then let him slide to the floor. She bent over him and with a deft forefinger drew back his eyelid.

"He's out," she said. "He'll be like that for an hour!"

Peter Spain nodded. He returned the spray to his pocket and as he did so there was a loud and peremptory knock on the door. He looked at the woman.

"Get him out of here," he said. "Open the windows. After that, get out by the back way!"

He went out of the room, along the hall and opened the door.

.

CHAPTER XVIII

SUPERINTENDENT MACNEILL was standing on the doorstep, a large and forbidding figure. He nodded as the younger man appeared.

"Mr. Spain?"

Spain smiled.

"You're MacNeill. I've heard Tommy Gavillan speak of you. I've seen you before. The day you came to the Close with Pat."

"Of course!" MacNeill said. "I'm here on another errand today. Not a pleasant one either."

Spain led him into the hall.

"Come along to the study, Superintendent. We can talk in private there." He indicated a door and when they stepped through it, MacNeill found himself in a small, untidy room which was cold and cheerless.

Spain was in no ways put about.

"I don't use this place much," he confided. "The old Admiral had it as his business room when he was here, but he had a lot of employees. I had the telephone taken out and put in the hall." He bent over to lift an electric radiator into a more central position, plugged it in and sat back to watch the elements begin to glow. "There you are. That's a bit better."

MacNeill had produced his pipe.

"I suppose you know why I'm here?"

Spain chuckled.

"I think I can guess. This attack on Gavillan last night!"

The policeman sighed.

"No, Mr. Spain. That was interesting and informative. Very informative, but that wasn't what brought me to Marks Malden. The Yard have been asked to take over the investigation of the murder of this woman whose body was found in Malden Mere the other day."

Spain looked surprised.

"I read about that. There was a photograph in the paper."

"This was it," said Superintendent MacNeill. He produced it from the depths of his pocket. "I'd like you to take a look at it, Mr. Spain. We're trying to find someone who may have known or even seen the woman."

Peter Spain stared down at the likeness of Mary Lou Slatter for a long moment.

"Quite young, wasn't she?"

"In her middle thirties. Have you ever seen her before?"

"No. Not to the best of my knowledge."

"You don't know who she is?"

"I do not."

MacNeill retrieved his picture with a sigh.

"Nobody does," he said, and his voice was unpleasant. "Now I've had to handle this routine work for a long, long time, Mr. Spain, and here's a thing I've always noticed. A funny, funny thing." He paused impressively and Spain listened attentively.

"What's that?"

"To begin with nobody knows the murdered party. They've never seen or heard of him; never knew he even existed—even if it turns out later on he lived next door to them all his life."

Spain chuckled.

"I suppose that's natural, Superintendent. Ordinary, everyday people don't like to get mixed up with police proceedings."

"I've noticed that too," MacNeill said. "But here's the queer part of it, Mr. Spain. Once the police do begin to pin down a few facts, and build up a bit of a picture—once we're in a position to go to So and So and say—'You knew this man', the whole picture changes. People come from far and near to tell us they once sat beside him at the Coliseum on the twelfth of May, 1927. They give us all sorts of details and information that you'd never suspect."

"By which you mean that if you can get a start here, the information will come rolling in?"

MacNeill nodded profoundly.

"So quickly we won't be able to keep pace with it."

Spain smiled, but there was no merriment in his smile.

"I'm afraid I can't give you that start, Superintendent."

The superintendent did not look unduly perturbed.

"Maybe not. Between you and me, Mr. Spain, we've got a little as it is. Just a very little, mind you—but as I told you that little grows and grows. It's like the hole in the dyke that the wee fellow put his finger into."

"I've heard the story," Spain said thoughtfully. "What have you managed to pick up?" He watched MacNeill with some curiosity. "I hope that doesn't sound nosy?"

MacNeill laughed loudly to indicate how little like "nosiness" it really did sound.

"No, it's no great breach of regulations to tell you that. In a day or so, it will be in all the papers. Anyway, as a matter of principle I always like to tell the folk that are most concerned first." There was a guileless note in his voice.

Spain's face was expressionless.

"Good. I'll be glad to hear about anything of interest."

MacNeill looked at him solemnly.

"First, she was an American. We know that by her clothing.

There were a few articles that had American labels on them."

Spain nodded.

"But that wouldn't necessarily have made her an American. Lots of English girls have been in the States."

"That's true. She must have been out quite a long time for she'd had quite a lot of dental work done. We took the opinion of a leading dentist in Winchester and he says that it was done in the States. They have a different technique out there and they use different materials."

"Yes?"

"She was probably a dancer," MacNeill said. "Dr. Blake tells me the muscular development of her legs proves that. I don't know much about the muscular development of girls' legs, so I took his word for it. A dancer or a chorus girl."

"That's something!" Spain admitted.

MacNeill nodded.

"Quite a bit. She'd also had a baby. There was the well-defined impression of a wedding ring on her finger. She must have worn it for some time. Presumably she was a married woman. The doctor is satisfied that she had had a child at some time. That's quite a lot to be going on with."

Spain smoked thoughtfully.

"You're correct there, Superintendent. I don't think you'll have much difficulty in finding out a lot more about her. Not with that to work on."

"It's quite a lot," the big man said. "We've got her description. We know she was thirty-five or thirty-six, married—and had lived for a long time in the States. We know she'd had a child several years before. Yes—it all adds up. One of these days we'll get her name. After that it's all plain sailing."

"I hope so," Spain said.

The big man took the pipe from his mouth.

"You've been in the States, Mr. Spain?"

Peter Spain agreed.

"I was born there."

"Been in England long?"

"I came over during the war. I was in the Army."

"I was in it at one time myself," MacNeill admitted. "A fine, fine thing the Army. Gives you something to do with your time. I was in the Argylls. Of course that was a long time back." He broke off his reminiscence briskly. "And you liked this country so much you stayed on, eh?"

"Something like that."

"Which part of the States do you come from?"

"Detroit."

MacNeill nodded knowledgeably.

"Where they make all the motor-cars and the like of that I've heard of it. Well, well, it's a small world too. What was your line of business over there?"

There was a little glitter in the younger man's eyes.

"I was in business—or at least my mother was. I was one of the lucky ones. I didn't need to work too hard."

"I've met folk like that," the Scot admitted. "It's a grand thing to be born with a silver spoon in your mouth." He knocked out his pipe and rose as he did so. "They tell me you've got a manservant here—a deaf and dumb man."

"That's correct. Silk has been with me for years. He's out at the moment. As a matter of fact, I think he's on the road to the village for he went out shortly before you appeared."

"There wouldn't be much point in me trying to get a statement out of him," MacNeill said pleasantly. "Well, I'll get on my way now, Mr. Spain. If you think you can give me any help, I'll be glad to hear from you."

"Are you putting up at Chyme Close?"

"No. I don't stay with friends when I'm on business. It gets to be awkward. I'm at the village inn. This is the way out, is it?" He pushed open the door and walked down through the hall. At the door to the long morning-room he stopped and sniffed the air suspiciously. "That's a funny sort of smell!"

Spain smiled his amusement.

"It's some stuff Mrs. Braddock's had," he said truthfully.

"Who's Mrs. Braddock?"

"She's a sort of nurse companion to one of our neighbours. Mrs. Klein, lives over at Blandfort. She keeps poultry and supplies the rest of us with eggs. Mrs. Braddock comes round with them every week. She was here this morning and she had a bandage on her hand. The place reeked of that stuff."

"I see," MacNeill said. He walked out to where the car was waiting for him. "Well, that's that, Mr. Spain. I'm glad I had an opportunity to speak to you. I was over at Mandell's this morning. I'm a little bit disappointed for Mr. Mandell said he thought you might have a little information for me."

Peter Spain did not rise.

"I'm afraid Mandell lets his tongue run away with him," he said pleasantly. "It's a habit a lot of people have."

MacNeill nodded pleasantly.

"And that's the truth. It isn't a fault of yours, though, Mr. Spain. I can see that. Good afternoon." He got into the car and drove away.

Peter Spain watched the car until it was out of sight, then, when the sound of it had died away he went back to the morning-room. He was closing the windows when he heard a footstep.

Braddock came into the room at his back. The big woman looked at him almost anxiously.

"What did he have to say, Peter?"

He frowned.

"I thought you were going away, Braddock?"

She shook her head.

"It wasn't too safe. I took Gavillan to the cellar. I didn't want to move out of it—not with that fellow around."

He closed the last of the windows.

"That infernal odour is still hanging around. Opening the windows didn't do much good. It just blew it back into the hall. MacNeill smelled it and asked me what it was. I had to hand him a bit of a line. I don't know whether he believed me or not."

She sniffed at the air.

"It's almost gone now. What did he have to say?"

"A lot."

"He doesn't suspect you?"

Spain smiled mirthlessly.

"I don't know. Gavillan may have spoken to him. I don't think he has. That, we can find out. But MacNeill's a smart policeman. I'll give him that much credit. He only came on the job yesterday and he even told me things about Mary Lou Slatter I didn't know myself. He knew she was an American and he knew she'd been on the stage. He knew she was a married woman and he told me she'd had a baby."

Braddock stared at him.

"I didn't know that."

"Neither did I. She never mentioned it. But the doctors wouldn't be wrong there." He paused for a moment. "She must have hated Cutten a lot. The baby helps me to understand what sustained her hatred of him. That used to puzzle me. Not many people can have a grudge over all those years."

Braddock was prepared to agree.

"It makes it a lot more understandable. Lee Cutten has a lot to answer for." She looked up at him. "What about Gavillan? I don't think it's safe to leave him here."

Spain considered.

"I think you're right. Damn him anyway! Somebody's always got to get mixed up in things, Braddock. What about Blandfort?"

She thought for a moment.

"I don't see why not. There's a wine cellar there that's never been used. You'll have to talk with him before you decide on anything."

There was a hard little smile on Peter Spain's lips.

"That's very true," he agreed. "I'll get him over tonight—just as soon as it's dark. I'll give him a shot of something to keep him quiet for half an hour or two. You'd better get back. Ada will be worrying. I wish she was out of it."

"She doesn't," Braddock said. "She's got a wonderful brain, that woman. It's a pity she's so crippled with arthritis. If it wasn't for that she'd show us all a thing or two."

"She may do that yet," said Peter Spain. He watched the big woman away and as she went, he pondered the remarkable intellect of Ada Klein who sat at her wheel chair before a window at Blandfort.

CHAPTER XIX

In the late afternoon, Superintendent MacNeill with a mission in view drove into Winchester and at Police Headquarters had an interview with the police surgeon.

"The information I gave you on the 'phone this morning is correct," he said. "I had Dr. Livesy from Bristol in here today and we went over the points at issue together. He agrees with me on every detail and I'm glad of that."

MacNeill chuckled.

"So am I, Doctor, for it fits in with my own ideas very well. In fact, it's made to order for them. Never knew so much unanimity on a matter of medical evidence in my life."

The surgeon smiled.

"Anyway, you can accept it as final. Livesy is one of the foremost specialists in forensic medicine in Europe." He talked for a few moments more, and when he had to leave to keep an appointment, MacNeill sought out Inspector Cleaver with a query.

Cleaver was pleased to see him, agreeable to his request.

"Solus is in a cell," he said. "He'll come up tomorrow before Mr. Daisborough, but we'll ask for a remand. We'll get it too. I'll have Tight bring him along at once." He rang for a constable, issued his instructions and sat back. "What do you think you'll make of it?"

McNeill looked thoughtful.

"I'm not sure yet. I think it's a bigger thing than any of us realized. I'm certain of that. It's a bit too early to make predictions."

Cleaver looked at him warily.

"The newspapers are making a lot of the fact that you've been put on this case," he suggested.

"The newspapers will make a lot out of anything," said MacNeill good-humouredly. "I've seen some of the articles. 'A Central Office Man in Winchester'. 'Shake up at Scotland Yard'. Then there was one that said, 'Who Takes Over Corporal Violet Case?' I tell you, Inspector, that's their bread and butter."

Cleaver smiled.

"I suppose there's something in what you say. We don't get so much publicity down here, and to tell you the truth I'm all the better pleased for it."

MacNeill was in complete agreement.

"The newspapers can make you, but they can break you too. Many a good man's lost his chances of promotion because the newspapers gave him bad publicity. I've seen it happen myself."

Cleaver had gone across to the office safe. He swung the door open and took out a large, brown envelope. This he brought over to the table.

"This is Lavery's stuff. There isn't a great deal that is likely to interest you, but there's a bit of a note."

He emptied the contents of the envelope on to the table and MacNeill saw a penknife, a silver pocket-watch, a handful of loose change, a cigarette-case and one or two odds and ends such as any man might carry.

The inspector picked up a well worn wallet, opened it and took out a scrap of paper.

"There was seventeen pounds in notes here," he said. "But what did interest me was this." He handed across a sheet of paper which had been torn from a pocket diary. On it, in a clear, round hand, someone had written:

Two gates but north will be shut. We'll not be later than eleven o'clock or earlier than ten. Take back road to Bramdean and to Petersfield. Change cars at Tim's and north to Sleaford. Rooms booked in Stag Hotel for two days. Wait here till clear call comes through. Drop Solus at Guildford. Go back alone.

MacNeill looked pleased.

"These were his instructions. I'm glad to see Solus mentioned. Every little helps. I want to put the weight on that man."

Cleaver had produced a driving licence.

"This is the one he had on him when we found him. It is made out in the name of Cannavan. You'll notice though that he's written his name on it here, and that the writing is the same as the writing on the note."

The Central Office man made a comparison and discovered that this was indeed the case. He tapped the scrap of paper.

"Lavery wrote this. I'd say he got his instructions by telephone. He took a note of time, place and detail like that. It's a pity there hadn't been a bit more to it."

There was a tap at the door. A uniformed constable entered with the information that Sergeant Tight was waiting with his prisoner.

"Send him in," said Cleaver.

Harry Solus was grey-faced and weary of eye. Overnight, the urgency of his position had been brought home to him and realization of Lavery's death had done nothing to supply emotional tranquillity. He looked at Superintendent MacNeill without malice, was almost prepared to hail him as an ancient ally.

"I'm glad to see you, Super," he said, "and that's the truth of it. I don't like this here place I'm in. A feller was telling me that the last man that was in my cell was hung. That's a fine thing to lie in your bed an' think at nights. Are you taking me back to the City?"

"The Hampshire Police have a prior claim."

"I'd sooner go back to London," Solus said. "I know the law there an' I know the police. This here place gets on my nerves. Do what you can for me, Super."

MacNeill nodded.

"Sure, I'll do what I can, Solus. A lot depends on what you can do for yourself, though. This attempted murder didn't take place in London. It took place right here in Hampshire. The Hampshire Police like to handle their own attempted murderers. That's right, Inspector, isn't it?"

"It couldn't be righter," Cleaver said.

Solus scowled.

"I don't know anything about no attempted murder."

"We found the gun," Cleaver said. "Maybe you've forgotten you made a statement last night."

Harry Solus had forgotten nothing. He capitulated suddenly.

"All right, Super. I'll give you and the gentleman here all I do know. It isn't much. I told you last night Lavery fixed it all up. I've worked the same sort of game before, but he always made the arrangements. He did it by 'phone."

"How do you know that?"

"He told me he did."

"So Lavery had worked for the crowd before?"

In the absence of Lavery in the flesh and in the knowledge that there was little to fear from his spirit, Solus became confidential.

"He did. Lavery did a lot of work for them."

"What about yourself?"

For a moment Harry Solus struggled to deny any implication of his guilt, then, of a sudden, he nodded.

"I've worked for them too. Twice. I was on the Bindloss steal last March. I'm telling you that and I don't have to; I was on that Keston job in Manchester last year. I'm telling you the truth there. Other than that, I don't know a thing."

"Who briefed you for the job?"

"Lavery."

Superintendent MacNeill sighed.

"The wrong man got killed. It's a pity it hadn't been your back that got broken, Solus. We might have got somewhere with Lavery."

Solus was inclined to be indignant.

"A fine thing that to say to a feller, Super. I'm telling you all I can. A man can't do better than his best."

"There's a world of philosophy in that," said Cleaver.

MacNeill returned to the questioning.

"Who briefed Lavery?"

Solus looked at him in silence for a moment.

"Lavery didn't know himself. He used to get 'phone calls from the feller when there was a job on. He always gave his orders over the 'phone. Lavery wasn't the only one that got them. Lew Friedsohn was fixed in the same way. So was the Mole. I'm telling you the truth, MacNeill, this feller was clever. He had a crowd of us on his list and when a job came along— you heard about it by 'phone. Nobody ever saw the fixer!"

"What about the pay-off?"

Solus shrugged.

"Lavery attended to that. He never told me how it was done. There's a lot of different groups. Lavery was the paymaster for our crowd. It always came through: cash—old notes at that. And always more than we figured we'd get."

"You knew who was behind this game?"

Solus nodded.

"We knew what we read in the papers. Corporal Violet! I never saw him—an' I'll bet Lavery never did either."

This was probably true. MacNeill had questioned other men and all of them had told a story which was substantially the same. Corporal Violet had indeed created an organization which was remarkable for its efficiency. How many groups there were, only he himself might know. There was one contact man, and for each group there was a fixer who took orders and recruited suitable men for the task in hand. Lavery was but one of a score of Laveries throughout the Metropolis. He looked back at the man.

"Lavery never told you anything about the 'contact' man?"

Solus said slowly:

"He talked about him, but he didn't know anything. He'd met him twice—when he started in on this game. Once it was on the Heath—and late at night. He came along in a car. Lavery was walking. The second time it was in a house in Lemon Street in Wapping. There was no electric light—just gas, an' it was screened down to a peep. He couldn't tell anybody what he looked like. I asked him about that a dozen times—maybe more. Lavery and me was good friends."

130

"But he couldn't tell you anything?"

Solus shook his head.

"He couldn't. I've heard him talk with Friedsohn. Lew was fixed like that too."

"And if they wanted to get in touch with the 'contact' man?"

Solus shrugged.

"They couldn't. That feller was too clever. When a job was coming along, he 'phoned every day at the same time. Lavery had to be around for that. That's how he got his instructions. We never saw anyone at all."

"What did Lavery call the 'contact' man?"

Solus sighed.

"I tell you I don't know no more than that, Mr. MacNeill. That's as true as I'm sitting in this chair. If I knew anything else I'd tell you that. You know me, Super! I'm the kind of feller that goes the whole distance. Once you've got me, you've got me."

MacNeill nodded.

"So you say. You never heard Lavery mention the 'contact' man at any time?"

"No!"

"You're certain about that?"

Solus looked upwards.

"If I should drop down dead this minute, Super, I didn't!"

MacNeill waited divine intervention. When nothing happened he said:

"That's a pity, Harry. A big pity. If you had happened to hear Lavery say something—it could help me a lot. Lavery must have had a name for him, whether it was his right name or not. Friedsohn and the Mole must have called him something! If I knew what that something was, I could help you a lot. After all, firing off a rifle is one thing—and murder is another."

"It all depends on the way you look at it," said Cleaver thoughtfully.

"And you didn't hit him," said MacNeill.

Cleaver nodded his agreement.

"You certainly didn't."

Solus looked from one to the other. Then he licked his lips. They were dry and hard and cracked but a wild new hope was stirring in his breast.

"Lavery's dead!" he said thickly.

"He's better dead," MacNeill said with quiet dignity.

Harry Solus dropped his voice to a thin whisper.

"I told you I didn't know anything about this 'contact' man. That was the truth. I told you Lavery didn't an' that was the truth too. But Lew Friedsohn figured he knew him. He told Lavery and me once he'd met him years before."

"Where was this?"

Solus looked at the Scotsman.

"Somewhere in the States. He never said where—all he said was he knew him an' he'd seen him before. Lew was in the States for years. He did a stretch there."

"That's right!" MacNeill said. He tried to keep his voice even. "What did Friedsohn call him?"

Solus swallowed.

"Cutten!"

The Scotsman stared at him.

"Cutten?"

"That's what he said. Lavery told him he was a damned fool to open his mouth about things like that. Maybe that was true. He was dead a month later. Somebody put a knife in his back down in Deptford. They said it was one of Gertie Hagin's boys, but I never figured it was. Neither did Lavery."

The superintendent nodded to Cleaver.

"All right, Inspector. That's all."

Sergeant Tight made his appearance a moment later, and removed his charge and as he went Solus looked back.

"Do what you can for me, Super. I've done all I can for you."

Tight pushed him ungently.

"None of your lip, feller. Get on your way."

The door closed behind them. Inspector Cleaver looked up at the big man, with little interest.

"That wasn't much help," he said. "Cutten? Who's Cutten?"

Superintendent MacNeill came to his feet.

"That's the first real break I've had in two years, Cleaver. Lee Cutten was a member of the old Sheldon gang."

Cleaver stiffened.

"The Sheldon gang! That was the crowd Gavillan ran with!"

"It was," said Superintendent MacNeill. "Cutten was one, Tyson was another: a third was Hans Speyer. They called him

132

'The Count'. There were one or two more. Sheldon was a grand organizer. One of the best."

"What happened to him?" Cleaver asked ominously.

MacNeill smiled coldly.

"I'd like to know that myself," he said. "I asked that question myself not so long ago—and I wasn't at all satisfied with the answer!"

He turned and made for the door and as he went his eyes were glowing.

Cleaver watched him go, puzzled.

"Was it Gavillan you asked?"

"It was."

"And what did he tell you?"

"He told me Sheldon was dead," MacNeill said, "but Gavillan isn't always careful about his facts—and I think this is one of the times when he lacks exact information." He opened the door and went out.

CHAPTER XX

IT WAS dark when Superintendent MacNeill drove into the courtyard of the Malden Arms. Rain pattered on the metal roof above his head, smeared the windscreen, and trickled from every surface of the big car. There was a comfortable glow in the room which had been delegated to them, and when he entered it, he heard Bolton moving on the stairs above.

The man came down in a moment more.

"There you are, sir. A nasty night. The young lady was down to see you about an hour ago."

"Miss Gavillan?"

"Yes. Mr. Till went back with her. He said he wouldn't be long, but I was to tell you where he was."

MacNeill considered.

"I'll get on the 'phone to him." He put through a call to Chyme Close. It was Flett who took the call and he was a worried man.

"It's Mr. Gavillan, Super. He hasn't been home all day."

MacNeill drew in a deep breath.

"Gavillan? That's a queer business. When did you see him last?"

"He went into Winchester this morning," Flett said. "Miss Pat was with him. He went to the bank and then he called round at the police station to see the inspector. He had something to put in a statement."

"That's right," MacNeill agreed. "I heard about that." Flett swore in his exasperation.

"They came in about noon and Mr. Gavillan went to the study. He asked me to bring in a fresh bottle of whisky. That was just after he came in. I put it in the decanter, and I know he had a drink out of that. He wasn't in for lunch an' nobody here has laid an eye on him since."

"What does Miss Pat think?"

"She's worried," Flett told him. "An' no wonder. I'm worried myself. Look at the things that's happened around here. I never knew the like in a Christian household. She wanted to see you about it and she went down to the inn, but it was the young Society feller she came back with."

"You mean Inspector Till?"

"That's his name," Flett agreed. "He looks less like a rozzer than any man I've ever seen in my life an' I've seen all sizes an' shapes of them, in every country under the sun, as the good Book says."

MacNeill considered this intelligence.

"Where are they now?"

"They went round to call on the folks at the Court," Flett said. "Miss Pat thought maybe he had gone round there. She 'phoned to them once already but Mr. Mandell was out. She spoke to the other gentleman—name of Hetty."

"And what did Mr. Hettche say?"

Flett could give no exact information on this score.

"He didn't tell her any more than that he wasn't there," the little man said. "Then she went down to the inn."

"Call me when they come back," MacNeill told him and hung up. He went through to wash and Bolton appeared to prepare the evening meal.

"Do you want to wait for Mr. Till, Superintendent?"

MacNeill thought not.

"He may be late. In any case, I want to go up to the Close as soon as possible. I'll have dinner just now."

He sat down to it, and over the meal he considered this new problem that had arisen. Tommy Gavillan was well able to take care of himself. There were few corners in which the Irishman was likely to find himself, from which he was not likely to extricate himself with a minimum of trouble, yet he felt oddly uneasy. Too many queer things had happened to the master of Chyme Close recently, and the man who had contrived them might have made another and more successful attempt.

He was finishing his coffee when he heard a car draw up in front of the inn. A moment later and a door slammed. Then the car pulled away. As it did so, he heard the sound of feet in the hall.

Inspector Till came in, shaking raindrops from his beautiful and well-cut raincoat. He nodded to his superior.

"Evening, Super. That's a stunning girl!"

"Miss Gavillan?"

Till had indeed been referring to Pat Gallivan.

"She's in the nursing line of business. I've known one or two of them in the same profession, but——"

MacNeill took his pipe out of his mouth.

"I'm not much interested in your amorous exploits, Till. What did you find out about Gavillan?"

Till became severely practical.

"Not a thing, sir." He took off his raincoat and hung it up with some considerable care. "Not a single thing. He came home from Winchester about noon and——"

"I've spoken with Flett. I know all that."

"Then you know as much as I do about him," Till said bluntly. "He went out after he came back from Winchester and nobody has seen him since then."

"Did anybody see him go out?"

Nobody had done so. He had been in the study when Flett had brought in a new supply of whisky. After that, his presence could not be accounted for.

"He drank some whisky," Till said. "There was a glass that had been used. I didn't see it myself for Flett took it away and washed it up, but he says it had been used."

The inspector sat down to dinner, talked while he partook of it.

"Miss Gavillan thought he might have gone over to the Court. She 'phoned even, but Mandell was out. She didn't want to talk to the servants about it, so she drove over. I went with her."

"Did you see Mandell?"

"No. He had gone up to London. They didn't expect him back until later tonight. We saw this fellow Hettche."

"What is he like?"

Till considered.

"Pretty quiet sort of chap. Rather slimly built. Five feet six or so, pale and dark. He was very pleasant but he didn't exactly welcome us effusively. I think he was a little surprised we had come there at all."

MacNeill puffed in silence for a moment or two.

"Tommy's been gone since noon then?"

"Yes. That makes it about eight hours."

"It isn't very long," MacNeill said. "There's no accounting for the ideas Gavillan might get into his head."

"Miss Gavillan says he wouldn't have gone away without telling her he was going—especially after what has happened recently."

The superintendent agreed. This was very likely to be true. Gavillan was well aware of the danger he was running, was keenly alive to the fact that he represented a menace to some party who was not particular as to the methods he used. In the face of such knowledge, Tommy was not likely to move too far without taking certain precautions. He looked over at the younger man.

"Did you call on Spain?"

"No. I figured you would be back. The girl said she would ring him up when she got back to the Close. I don't think she's very fond of Spain," he added thoughtfully.

MacNeill sighed.

"Maybe not. I wasn't too fond of him myself. He's a pretty capable article. I wouldn't like to say that he was altogether too scrupulous, but that's neither here nor there at the moment." He knocked out his pipe. "I'm going over to Chyme Close for an hour. You can wait here. There may be a message from Central Office and if there is I'd like you to receive it."

He made his way into the hall, drew on a heavy raincoat and went to the door of the inn. When he pushed it open he heard the gentle hiss of rain on the cobblestones of the courtyard, the gurgle of water in the choked gutters. He stood for a moment in contemplation of these delights, then made for the car which he had left at the rear of the building. He started up the engine and drove as far as the police station. He stopped here and went inside.

Police-Constable Pitman was in his small and comfortable sitting-room, preparing a charge-sheet for the benefit of his inspector, and his eyes were glassy with the efforts of composition. He laid down his pen and rose to welcome the superintendent when his wife ushered him through.

"Good evening, sir. I'm glad to see you indeed. Was there something you wanted from me? Some information of some sort?"

MacNeill indicated that there was.

"I suppose all of the telephone calls here go through the post office?"

Pitman agreed that this was so.

"So that it wouldn't be very safe to put through a confidential call? Not a highly confidential one at any rate?"

The policeman grinned.

"Old Miss Caple has the name of knowing most of the things that go on locally. I say she has the name of it, sir. It may not be true because people always say that sort of thing about country post offices. But if it was highly confidential, I wouldn't like to risk it."

"That's what I thought," MacNeill said thoughtfully. "I want a message sent through to the Yard, Pitman, and I don't want anyone in this part of the countryside to even suspect what I'm doing."

"You'd better send it from Winchester then, sir."

MacNeill considered.

"I think you're right. I want you to take it in there. You've got a motor-bike. I'd like you to 'phone it through yourself."

Pitman was agreeable to this suggestion.

"I'll get my things on right away, sir. What's the message?"

"Call Central Office, identify yourself and ask for Inspector Kelly. Tell him you're calling for me and that you want any information he can give you about Lee Cutten."

"Lee Cutten!"

MacNeill spelled it for him.

"Tell Kelly it's important. I want it delivered by hand as soon as possible. I don't want him to telephone me—and I don't want him to send a letter. I want the information delivered by hand."

Pitman was impressed.

"Very good, sir. I'll get away at once. I'll drop in at the Malden Arms on the way back."

"Excellent," said MacNeill. He took his leave, drove up to Chyme Close where he found Pat Gavillan a worried girl.

She came into the hall to greet him and he saw the little lines of dread around her eyes.

"It's you, Uncle Mac. I—I wondered if it was Daddy."

MacNeill drew off his coat.

"I wouldn't worry about Tommy if I were you," he said kindly. "Tommy can take care of himself as well as anyone I know."

Pat shook her head.

"I can't help worrying, Uncle Mac. Not after what has happened."

He led her back into the library.

"Sit down. I'll have a smoke. It's after nine o'clock and it's high time I had one. No, I'm not unduly worried about Tommy. I've heard Flett's story and I've heard Till's. We'll go over it again. Tell me all that you know and leave nothing out at all."

Pat did as he requested, told him of the trip they had made together into Winchester in the morning, of their return to the Close. To it all, MacNeill listened with interest, then:

"What sort of mood was he in?"

She frowned.

"A little quieter than usual. You know what Daddy was like, usually joking and having fun. He seemed more serious."

"Did he meet anyone in Winchester?"

"Not unless it was at the police station."

"You're certain of that?"

"He drove me around," she said. "We had a few calls to make. He didn't leave the car at all, except when he went in to see Inspector Cleaver. No—I don't think he saw anyone or spoke to anyone."

"He didn't suggest going away at all?"

"No. What he did suggest was my going away. He wanted me to go back to work, but I told him I couldn't while all this was going on. That's the truth too. I couldn't bring myself to go and leave him. I told him that too."

138

"What did he say?"

She looked at him with some exasperation.

"You know Daddy. He made a joke of it all. But I'm frightened, Uncle Mac. It isn't like him to do that—and I can't get those other things out of my mind. They tried to send him to prison then when that didn't work they tried to kill him." She caught hold of his arm. "Who is it, Uncle Mac? Daddy won't speak about it to me. I've begged and pleaded— but he's so stubborn. He just won't tell me a thing!"

MacNeill looked down at her.

"And he won't tell me either, lassie."

"But you—you have an idea?"

He sensed the worry in her voice and felt a little surge of sympathy. He put his big arm around her shoulders.

"I wouldn't worry about it too much."

"But I can't help worrying, Uncle Mac, if I knew what it all meant! Who was behind it! Tell me what you do know!"

He swore softly in his exasperation.

"That's the damned thing, Pat, I don't know anything. I suspect a lot—a good deal more than even Tommy thinks. But I don't know anything. He won't speak—and why he won't speak I can't understand. The man who is behind this thing is evil. The worst man in England—the cleverest criminal we've met in thirty years!"

She looked up at him.

"Who is he?"

"The newspapers call him Corporal Violet."

There was a little silence.

He said slowly:

"We don't know who he is. So far he has been clever enough to keep his identity hidden. That's a difficult thing to do— especially in a little country like England. We've been after him for three years now. When we get him we'll hang him— but so far we haven't got very close to finding him."

She looked up at him.

"Of course I've read about him. Corporal Violet! Why do they call him that?"

MacNeill shrugged.

"They've got to call him something and the newspapers always like to get a touch of drama into everything. They used to call him the 'Napoleon' of crime, and then somebody discovered that one of Napoleon's nicknames had been 'Corporal

Violet'. There was a bit in the paper about it at the time. It told you how the folk used to call him that and toss bunches of violets at him when he rode through a town." He chuckled pleasantly. "It seemed to fit this fellow too, for the men he employs always wear silk stockings over their faces and that gave them a sort of violet colour. Anyway, they gave him the name and it stuck. We call him that ourselves now—officially!" He rose as he spoke. "I'll have to get back now, Pat. But I don't want you to be worried about this. I'll——"

She put up a small white hand and caught at his large one. When she tightened her grip her fingers dug into his flesh.

"Uncle Mac, tell me one thing more!"

"What's that?"

She said woodenly:

"I know the sort of life Daddy lived at one time. He told me about it and he didn't keep anything back. I've always admired him for telling me."

MacNeill's eyes held hers.

"Yes. It took a bit of courage."

She said slowly:

"Knowing that has made things look different to me. I hate to think he did those things, but I don't feel so terribly shocked about it, because I know what he's like now."

"Well?"

She heard her own voice, very small, very far away.

"Tell me the truth, Uncle Mac. Please tell me! You don't think that—that Daddy is Corporal Violet?"

There was a long, long silence. MacNeill looked down at her with an odd gentleness in his grey eyes. Then he smiled.

"No. I don't think that, lassie—but what I do think is that Tommy knows who Corporal Violet is! I'm positive he does— but he's got a queer sense of loyalty. He won't talk—he won't tell. I can't understand that. He can't respect a man with a record like that. That's what puzzles me. Why does he cover him up? Corporal Violet has done his best to put him away twice now. I'm certain I'm correct there. If I'm wrong in that, my whole idea and concept of the case is wrong!" His genuine mystification at the peculiar conduct of Tommy Gavillan brought a little touch of anger to his voice. Queerly enough, it had the effect of breaking the tension as nothing else might have done.

Pat laughed a little bitterly.

"Don't get angry with him, Uncle Mac."

MacNeill's good humour had returned.

"I won't," he said. "I'm getting back. I'll send Till up here in case anything does happen. If Tommy comes back, Till can let me know at once. Good night, Pat."

"Good night," Pat Gavillan said.

She followed him out into the hall, very small, very wistful.

"Good night," she said again. She turned away very quickly, lest he should see the hot tears which flooded her eyes.

CHAPTER XXI

IT WAS still dark next morning when Superintendent MacNeill left his comfortable bed, shaved, dressed and prepared for the events of the day. He was sitting over his breakfast when he heard the sound of a car arriving at the inn, and a few moments later Inspector Till presented himself wearily.

"Nothing doing, Super," he said. "I hung around all night. Slept a bit in the library, and it was pretty cold too."

"And Gavillan didn't come back?"

"He didn't. Miss Gavillan went to bed about one o'clock! I guess she was pretty well bushed. I told her to get off then. Flett sat up till two and I got him off." He pulled off his coat and sat down at the table. "This coffee looks very nice. I can do with some for my head feels as big as a haystack."

MacNeill watched him in silence. After a moment or so the younger man looked up.

"Where do you think he's gone?"

The superintendent scowled.

"I can't say. Gavillan is unpredictable. At the same time it's not like him to do a thing like this. He knows Pat will be worried and he knows I'll be curious, and I've got enough on my mind at the moment without any additional worry."

Till nodded his agreement.

"That's my opinion too. I think it's very queer."

MacNeill said thoughtfully:

"He didn't take the car or the brake. That means he didn't go very far. That's a bit of a puzzle in itself."

"He didn't hire from the village," Till said. "Or from Lower Oxley or from Meredale. I checked up on all of them."

MacNeill rose abruptly.

"You'd better take a couple of hours, just now. We'll have a busy day. If Gavillan doesn't turn up this morning I'll have to notify the Hampshire Police."

"Why not notify them now?"

The Scotsman frowned.

"Because I'm not satisfied," he said slowly. "Gavillan is just the sort of fellow to dive off on some hare-brained scheme of his own. I don't say that's what has happened—but it could be. If it was, he told no one. He didn't tell Pat—he didn't tell me. That means it was a highly confidential business. If it had any bearing on this case, I don't want to spoil things for him."

Till poised a cup of coffee in his hand.

"You're giving him an awful lot of latitude, Super."

"That's true," MacNeill admitted grudgingly. "And I don't know that I'm entitled to do it." He watched the young man for a moment, then:

"I'll take a run out to the Moorings just now to see Spain again. You'd better get a little sleep!"

Till laughed the suggestion to scorn.

"I could go for a week without it, Super."

"Most folks can," MacNeill said drily. "But when they do they aren't much use in an emergency. You've got time for it—get it."

He left his subordinate with this tender suggestion and drove to the Moorings. The grey light of day was filtering through the trees of the avenue, and shaded lights shone in the windows of the rambling old house as he approached it. He left the car, rang the bell and waited.

It was Silk who received him, and if the manservant was surprised to see a representative of the Constabulary at so early an hour, he gave no evidence of it.

MacNeill nodded to him.

"You're Silk. Can you hear me?"

Silk shook his head. He took a small writing-pad from his pocket, wrote something on it and pushed it across.

I CAN LIP READ. SPEAK VERY PLAINLY

MacNeill glanced at it and nodded.

"I want to see Mr. Spain."

Mr. Spain was at breakfast and received him in the comfortable little dining-room. There was a fresh fire burning in the wide fireplace, logs crackled in it and in the air was the pungent odour of freshly brewed coffee.

Spain waved him to a chair by the fire.

"What brings you along at this hour of the day, MacNeill?"

The policeman smiled.

"Duty, Mr. Spain. Unpleasant duty. I'm looking for Gavillan."

Spain looked at him curiously.

"What's happened to him?"

"I'd like to find out," MacNeill confessed. "He left home yesterday morning—a little after noon it was—and he left to come over here. Nobody's seen him since."

Spain stared.

"He left to come over here!"

"So he said," MacNeill said gently. "Just before lunch, it was. I've been thinking things over. He must have come here just about the time that I was here myself."

The young man's face was troubled.

"Who told you that?"

MacNeill rubbed at his ear.

"It may have been Flett, it may have been Pat. I'm not too sure about it myself. Anyway, it's obvious he didn't go very far. He didn't take the car—or the brake. Either he went to the Court or came here. What do you think?"

Spain shook his head grimly.

"He didn't come here wherever he went. I was here with Braddock yesterday and then you came along. When you left I went into Meredale for some stuff for Silk." He pushed his chair back from the table. "Tom's caused a lot of trouble to everyone," he said with patent exasperation. "I'd like to give him a bit of my mind."

"You're not the only one," MacNeill said with fervour. "Anyway, this is an awkward position for Gavillan to be in. It's awkward for me too. I'll tell you about it."

Spain listened while he gave a brief accounting.

"I don't know why anyone said he came over here," he said bluntly. "I haven't seen him. I'll bet Pat is worried."

"Very worried," the policeman said. "I've been over to

see Mandell. When I say I've been, I really mean my inspector has. He went over with Pat, yesterday."

"What did Mandell have to say?"

"Nothing. He wasn't at home. They spoke to Hettche."

Spain considered.

"And Hettche couldn't tell them anything?"

"He couldn't."

The younger man tossed his napkin on to the table.

"I'm glad you came over, MacNeill. I'll go across and see him. But I wouldn't worry a great deal about Gavillan. I've got the idea that he can take care of himself pretty well."

"If it were left to himself he could," the Scot said pensively. "The trouble is, you don't know the daft sort of things a fellow like Gavillan is likely to do. Anyway, if you haven't seen him, you haven't seen him."

Spain shook his head.

"I haven't. It's damned queer."

"Queer indeed," said Superintendent MacNeill. He took his leave, drove down to the main road and here he pondered an ordnance survey map. He studied this for a moment or two then drove off in the direction of Meredale.

Blandfort, he discovered, was a mile removed from the main road, and he found it nestling in front of a mountain of verdure, for the sun was on the pine slopes so that all that was fresh and green was picked out in the full glory of the December day. The house was larger than he had imagined it to be, and on the lawn in front of it an aged gardener swept leaves into a little circular pile. He desisted from his labour as Superintendent MacNeill left the car and came towards him.

The policeman nodded.

"Good morning. Is this Blandfort?"

The old man agreed that it was.

"You'll be wanting to see Mrs. Klein?"

MacNeill indicated that such was his errand.

The gardener looked up towards the house.

"She don't rise too early, sir. Poor lady is an invalid. You'll maybe have to wait a spell. Usually she sits at the window there, but she ain't up this morning."

"I see," MacNeill said. He walked across towards the house and from behind the thick glass of the windows, Braddock watched his approach with a little uneasiness.

"It's MacNeill," she said.

144

Ada Klein drew the dressing-gown which she wore around her thin shoulders. She looked up at the big woman with a shade of amusement in her eyes.

"You're not afraid, Braddock?"

"I'm not afraid—but I'm suspicious," said Braddock crisply. "I think Peter went the wrong way about it. I've always thought that. These English police won't show much consideration for us. I know them of old. The main thing was to avoid attention from them. We haven't been able to do that."

"That was Mary Lou's fault," Mrs. Klein said.

Braddock scowled.

"It was Peter's. He shouldn't have let her come here."

"She came from America," Ada Klein said mildly. "Peter didn't know she was coming until she walked in on him. After that, he did the best he could. He couldn't let her come over here. She didn't know that we were in the country."

Mrs. Braddock was not impressed.

"I still think we were wrong." Her eyes narrowed. "I wonder what he had to say to old Cole?"

Ada Klein laughed.

"Most probably he was asking if this was Blandfort," she suggested, and was closer to the truth than she knew.

The doorbell rang as she spoke. Braddock looked down at her.

"You don't want to see him?"

"No, I think not. Peter said it wouldn't be wise."

The big woman walked out and made her way downstairs. One of the girls had gone to the door. She had admitted Superintendent MacNeill and now he stood watching her approach. He did not speak until she had reached him, then:

"Good morning, ma'am. You're not Mrs. Klein?"

Sme smiled faintly.

"No, I'm her nurse, Mrs. Braddock. You're the gentleman from the police. I saw you in the village yesterday."

MacNeill agreed that such was the case.

"I came along to have a few words with Mrs. Klein."

She looked suddenly serious.

"I don't know if you'll be able to see Mrs. Klein. She's had one of her bad mornings and I gave her a sedative half an hour ago. She suffers a lot and was quite worn out this morning."

He pondered this information.

"I didn't know she was as bad as that, poor lady."

Mrs. Braddock nodded.

"She comes and goes. She's troubled with arthritis. You know what that means, Sergeant."

"Superintendent," suggested MacNeill. "It's a long, long time since I was a sergeant. Yes, I've a fair idea. A bad, bad complaint. I'm sorry I couldn't see her; you'll maybe do yourself."

She had taken him into the little morning-room and MacNeill sat down in a very low chair and thrust his legs out in front of him. He looked up at her with some interest.

"I meant to get across before this," he said, "but I've been a busy man. As a matter of fact, I told my inspector to come over, but for some reason he didn't get round to it. You know what these young folk are like nowadays."

Mrs. Braddock was prepared to agree that she knew full well what they were like, and that the knowledge brought her little comfort.

"Things have changed since I was a girl, Superintendent. In those days we had some liking for hard work and a proper respect for our elders. That's all gone nowadays."

"It is indeed," said MacNeill and, the ice having been broken, became official. He took a photograph from his pocket and passed it across to her.

"This is the unfortunate woman who lost her life. You don't remember ever having seen her before?"

"No. She's a stranger to me."

MacNeill sighed.

"She's a stranger to everyone," he said wearily. "She's an American—the same as you and Mrs. Klein."

The big woman permitted herself to show surprise.

"An American. I didn't know that."

"Few do," said MacNeill. "But if you don't know her, you don't know her." He rose abruptly. "Miss Gavillan was visiting here on the day her body was found."

Braddock was on her guard.

"Yes. She came in to see Mrs. Klein. She often comes over."

"Does Mr. Gavillan ever come over?"

"Mr. Gavillan?" The big woman smiled at the ridiculous nature of the question. "No—I don't think he'd find much to interest him here. Not that he isn't a very nice gentleman

146

indeed—but he's more of a man's man, if you know what I mean by that."

"I think I do," MacNeill said shortly. He moved towards the door, then: "You haven't seen Gavillan within the last twenty-four hours or so?"

"No. I haven't seen him for several days."

"He hasn't called here?"

"He never does. Why do you ask?"

The Scotsman stepped into the hall.

"Gavillan seems to have disappeared," he said slowly. "He walked out of his house yesterday. Since then he hasn't been seen."

Mrs. Braddock drew in her breath.

"That's extraordinary!"

"I thought so too at first," said Superintendent MacNeill. "Now, I'm not too sure: not so sure at all." He went out to the car and she watched him get into it and drive off.

When the last sound of it had died away in the distance, she went upstairs to where Ada Klein awaited her arrival. The older woman looked up eagerly.

"What did he have to say?"

"Not very much," Mrs. Braddock said, "not very much at all." She was silent for a second or two. "But Peter was right. He's deep. He's got the knack of making you feel uncomfortable—and that's a handy knack for a policeman."

Something crashed to the ground in a room above.

Ada Klein looked upwards, startled.

"What was that?"

Mrs. Braddock smiled.

"I'm not certain, but it sounded like Gavillan. He isn't very discreet and he's as clumsy a man as ever I came across. That's saying a great deal." She left the room and went upstairs. A door opened above and Ada Klein heard the muted tones of the man raised in protest. She sighed, drew the gown more tightly around her and waited for the nurse to return, for this was indeed to be a busy morning for the occupants of Blandfort.

CHAPTER XXII

THERE was a motor-cycle in front of the Malden Arms when Superintendent MacNeill returned, and when he went inside he found a uniformed man, his hat off, and a pewter mug in his hand.

Police-Constable Sheer was considerably discomfited to be discovered under such circumstances.

"Begging your pardon, sir. I was as dry as a lime kiln."

Inspector Till offered corroborated detail.

"So was I. It was the fish I had for breakfast. Bolton keeps a very good draught ale, Super. You should try it."

"I have," said MacNeill. "But not when I was on duty."

The policeman had a dispatch-case strapped to his Sam Browne belt. He opened this and produced a stout, buff-coloured envelope.

"Here you are, sir, with Inspector Kelly's compliments."

MacNeill put it into his pocket and retired from the room. He went upstairs, sat down in an armchair and with his knife slit open the envelope. There was a covering letter together with photographs and two pages of typewritten information concerning Lee Cutten. He read over this carefully. Much of it he already knew, but it was interesting to have detailed information at hand.

Inspector Kelly's note was brief.

Central Office.

Superintendent J. MacNeill.

Sir:

I am enclosing herewith the information concerning Lee Cutten for which you asked. This man has never served a term of imprisonment in this country. However, in 1938 he came to England and lived for seven months in London. In March 1939 he went to Paris and in August 1939 he was known to be in Berlin. The American F.B.I. supplied us with the information which you will find here.

I am, sir,

Your obedient servant,
Dennis Kelly.

He laid it down to lift the photographs. There was a full-face picture of Lee Cutten and two profile pictures. They showed a man in his early twenties, hard-faced, lean, and with a certain ruthlessness about him. For a moment or so he studied them, then lifted the typewritten sheets.

LEE CUTTEN

Cutten was born in Chicago in 1906. His father Oscar Stegel Cutten was the proprietor of a second-hand furniture store. He died when Cutten was eleven years of age after which his mother remarried. Educated at the School of Sacred Heart where he was classed as an incorrigible. In 1920 when he was fourteen, Cutten was sent to the Maxwell Institution by District Judge Elmer P. Wayne. He spent four years here. In April 1925, Cutten was picked up by the police and questioned concerning a hold-up in Delaware City. He was released for lack of evidence. A year later he was known to be running around with the Monato gang who were engaged in rum-running. He was twice arrested by the Chicago police during this period. On each occasion he was discharged as evidence which might have placed him before a court was lacking.

In June, 1929, Cutten was arrested by Government Agent Leo Maynell in New York. He was charged with robbery of a Post Office in New York State and was sentenced to two years' imprisonment which was served in the Federal Penitentiary. This has been his only conviction. On his release he went to California where he opened a film agency. He lived in Cataraqui Heights, Los Angeles, until 1938. In February of that year he returned to New York and subsequently went abroad. He spent several months in England, in Paris and in Berlin, returning to New York two days before the outbreak of war in 1939.

During the period he was resident in California, Cutten was never in the hands of the police although it was suspected he was working with the Sheldon gang which was operating in New York, Detroit, Chicago and the major cities.

In June, 1936, Cutten married Mary Lou Slatter, a dancer at the Torrid Club. In the spring of 1937 this marriage had broken down. Mary Lou Slatter left the city and later brought suit against Cutten. He was ordered by District Judge Homer Balden to pay $3,000 alimony. Our information is that this was not done but that a private settlement was reached. No trace of Cutten has been found since the war. His old connection with the Sheldon gang probably broke down when the Sheldon crowd were dispersed. In view of his early record of violence, this man is considered dangerous.

He folded the sheets together and placed them in his wallet. There was little here that was new to him, save the knowledge that Cutten had been married. He was completing a brief report when there was a tap at the door and Till appeared.

The young inspector sat down.

"Anything fresh, sir?"

"Nothing at all."

"Gavillan hasn't come back."

"If he has, I haven't heard of it," MacNeill said. "I had a few words with Spain. He swears he hasn't seen him. I also went over to Blandfort to see Mrs. Klein."

"She's the American lady?"

"She is. I didn't see her. She was indisposed. I saw her nurse instead—name of Braddock."

Till shuddered.

"I saw her in the village. She drives a little car around and sells eggs to folk—big folk such as Mandell and Gavillan and so on. What a woman! I wouldn't like to get a clewer on the side of the ear from her." He fumbled for a cigarette, lit it, then: "What was the news from Central Office, Super?"

MacNeill produced the information .

"Read it. It will improve your general knowledge, Till, and that's a thing you can afford to keep on doing as long as you're a policeman." He passed it over.

Till inspected the contents of the envelope.

"Lee Cutten. I never heard of him."

The big man chuckled.

"You haven't read up your case-books then. Lee was a member of the Sheldon gang. Any of the old-timers could have told you that. He handled the eastern end of the business. He was never arrested—at least not while he worked for Drew. Sheldon was a good master. He took care of his men."

Inspector Till was considerably interested.

"Then Gavillan would know him?"

The Scotsman pondered.

"I don't know. I never heard Gavillan mention him, but then Tommy never mentioned any of them." He was silent for a second or two. "It's an interesting point. I wish I knew the answer to it myself. Gavillan worked mostly in the east—in New York, New Orleans—Philadelphia—and in the midwest—Chicago and back to Detroit. I don't think he was ever much farther west than Detroit. I've heard him say that more than once. Gavillan wasn't the man to lie. It may have been true. Gavillan himself is the only one who can give us any information about that."

Till read through the closely typewritten sheets.

"It's pretty general information they give you, Super."

"It is," MacNeill said. "I knew most of it already. We had occasion to check up on Cutten when he came to England in 1938. The American authorities tipped us off that he was on his way."

"And you saw him?"

"No. Inspector Kirk saw him. Kirk was in my department. He turned in a report. I'd have liked a look at him myself for the Sheldon crowd always interested me. However, I never had the opportunity. I was in Northern Ireland for a few months and by the time I got back he was gone."

Till pondered for a moment.

"And where does he come in here?"

"Solus squeaked!"

There was a little silence. Till's eyes came up, blank and surprised. He stared at his superior for a long moment, then:

"Solus did? You didn't tell me, sir!"

Superintendent MacNeill was used to the tone of righteous indignation employed by injured subordinates at such moments.

"I didn't," he agreed genially. "If it will be of any solace to your ego, I'll give you this much satisfaction. I would have told you when I returned last night—only Gavillan's disappearance put it out of my head. It was still out of it this morning."

Inspector Till was a little mollified.

"Thank you, sir. What did Solus say about Cutten?"

"He named him as the contact man for Corporal Violet!"

Till's eyes were excited.

"He did? That's the first real break we've got, Super. "What did he have to say?"

"Not very much, I'm afraid. But on that account I think the more of it." He told the younger man what Harry Solus had been able to impart. "Solus didn't know who Cutten was. But Lew Friedsohn would know. Friedsohn had been in the States for several years and he'd moved around. He must have met Lee Cutten there."

"Which links Corporal Violet up with the Sheldon gang?"

MacNeill smiled grimly.

"It does. I've had an idea for the last year or so that that was the case. That was where Gavillan came in. Tommy was in the clear. They must have known he suspected them. It may have been Cutten—it may have been someone or something else. That was what brought Gavillan into it!"

Till's eyes were alert.

"Of course. And they tried to put him away. That looks as though they were afraid of him."

MacNeill was perplexed.

"It does but not very much. In prison he could still talk. They weren't afraid of him talking. What was it they were afraid of? That's what beats me. When the frame fell through, they decided to put him down. Why? What did he know?"

"Cutten?"

"I doubt it."

The telephone rang as he spoke. They heard Bolton go through to it. A moment passed, then the landlord's voice reached them from the foot of the stairs.

"Telephone call for Superintendent MacNeill. It's from the City—a trunk call."

MacNeill went down to take it and Till lifted up the photographs and inspected them again. There was little about these plain prints, however, to appeal to the casual eye. If this was Lee Cutten, there was little to distinguish him from a thousand other Lee Cuttens who walked the streets of the city. He laid them down on the desk and as he did so, he heard the heavy tread of MacNeill's feet on the stairway.

The Scotsman came into the room. There was a glint of triumph in his eyes, and Till, who had seen that look before, came to his feet.

"Something new, Super?"

MacNeill nodded.

"Yes. Central Office had a reply from New York on the fingerprint query. The woman had been through the hands of the police—in 1934. It was Devine who spoke to me just now. He tells me that according to the American cable she was involved in a blackmail case out in Utah. She served seven months in prison and the remainder of her sentence was revoked!"

Till's eyes lit up.

"And were they able to name her?"

"They were."

"That was a stroke of luck. Who was she?"

Superintendent MacNeill smiled benevolently.

"Her name was Mary Lou Slatter!"

CHAPTER XXIII

"MARY LOU SLATTER!"

Inspector Till was considerably surprised.

MacNeill rubbed his big hands together.

"Nobody else. Imagine that now! It's a small, small world as I've often had cause to remark."

"And Mary Lou Slatter was married to Lee Cutten!"

"She was. And divorced from him. And here she turns up in Marks Malden." Superintendent MacNeill was suddenly grim. "There's a lot more beneath all this."

"It means that Harry Solus was right."

"Very probably so. It means a lot more than that," said the big man. "That's the way of life. You're always learning. I wonder if Gavillan knew. He went in to see her. That might have been curiosity. If he didn't know Cutten, it's odd that he should be interested in the woman. I'd give a year's pension to have him here just now." Of a sudden he became brisk. "Take the car and go into Winchester. I want you to take this information to Cleaver. You can tell him what I've told you—but it has to go no farther than Cleaver. Tell him not to use the telephone either, if he wants to discuss the matter."

"What's wrong with the telephone?"

"Nothing. It was a grand invention, but if I'm as close to Corporal Violet as I think I am, I don't trust a country exchange."

Inspector Till rose to prepare for his journey.

"I'll be back straight away, sir. What do you propose to do next?"

MacNeill yawned.

"Write a report. If I haven't heard of Gavillan by the time I've finished it, I'm going to let Cleaver know."

When the younger man had gone, MacNeill settled down at the broad, old-fashioned desk. Here indeed was more luck than he had ever anticipated. The dead woman was Mary Lou Slatter and Mary Lou Slatter had been the wife of Lee Cutten. This was too much to be coincidence. Lee Cutten was in the vicinity and this grim man was the magnet that had drawn the woman. Was Cutten the man for whom the police were seeking? Was Lee Cutten the Corporal Violet whom he had been pursuing for more than two years now? If Harry Solus was correct, Cutten was the contact man. That was something which Solus could not have been in a position to know.

The old Sheldon gang had broken him into the game. Cutten had served under a good master. Drew Sheldon had been one of the slickest criminals of the age. Then had come his disappearance. That in itself was something that had always puzzled him as it had puzzled a score of other eminent thief takers and police chiefs. Drew had disappeared from the eyes of man. Gavillan had said that he had died, and added that he had been present at his death. In some odd fashion he found this difficult to believe. Gavillan would not lie readily, but would not be above equivocation to preserve a loyalty. Tommy was no squeaker!

He picked up his pen and began to write. For an hour he sat at the desk, then he pressed the blotter over what he had written, read it over and enclosed it in an envelope. On the outside of it he wrote:

COL. H. M. CAMERON,
Commissioner of Police,
New Scotland Yard.

He placed the report in an inner pocket and went out of the room. He stepped into the darkened hall and something moved ahead of him. He heard a door close softly and then the sound of a quick-moving footstep. He walked quickly as far as the door, opened it and went into the passage beyond. This was narrow and dark, connected the kitchen with the back door of the inn. At the end of it, another passageway branched off, and from it there was a corridor which led to the public bar.

He walked through this, and when he reached the end of the corridor, heard a mumbling of voices. There was a glazed glass door. When he pulled this open he stood in the public bar. In one corner were three of the locals, but it was the man who stood at the bar who engaged his complete interest.

Billy Mandell held a pewter mug in his hand and appeared the spirit of English conviviality. He watched the man for a moment, then stepped out into the light of the room.

Mandell turned round towards him and his face lit up.

"Hello, Super. Where did you come from?"

MacNeill indicated the door at his back.

"From the house. Have you been here long?"

The younger man looked surprised at the question.

"About ten minutes. Have a drink?"

For a second it seemed that the big man would refuse, then:

"I think I will. A lager, if you don't mind, Bolton."

He took it and raised the glass.

"Good luck, Mandell." He drank it off at a gulp. "It's a fine thing a spot of lager when you can't get anything stronger."

Mandell was prepared to agree.

"I've just got back from the City, and I stepped in to have one." He laughed ruefully. "Hettche won't touch the stuff and I don't like drinking alone." He leaned one elbow on the zinc-covered bar. "What has been happening about the place?"

MacNeill raised his grey eyes to meet the blue ones.

"Gavillan has disappeared."

If he had expected to see the man show surprise, he certainly succeeded, for Mandell's heavy jaw sagged open.

"Gavillan! When did this take place?"

MacNeill pushed away his glass.

"Yesterday. He went out at noon. Nobody has set eyes on him since."

"That's queer!"

"It's very queer. I don't like it either. Not with the trouble we've been having around the place. Gavillan's a damned nuisance." He spoke vexedly and Mandell nodded his agreement.

"I've said that myself, Super. He's an unpredictable kind of feller. I'll bet Pat's pretty worried."

"She is."

"I'll go around and see her," Mandell said. He glanced at his watch. "I've got time for that. Hettche isn't expecting me much before dinner." He lit a cigarette. "What about your murder?"

"We've found out a little more about the lady."

The younger man was inquisitive.

"Have you found out who she was yet?"

MacNeill nodded.

"We have—and it wasn't easy. I won't say that we didn't have a bit of luck, but then you never would get anywhere in this world without it. That's my opinion of it anyway, Mandell."

Mandell was of the same point of view himself.

"Luck counts for a lot, Super. What did you find out about her?"

The Scot closed one eye.

"Everything we need to know. I can't tell you any more."

"It's confidential, is it?"

"Highly," the big man said. "It couldn't be more so. In a day or two you'll maybe hear a little about it. I'm not even sure that you will then. There's certain difficulties in the way of it. We've got to wait till we hear from the American Police."

Mandell stiffened.

"The American police! What have they to do with it?"

Superintendent MacNeill was heavily mysterious.

"That's one of the things you'll have to wait and see," he said softly, and Mandell gave a sigh of annoyance.

"You're an exasperating devil, Super. Really you are. Well, I won't be around for a couple of days. There's a meet tomorrow at Low Oxley and I'm going across. I wonder if Pat would like to go. I'll have a word with her." He tossed a half-crown on to the zinc-covered counter.

"There you are, Bolton. Good-day!"

MacNeill watched him go out. When the car had started up and he had driven away, he saw Bolton at his elbow. The landlord was smiling pleasantly.

"A very nice gentleman, Mr. Mandell. Mind you, he's got a temper—especially if you cross him. I've seen him fair wild with a man for opening a gate to him at the Hunt. Curse you as soon as look at you, but next minute he'd buy you a pint of beer, and as quick to do the one thing as the other."

"A fine fellow," agreed the policeman. "Had he been long in the bar when I came in?"

Bolton considered.

"A minute or two. He went through to the lavatory when he came in—then he came back and ordered a pint."

"Where is the lavatory?"

Bolton pointed to the door through which MacNeill himself had come.

"Through there and you turn to the left."

"Does that take you into the house itself?"

Bolton agreed that it did.

"There's a door that we usually keep shut," he admitted, "but it's open as often as not. It takes you on to the landing where the stairs are. Everybody knows it's there but nobody ever gives us any trouble."

"I see," said Superintendent MacNeill. He took his leave and walked in the gathering darkness as far as the police station. As he went, he turned over in his mind this new and interesting occurrence. Had it been Mandell he had heard on the landing? It was impossible to say. The corridor was connected with the back door of the bar. An enterprising man could have made an entry from that quarter.

He pushed open the gate that led to the police station and as he approached the door it opened. Pitman held it wide for him to enter.

"I was at the window, sir, and I saw you approaching. A nice night. A touch of frost now, and I hope it will hold." He led his visitor into the comfortable little room. "It's not too tidy. The wife's gone to Southampton for a day or two."

MacNeill sat down.

"I've got a little job for you, Pitman."

"What's that, sir?"

"I've prepared a dispatch. I want it to go into Winchester tonight."

The constable nodded.

"I'll get the bike out at any time you want, sir."

MacNeill smiled.

"Fine. I don't want you to leave here till Till comes back. I'd give him an hour yet." He laid a stout, brown envelope on the arm of the policeman's chair. "Keep your wits about you, Pitman. This crowd are pretty desperate and I'm looking for trouble."

"I'll watch my step," said Pitman. "Anyway, I've handled a few pretty rough assignments in my day." For half an hour he spoke of the rough assignments he had handled, and MacNeill listened approvingly to these tales of inspiring valour.

"I'm glad to hear it, Pitman, for I'm expecting trouble tonight."

Pitman was a little surprised.

"What do you think will happen, sir?"

"Ambush," MacNeill said. "They've used those tactics before and Corporal Violet repeats a thing if it works."

"Corporal Violet!"

MacNeill nodded grimly.

"Corporal Violet. I'm giving you that information in case you have the idea I'm a bit of an alarmist. Incidentally, you've got a revolver here?"

Pitman agreed that he had.

"I'm not supposed to use it without letting the sergeant know."

"Never mind the sergeant," the Central Office man said. "Take it on my authority. Use it too, if you need to." He rose. "I'll give you a call when I'm ready—an hour at the most from now. Probably less."

Pitman escorted him to the door.

"You can rely on me, sir," he said, and retired to make his preparations.

CHAPTER XXIV

BOLTON was preparing the long table for dinner when Inspector Till returned, a satisfied man. He came into the room, tossed aside his gloves and prepared to impart to Superintendent MacNeill the result of his labours.

"I saw Cleaver and told him what I could. He was pretty well excited by it. When I left him he was going up to call on the Chief Constable to put the matter to him."

"What about the men?"

"You can have as many as you need."

MacNeill knocked out his pipe.

"We may need them a bit sooner than we imagine. Right, we'll have a bite of dinner. After that there's another job in hand, and it may be a bit trickier than we expect it to be."

Till was not to be intimidated by difficulties.

"What's that?"

For the space of two minutes the superintendent spoke very quietly, and the young inspector listened. Then, when his superior was finished:

"You think that Mandell was in the corridor, then?"

"Somebody was. I don't say it was Mandell. All I know is that he was in the bar, and that he'd left it for a few minutes. Anyway, I'm sending Pitman to Winchester with a report for the Commissioner at New Scotland Yard. I've warned him that the job is dangerous, and he's going to carry a gun."

Till frowned.

"You think he'll be ambushed?"

"I'm pretty sure of it."

"Don't you think that's a bit risky, Super? These fellows kill at the drop of a hat." Till looked a little concerned. "I wouldn't like to think old Pitman would get knocked off just to prove a theory."

MacNeill pondered this point of view.

"I believe you're right."

"I know I am, Super." Till pressed his advantage. "He's a married man too. It wouldn't be fair."

"That's correct," said Superintendent MacNeill. "I didn't think of it that way. You'd better go in his place!"

Inspector Till squeaked his indignation.

"Me?"

"It has to be done," MacNeill said evenly. "Naturally, I didn't like it. I told Pitman that, and he didn't object. To tell the truth, I thought he was quite keen on the job. To take the sting out of it, I meant you and I to follow on behind in the car."

Till sighed his relief.

"That makes it different, Super."

"Naturally," said Superintendent MacNeill. "This looks like Bolton with the soup. Draw in your chair."

They sat down to dinner and when the coffee stage was

reached the superintendent left the room to put through a call to the waiting Pitman. The constable had already finished his meal, had stored the revolver in a holster which was strapped to his side. So much he informed MacNeill with some firmness.

"I'm ready for whatever can happen," he said. "Don't you worry about me, sir. Forewarned is forearmed. I read that in a book once. I know these roads. I can get to Winchester any one of a dozen ways and fool half the county. If I do run into trouble, I'll use my fists."

"If you run into trouble use your gun," MacNeill said grimly. "We'll expect you in ten minutes."

He hung up, went through and swallowed down a cup of coffee. Till was already buttoning up his coat. He watched the superintendent produce two Brownings, accepted one of them and weighed it in his hand to get the feel of it.

"I used to be a dab hand with one of these things."

MacNeill surveyed him without enthusiasm.

"Maybe so. Put it out of the way before it bites you."

They were in the hall when they heard the sound of the motor-bike, and MacNeill took a stout, brown packet and looked at it. He handed it to the younger man.

"This is for Cleaver. He'll send a man to London with it."

Inspector Till looked at the inscription.

"Pitman doesn't know that we're following up behind?"

"No, and I don't want him to know. Tell him I've gone up to the Close. I don't want him to get any ideas of his own. Tell him to be careful of his speed too. No more than forty miles an hour. We don't want to lose him."

"Trust me," said the inspector. He went outside, drew the door behind him and met Police-Constable Pitman in the courtyard, lifting his motor-bike on to its rest.

The constable raised his hand to his crash helmet in salute. He wore his uniform tunic, and one pocket bulged significantly.

Till surveyed him admiringly.

"Ready for action, eh, Pitman!"

The policeman slapped his pocket with a gloved hand.

"Right. Here you are. It's important as you know. Put it away carefully." Till handed him the envelope and watched him stow it into an inner pocket.

The man drew on his gloves.

"Right, sir."

"One thing more," said Inspector Till severely. "Don't try to be too quick on this job. The more hurry, the less speed, Pitman. Don't travel any faster than forty miles an hour. If you hit a rope at that speed even, you'll feel uncomfortable about it. And keep to the main road!"

Pitman nodded and adjusted his helmet more comfortably on his head.

"Trust me, Inspector."

He went over to the bike, straddled it and kicked the motor to life. With a roar he ripped out of the courtyard along the open road.

MacNeill had pushed open the door of the inn.

"All right, Till. Into the car."

In a moment more they were on the highway, the big car running without lights. Half a mile ahead of them they could see the streak of white light on the roadway, then the motor-cycle swung between the woods and the night was black again.

Till settled himself down to drive. For five minutes neither of them spoke, and the younger man kept his eye rivetted on the road, then:

"We ought to see him in a moment or so, on that long, bare stretch along the Ede."

MacNeill nodded his agreement. They drove on, but when they reached the long, flat stretch which flanked the river, there was no sign of the man ahead.

Till trod down on the accelerator.

"I hope the silly devil hasn't switched off into one of these back roads. If he's done that we'll never find him."

"You told him to keep to the main road?"

"I did. I was emphatic about that."

"Then if he carried out your instructions we'll find him," the big man said. He lapsed into silence, his eyes searching the road ahead for a glimpse of the motor-cyclist's light.

They had travelled some six or seven miles before they saw a car approaching. When they did so, MacNeill said:

"Draw across the road and stop this fellow. We'll question him."

When the approaching car was close at hand, Till slowed down across the road and blocked the way. He applied the handbrake, cut the motor and climbed out.

MacNeill was already at the side of the other car, and

the driver, a pallid-faced man, shrank back in the glare of the headlamps.

The superintendent allayed his fears.

"Sorry to trouble you," he said. "It's a police job. Did you pass a motor-cyclist on the road between here and Winchester?"

The man cleared his throat.

"I—I think I did. Two of them. One behind the other."

"Where was this?"

It had been some two or three miles along the road. The man had noted the occurrence because both motor-cycles had been travelling at high speed.

"They fairly whipped past me," he said. "Made me think twice about taking a blind corner with fellows like them on the road."

They thanked him and returned to the car and Till was aggrieved.

"I told him not to go over forty," he frowned. "We'll have to step on if it we want to catch up on them. I wonder who the second man was. That's what's puzzling me."

It was puzzling Superintendent MacNeill too. When they came to a village, he had the car stopped, put through a call to the Winchester Police and spoke to Inspector Cleaver. In a few moments he had returned.

"We'll try to overtake them," he said, but although Inspector Till sat with his foot resting on the floorboard, the lights of Winchester appeared and they entered the town without catching sight of the erring Pitman. Till drove slowly through the streets to the police headquarters. They alighted here, and MacNeill went through to have a word with Inspector Cleaver.

Pitman had not appeared as yet; a patrol, acting on MacNeill's telephoned instructions had been on the road to meet him. They had failed to do so, but were scouring the roads.

Till swore feelingly.

"What about the two motor-cyclists who were on the road?"

Cleaver shook his head.

"We got them. They were the Levison brothers. They're well-known motor-cyclists. They go in for speed trials and the like, and they were out for a trial spin."

Till stared.

"Then where is Pitman? He should have been here before us!"

Cleaver was grim.

"It looks like they've got him on the road. He was warned, you say, about the sort of job this was?"

"Warned and armed," MacNeill replied. A great light was dawning on him. He swore very softly. "That damned fellow was smart." He came to his feet. "All right, Till—back to Marks Malden as fast as you can manage it. Inspector, I'd like you to bring a couple of men and come along too."

Cleaver was willing to oblige.

"What do you expect has happened?"

The Scotsman scowled.

"What I might have anticipated. You can keep your men on the roads just now in case I'm wrong—but I don't think I am. We'll get back to Marks Malden at once."

He led the way out to the car. Inspector Till got into the driver's seat and watched the Winchester car follow him out to the street. He drove slowly out of the town, but on the open road trod heavily on the accelerator, aware that Superintendent MacNeill sat beside him, grim and unsmiling.

The big man did not speak at all until Marks Malden was reached, then, when they were running into the village:

"Drive to the police station."

Inspector Till pulled up in front of it and MacNeill was on the way to the gate before the car had stopped. He brushed through it, went up to the door and knocked heavily.

There was no answer!

Till was watching curiously.

"Where's Mrs. Pitman?"

"She's gone to Southampton for a couple of days. Pitman told me that tonight already." MacNeill walked round to the little pathway towards the garage where the policeman kept his motor-cycle. It was neat and trim, and the sliding doors were held together by a chain and padlock. He put his big hands round the end of one of the doors and exerted his strength. It ran along the steel grooves, then grounded in the soil of the garden, but the opening which it left was wide enough for his purpose. He squeezed his vast bulk through.

Inspector Till followed him, a torch in his hand.

"What is it, sir? What do you——!" He stood stock still his eyes on the man who lay on the ground at his feet.

"Pitman!" he gasped.

MacNeill nodded grimly.

"Pitman! I figured on an ambush but Corporal Violet was just a jump ahead of me. I expected it to be after he left Marks Malden. Instead of that, it was before he arrived at the inn!"

There was a little silence. Inspector Till drew a long breath.

"You mean that it wasn't Pitman who came to the Malden Arms?" There was a queer note of incredulity in his voice.

MacNeill had dropped to his knees beside the constable.

"It certainly wasn't. Pitman's been here for a couple of hours."

Till said wearily:

"Well, I'm damned, Super. If he wasn't Pitman, who was he?"

Superintendent MacNeill laid a big hand over the man's forehead. He lifted his wrist and groped for the pulse. For a moment he did not speak, then:

"Who was he? My guess is he's the man we've been looking for. Lee Cutten!"

CHAPTER XXV

"CUTTEN!"

There was chagrin in Till's voice. "You mean I was standing there talking to the fellow and I let him walk away from me." He swore loud and long. "Take your foot and kick me, Super. I deserve it."

"I deserve it myself," MacNeill said. "I might have anticipated something like that. Hold the torch lower." He made a brief examination of the injured constable.

Pitman was breathing heavily. There was blood on his head, but when MacNeill wiped it away, it seemed almost superficial. He sighed in his relief.

"There's a lump on his head as big as an egg, but I don't think his skull is fractured. However, that's for the doctor to say."

The second car had arrived. Cleaver's voice could be heard from the garden. The inspector came through, considerably perturbed. He listened to MacNeill's explanations, then:

"A wily devil. We'll take Pitman back to Winchester with us."

MacNeill demurred at this.

"You'd better have an ambulance. He may be worse than you think. I shouldn't move him at all until the doctor has seen him. He's fairly comfortable where he is."

This was true. The policeman lay on a heap of sacking, and one of the officers dropped a topcoat over him.

Cleaver had gone through, forced the door and put through a call to headquarters. In a moment or two he returned.

"Where's his wife?"

"In Southampton—fortunately. He told us earlier in the evening that she was going there. From her point of view that is a very good thing indeed. Corporal Violet is no respecter of persons."

"How do you think it happened?"

MacNeill laughed coldly.

"Our man was watching me," he said. "He must have followed us here and anticipated my design. He might have attacked me—but probably he figured he was taking too big a chance. Marks Malden isn't Piccadilly, but there's a certain amount of stir about it. Anyway, he came out here and waited for Pitman to come for his motor-cycle. When he did, he let him have it, stripped him and took his place."

Cleaver scowled.

"I suppose you're right. With the crash helmet and goggles, you wouldn't be likely to suspect him. Did he come into the inn?"

"I went out to him," said Inspector Till. "And I can tell you, sir, I didn't suspect he wasn't Pitman. He was the same build, height—even his voice was perfect."

"If they weren't perfect, they were good enough," MacNeill said. "A man's height and build are difficult to gauge in that rig-out, especially in the darkness."

One of the uniformed men was on his knees beside Pitman.

"He's coming round, sir," he said.

MacNeill dropped down beside him. Sure enough the constable's eyes were open. He looked ahead of him with an odd fixity, then groaned a little and tried to pull himself up.

MacNeill laid a hand on him gently.

"Take it easy, Pitman. This is MacNeill. You've had a bad knock."

The man brought his hand up to his head.

"What happened?"

"Somebody was waiting for you," the superintendent said, "with a cosh. He let you have a heavy one."

Cleaver leaned over.

"You didn't see him, Pitman?"

The man groaned.

"No. I was at the door when something hit me."

MacNeill came to his feet.

"Don't try to talk. You've had a nasty wallop, Pitman. We'll have the doctor along directly. In the meantime, keep quiet."

Till had been inspecting the rear of the house.

"Plenty of footprints there," he said. "There's a bit of a vegetable garden at the back and someone has walked across it. That wouldn't be likely to be Pitman."

They made their way into the house; here Cleaver found a stretcher, a legacy of wartime equipment. With this they carried the injured man indoors, and by this time he was recovering considerably.

"I remember you calling me on the 'phone, sir," he said to MacNeill. "I came back and got on my belt and coat. Then I went round to the garage. There's a big holly tree there. He must have been standing behind that. Anyway, I remember putting the key in the lock—and then he must have clipped me. What happened after that?"

"He took your tunic and your helmet and goggles," Cleaver said, "and he rode round on the bike to the inn for the superintendent's despatch. A cool fellow he was."

Pitman supplied another description qualified by a sanguinary and blunt epithet and the local inspector nodded in agreement.

"He was all that."

Till, an interested listener, added his opinion.

"All that and more. It's a damnable pity he got the report."

MacNeill chuckled.

"He didn't get the report, Inspector. Pitman was the decoy and we were the smashing party. You don't hand reports as important as that one was to your decoy. I carried the report myself. I handed it to Cleaver in his office at Winchester."

"It's on its way to London now," Cleaver said. "There's some satisfaction in that at least."

Inspector Till was considerably annoyed.

"You didn't tell me that, Super."

"I didn't tell anyone," MacNeill said.

"Here I've been cursing my carelessness," Till said bitterly, "and all the time that's the sort of life I've let myself in for. A man would be better off selling soap powder."

MacNeill nodded his sympathy.

"It's a fact. That's the sort of thing I've been trying to live down for the last thirty years. But you'll get over it. We all do."

The door opened as he spoke. A uniformed constable appeared.

"That's the doctor now, sir."

A short, cheerful man came in, a small case in his hand.

"Hello, Pitman. What's the game?" He made a painstaking examination of the policeman's head, looked a little thoughtful. "You've had a nasty knock. What was it?"

"Cosh," supplied Inspector Cleaver.

"You've been struck twice at least." He asked a question or two. "You're a fairly tough nut. I've told you that before. No—I don't think you've got any more than a bad concussion, but you'd better come back with me to the County Hospital. I'd like an X-ray done. There may be a fracture."

Pitman grimaced.

"I was hoping I could go to bed an' call it a day."

"You'll go to bed all right," the doctor said. "I'll take you back with me." He looked at Cleaver. "Look out a case for his clothing. I'll run him along. I was going up to the hospital in any event. I've got a patient there who's pretty far away tonight."

Pitman gave explicit instructions and they located a case, clean pyjamas, his razor and certain essentials which he deemed necessary. When the doctor and Cleaver had taken him to the car, MacNeill rose.

"We'll get back to the inn," he said. "This hasn't worked out just as well as I expected it would."

Cleaver came back as he was speaking.

"That's that. Pitman has had a nasty crack. He's a tough

167

sort of chap—as hard as nails. I'm glad it isn't any worse. You think it was this feller Cutten who did it?"

MacNeill nodded, a little frown on his face.

"I think it was. There's no way of proving that for the moment, of course, but I'm convinced I'm right."

"Then Cutten is in the neighbourhood?"

"He must be. It's always worth something to know that." The Winchester man was jubilant.

"This is a much bigger thing than we imagined, Superintendent. It's queer to think those fellers have been in our territory with every policeman in the country looking for them. But I suppose they have to be somewhere." He pondered for a moment. "That was a pretty good job you did. The woman turned out to be Cutten's wife."

"Mary Lou Slatter? Cutten's former wife."

"I wonder what brought her here," Cleaver said thoughtfully. "If she knew the kind of feller he was, you'd think she'd have kept as far away from him as she could."

MacNeill smiled his grim smile.

"Women are pretty difficult to figure out, Inspector. They don't seem to reason things out in the same way as a man does. I'd have said Cutten was poison. If she was rid of him, she was well rid of him. Apparently she didn't think that."

Cleaver searched the recesses of his mind.

"You said there was a baby?"

"The police surgeon said that. There was nothing in the record about it, but of course the record is far from complete."

Inspector Till had an opinion to offer.

"She came over here to make it up with him. You mark my words, that was the way of it. She had maybe left him, but there may have been more between them than we know. Anyway, she came over to see if she could have a reconciliation."

"If she did, she didn't have much success," said the practical Cleaver. "She took a mighty big chance. I'd sooner be single than dead myself," and there was a sardonic grimness in his voice.

MacNeill puffed methodically at his pipe.

"We won't know about that until we get the bits and pieces together. That's the sort of thing nobody can say much about, because it's purely a personal problem. My guess is that Mary Lou was on the make and came over to see what the chances were like."

"Blackmail?"

"Something like that. It was either that—or revenge. She knew Cutten was in something that was pretty big, and she came over to put a spoke in his wheel." He glanced at his watch. "Look at the time! It's coming on for midnight."

Inspector Cleaver yawned.

"So it is. That's the worst of good company. You hate to break up the party. All right, Hinchbrook. Get her started up. I'll be out at once."

He took his leave of the constable he had delegated to remain in Marks Malden, and went out to where his car waited.

"Cooper is a sound man, and he can handle himself in any sort of trouble you're likely to have. By the way, Solus is travelling up to London tomorrow. I'm sending a strong guard with him."

"Excellent," said MacNeill.

When the local man had driven off, he got into the car beside Inspector Till, and that young man was curious.

"You didn't mention Gavillan to him."

MacNeill grunted.

"I didn't. And I was scared stiff that you might."

"I nearly did," said Till frankly. "I thought you had forgotten all about him, what with the trouble we've had."

The Scotsman grinned sourly.

"If you had, your chances for promotion for the next fifteen years would have gone west," he said drily.

Till drove the big car straight into the garage, switched off the engine and got out.

"You're not so worried about him as you were?"

MacNeill shook his head.

"I'm not. I don't know where Gavillan is, but I know now why he left Chyme Close—and I think he showed a lot of wisdom in going when he did. Corporal Violet is on the run, and Gavillan is the man who helped to flush him!"

Till was on the steps. He stopped now and looked round.

"You mean that?"

"I do," said MacNeill. "This thing is coming to a head. Go in and go to bed. You young fellows need a lot of sleep."

Inspector Till went inside, grumbling. There was a light in the corridor, and at the sound of their voices, Bolton appeared in his pyjamas, a thick woollen dressing-gown wrapped around him.

"Evening, gents. A nice night, but a bit frosty they tells me. There was a telephone call for Mr. MacNeill an hour ago."

"From Miss Gavillan?" the Scotsman asked.

Bolton looked surprised.

"Yes, sir. Did you call her?"

"No. I wondered if she might ring up. What was the message?"

Bolton hitched his robe around him.

"There wasn't much to it, sir. All she said was, 'Tell Superintendent MacNeill everything is all right.' What was all right she didn't say. I asked her myself, but she maybe didn't hear."

MacNeill drew a long breath.

"Fine, Bolton. You can get off to bed now."

The landlord made his way to the stairway. On it, he turned.

"I took the liberty of putting a half-bottle in your room, Superintendent," he said. "It's the real stuff. The genuine Glen Livet. There's a tumbler on the stand. A little whisky's a fine thing on a cold December night."

"Grand," said MacNeill. He went up to his room and Till followed at his heels.

"Did Pat Gavillan mean that Tommy had come back?"

MacNeill felt for his knife. It was an old-fashioned one equipped for opening bottles and performing divers other operations. He manipulated the corkscrew, and there was a pleasing report.

"Pass me that tumbler, Till."

Inspector Till obliged. He watched the big man pour out a measure.

"You haven't answered my question, Super."

MacNeill held the glass up to the light.

"Look at the bead on it, Till. Here's my respects. What's that you said? Is Gavillan back? I don't know. I hope not—but I'll lay you my pension she's heard from him. We've learned a lot today."

Inspector Till beamed.

"That's the best news I've had for a long time." He pondered for a second or two, then: "I think I'll take a spot of that myself, Super."

MacNeill looked at him, surprised.

"I thought you were a Rechabite."

"There are occasions," said the inspector with dignity.

Superintendent MacNeill put the cork in the bottle and drove it home with a mighty blow of his palm.

"There may be. This isn't one of them. Do your drinking with men your own age, my lad. That's the best advice I've got for you." He pushed the bottle aside. "Go to bed, young fellow. I'm going out."

CHAPTER XXVI

THE day had dragged itself through for Pat Gavillan. At a later date she was to remember the grey horror that had been in her heart: now there was only a chill sense of numbness and shock. There had always been a gay sense of irresponsibility about Tommy Gavillan, but he had never been neglectful or thoughtless so far as her peace of mind was concerned. Recently, they had been drawn much more closely together than ever they had been, and the nagging little devil of uncertainty within her laid its fingers more surely on her heart.

At noon there had been a break that was more than welcome, for a flustered young man had come up from the village to seek her assistance. A baby which had not been expected for another fortnight had sent out certain signs of imminent arrival, and in a perspiring and palpitating nervousness which did a great deal to settle her own agitation, he explained the urgency of the situation.

"The doctor's in Winchester, miss," he said. "At an operation. He said to get Dr. Bentley from Meredale and he's out on a case, and the District Nurse is over at Black Hall."

She calmed him in a moment or two.

"All right, Sparr, I'll go down with you. I'll call Dr. Fern and tell him. I'll be with Mrs. Sparr until he comes back. I've got as much here in my case as we'll probably need."

She completed the one or two necessary tasks, had a word with Flett and led the young man out to the brake.

His cottage, he explained, was two miles away. It was off

the main road and they could not drive the car up to the door, for there was a stream that could only be crossed by a footbridge. She listened to these details as they went on their way and in less than twenty minutes arrived at the cottage.

There was an elderly and alarmed woman present.

"I'm Ethel's mother, miss," she said. "Such a to-do and everything arranged so nicely for the first week in January at St. Margaret's Nursing Home. Her father and me were paying for it. You know how it is with your first grandchild. She's in here."

Pat Gavillan went through to where the girl lay, and in a short time she had brought the full benefit of her training and practice to bear on the situation. She had specialized in midwifery, had found this particular branch of the work singularly engrossing. Now she was thankful for the experience she had had.

It was late afternoon before the child was born. It was six o'clock before the doctor turned up, and by the time he did appear, Mrs. Sparr and her son were more than reasonably comfortable.

Pat sat on the end of the bed, a cup of tea in her hand and a little feeling of elation in her heart, for the doctor was more than fulsome in his praise.

"You've done a grand job, Miss Gavillan. What you've done today makes more than worth while all the months and years of training and effort you put into it. I'm sure you feel that too."

She nodded.

"You've put it very well, Doctor," she said. "That's exactly what I was thinking when it was all over."

He chuckled.

"I know. Every person in the profession thinks it a thousand times in his career. I've been practising for thirty years and I still feel like that every time the miracle happens."

Later, when he had gone and her patient had been settled comfortably, she went out and drove back to Chyme Close. She was limp now, exhausted physically and mentally. The reaction after the tenseness of the day had set in and it had left her weak, collapsed.

Flett admitted her glumly.

"No, Miss Pat, we've had no word yet."

She stared at him through a mist of tears.

"No word, Flett?"

"Nothing at all."

She walked wearily to the library and he followed her.

"Did Uncle Mac come up?"

Flett shook his head.

"He didn't come up. He rang up twice in the afternoon. The other young feller rang up too."

"Mr. Till."

"That's the one. He sounded very upset."

She could think of no adequate reason for undue agitation on the part of Inspector Till.

"What was wrong with him?"

Flett coughed apologetically.

"I think he was worried about you, miss."

"Oh?" She was a little surprised. "What did he say?"

Flett was not exactly sure.

"He seemed annoyed," he said. "He wasn't the only one. Mr. Spain was in this morning not ten minutes after you went out with the feller that was going to have the baby."

She looked up.

"Spain? Did you tell him where I was?"

"Yes. He said it was the best thing that could have happened to you."

For the first time since she had known him, she felt in accord with sentiments voiced by Peter Spain.

"He hadn't seen Daddy?"

"Not him. But he knew all about it. The Super had been over to see him. He wanted to know a lot of things. I told him to come back later. He didn't come back, but he 'phoned about about six and I told him you were still at the Sparr's place." He paused for a moment. "Was it a boy?"

She nodded.

"It was. Eight pounds four ounces."

"Ain't that nice," said Flett romantically. "They wanted a boy."

For a moment she was amused.

"I didn't know you knew about these sort of things, Flett."

The little man nodded.

"It's been the talk of the place for a month, Miss Pat." He took her coat and became severely practical. "I'll get you a glass of sherry now and I've got a tray set. Soup an' some tongue sandwiches. I'll make you some coffee an' bring it all here."

"That would be wonderful," she said. She went upstairs, ran a bath and got into it. When she came out of the bathroom, she felt immeasurably better, for the heat had drawn the fatigue from her and had left her relaxed. She put on a house-coat, brushed her hair for a moment or two then went down to the library.

Flett was tidying up the hearth. He had built a new fire, had piled the logs high. Now he flicked the last fleck of ash away.

"Well, here you are, Miss Pat. You look grand. I'll be back in a minute. There's the sherry at your very elbow so to speak."

She sat down and lifted the glass, sipped the wine slowly. It was seldom that she smoked, but now her nerves demanded the soothing influence of tobacco, and she lit a cigarette then lay back, a pleasurable little wave of somnolence gripping her. How long she had remained like that she never knew. It was a gentle movement close at hand which caused her to open her eyes, and when she did, Flett was crossing towards the fire-place. She sat up with a little start.

"Goodness, Flett, I've been asleep."

He chuckled.

"That's right. You were sleeping when I came in with the tray so I took it back. I'll bring the things through again." He went out, to reappear in a matter of moments with his tray. "There you are, Miss Pat. Chicken soup as thick as a jelly when it was cold. Do you a world of good. Do you want your coffee black or white?"

"Black," she said, "and very black."

"I know just the very shade of black for it," he said

When he brought it she lit another cigarette and lay back to consider anew the problem which had been holding her over the past thirty-six hours. It was queer that Superintendent MacNeill had not led an investigation in person. She imagined that he would have brought up a force of men and that the woods would have been drawn, although the woods were the very last place in which Tommy Gavillan would have been at all likely to have been discovered.

She laid down her coffee-cup and rang for Flett. When the little man came, she said:

"That was wonderful, Flett. I don't know when I've tasted such coffee. You must teach me the trick sometime."

He winked one eye.

"Learned it in France, Miss Pat. During the war. The first one that we did all the fighting in. That was a war."

She watched him go out, heard the door of the kitchen close. As it did so the clock in the hallway chimed once!

"Ten-thirty!

She had not realized that it was so late. Curiously enough, all her fatigue had departed now, and mentally she was un-pleasantly alert. It was a sensation that she dreaded. Over-powering weariness would have been a blessing tonight. She tossed the cigarette from her, and as she did so, without warning, the lights went out and she sat in the wan glow of the fire!

She looked around her almost curiously. A fuse had blown. That the lights were off elsewhere in the house, she knew, for she heard a door slam in the region of the kitchen. Then came the voice of Flett from beyond:

"It's all right, miss. It must be a fuse. I'll get down to the cellar and fix it. There's some fuse wire in the cupboard here."

She went across to the door, opened it.

"It's all right, Flett. I've got plenty of light from the fire."

She heard him moving about on the stairs, then there was silence. She turned back to the room and as she did so, something moved in the hall!

She swung round, a cold, icy finger touching at her heart. She saw a black shape move silently towards her, and shrank back against the door. She opened her lips to scream. Then, from the darkness she heard a low, soft chuckle.

"Patsy, lass!"

She stared wildly into the blackness.

"Daddy!"

In a second more she was in the arms of Tommy Gavillan!

CHAPTER XXVII

FOR a long minute he held her very tightly, then she felt his grip relax. Her face was against his cheek, and he felt the hot tears as she brushed against him. His hands tightened on her shoulders.

"Bear up, soldier!"

She laughed softly but hysterically.

"Daddy, you've come back! You've really come back! I was so frightened! I was terrified and——"

He said quickly:

"Listen to me, Pat. I want to talk to you seriously. You're a sensible girl and I'm not trying to fool you. This is a dangerous place for me. Damned dangerous! That was why I put out the lights."

She stiffened.

"Oh! I thought a fuse had blown."

"I got into the cellar," he said calmly, "and rigged the fuse box. I didn't want even Flett to see me, but I had to see you."

"Where have you been?" she gasped.

"Never mind that. I'm safe enough where I am. I came here tonight to see you because I knew you were worried. I didn't want to see you. I tried to get word to you today, but you were out on that case and I couldn't do anything myself."

She caught at his arm.

"You're not going away again, Daddy?"

Gavillan kissed her.

"I am. But it won't be for long, Pat. A day or two more— and this is all going to be over. I promise you that. I'm not lying to you. I've never let you down. A day or two more and I'll be back here. We'll go away for a month to the City and celebrate!"

She laughed weakly.

"But I don't understand."

"You don't need to," he said softly. "Listen! Is that Flett coming back?"

She listened but could hear nothing.

Gavillan's body was tense. He was silent for a second or two, then:

"That's that. I've got to get out of here. Don't mention to Flett that I came here tonight. That's important—very important."

"Don't you trust him?" she gasped.

Gavillan laughed softly.

"Flett's as honest as any man in the country, but he's got no head. He'd shout the good news no matter how you cautioned him—and I've had to duck enough bullets. I'm telling you the truth, Pat—I'm in a dangerous spot. You can realize that. In a day or two things are going to be different." There was a grimness in his voice she had never heard before. "That's a promise. Now I've got to get out of here before the lights go on." He tightened his grip around her, kissed her once. "Good night, Pat!" He walked across to the window, slid the catch.

She had followed him across.

"Take care of yourself, Daddy."

Gavillan laughed softly.

"Whoever heard of an Irishman who didn't look after Number One." He squeezed her shoulder. "One thing more. You can tell Mac I called here. See him if you can. Don't telephone him. I'm not too sure about the 'phone in a place like this. If you do call—don't mention me by name. Tell him everything is all right."

"Yes," she said.

She thought a shadow moved in the darkness. When she looked again, he was gone. There was a puff of cold wind from the open window, and the room was strangely silent.

She closed the fastener, locked it. When she went back to her chair her heart was thumping wildly and madly. Tommy Gavillan had come back! All the dread, grim fears which had held her in their grip had dissolved in the knowledge that he had stood in this room and spoken to her.

She went back towards the door. As she did so the lights suddenly went on again. She stood there, blinking, then she heard Flett's feet on the stairway at the end of the hall.

"Everything in order, Miss Pat?"

He came up, brushing dust and cobwebs from his head. There was a streak of dust on his cheek and she laughed almost buoyantly.

"You've got a smudge on your cheek, Flett."

He rubbed at it with a grimy hand.

"It was a fuse all right. Well, it's fixed now. You're looking a lot better I must say." He fixed her with a thoughtful look. "Do you want me to sit up again tonight, miss?"

She considered. For a moment she was about to suggest that this was hardly necessary, when her caution reasserted itself.

"I'll take my turn tonight, Flett. I'm as wide awake as can be."

He did not look displeased.

"Very well, miss. I'll get things put into order." He went back to the kitchen, and when she was alone she sought the 'phone.

It was Bolton who answered her call.

"Mr. MacNeill, the police gentleman? He's out, Miss Gavillan. So is the young, thin one as well. If you want to leave a message, I'll take it for him. Mr. MacNeill gets a lot of messages left."

She hesitated, then:

"Just tell him I called, and that everything is all right."

He coughed.

"What's that, miss? What's all right? It ain't very clear."

"Everything is all right," she said. She hung up. For a moment she stood by the telephone, then crossed to her chair. There was a magazine on the table at her hand. She lifted it and leafed over the pages. She had started to read an article dealing with the international value of sea food when she heard the sound of a car on the driveway outside.

Could this be MacNeill? She rose and was crossing to the door when she heard Flett's voice in the hall.

"Come in, Mr. Mandell. The door was locked. I just put on the chain five minutes ago. Miss Pat's in the library. She'll be glad to see you, sir." He opened the door. "Mr. Mandell."

Billy Mandell came into the room.

"Hello, Pat! What a damnable business about Tommy! I just heard about it today. I came over as soon as I could."

She swallowed.

"Sit down, Billy."

He looked around him.

"I could do with a drink. You don't mind, Pat. A thing like this upsets me more than you could believe." There was a decanter on the cabinet. He went across, poured out a drink and held it up. "Here's to Gavillan's good luck."

She watched him drink it.

"You've been in the City, Billy?"

He nodded.

"That's right. Business. I don't go up any oftener than I can help, but this was different. Anyway, MacNeill told me the bad news today. I meant to come over before this but I had to go back to Winchester with Hettche. But that's not what brought me over. You've had no news from him?"

178

She looked into his blue eyes.

"No, Billy."

"That's damnable!" he said again. "Perfectly damnable. Excuse the language, Pat. I'm upset more than you know. It isn't like Tommy to clear out without a word like that."

"It isn't," she said softly.

"I could hardly credit it," he said. "Maybe he's gone up to the city. Gavillan's got interests there. That would account for it."

"It wouldn't account for him not telling me."

"That's true," he said gloomily. He looked at her grimly. "What does MacNeill say about it?"

"He's puzzled just as much as I am."

He rubbed at his full cheek.

"That's queer. I didn't think the Super would be puzzled like that. Couldn't he have put some men on the job?" There was a little indignation in his voice. "After all, that's what police are for, isn't it?"

She smiled her amusement.

"Apparently Uncle Mac doesn't think so. He's called up once or twice today. I haven't been at home much. I had some nursing to do in the village. I was glad of it. It kept me from thinking."

He was interested.

"Nursing? What happened?"

"There was a confinement which didn't wait for confinement," she said calmly. "Fortunately they remembered I was at home. I'm very pleased they did. It was a boy—rather a darling little boy—and very fair."

Mandell coughed.

"Quite, Pat old girl. I'll bet you did a grand job." He looked up as the clock on the marble mantelpiece began to strike.

"Eleven-fifteen! I'd no idea it was so late! You must be exhausted after it all. I'll get away back now. If you hear from Tommy, you'll let me know at once!"

She was aware that his blue eyes were fixed on her searchingly, and she felt a little discomfort in his level gaze.

"Yes, of course, Billy."

"That's good," he said. "I've been worried all day about you. I don't like to think of you here—alone like that."

"I've got Flett and Lena."

He nodded vaguely.

"Naturally. That's not what I mean at all. You know that. Only these days I——" He stopped abruptly. "Well, I'll be back soon at any rate."

Flett had appeared in answer to her ring.

"Yes, Miss Pat? Mr. Mandell's going, eh?"

"He is," said Mr. Mandell. "Good night, Pat."

He went into the hall and the little man escorted him to the door. At it, Mandell stood for a moment, his weight against it.

"Miss Pat doesn't look too bad, Flett," he said approvingly. "I thought she'd be all broken up about Gavillan."

Flett smiled a private smile which hinted at secret knowledge.

"She's been pretty upset, Mr. Mandell. Don't you think she hasn't. As white as a ghost and never slept night or day or ate any more than a pick at her meals. She's changed all at once. I noticed it myself tonight. She was laughing when I went in—joking too. I was going to ask her if she'd heard from Mr. Gavillan, only I knew she hadn't because there's been nobody here since she came back from the Sparrs'."

Mandell considered.

"Maybe he 'phoned?"

"Not him. I would have heard it. I've been in the house all night." The little man pondered for a moment. "Maybe it's just the job she did today. She was all out when she came back. She had a bath and a meal. I made some strong coffee for her. She's a different woman."

"That's a blessing," said Mandell. "Good night, Flett." He went down to the car, got into it and drove away. There was a thoughtful glint in his eye as he drove across to Malden Court. Matters were coming to a head more quickly than he had anticipated. The disappearance of Tommy Gavillan was ominous indeed. He swung up the driveway that led to Malden Court, saw the lights in the windows to the right of the doorway which indicated that Hettche had not yet retired. He drove the car to the garage for the night, got out and locked the door. He walked up to the big house slowly.

The moon had crept out now. Its silver light softened the harsh lines of the gaunt old buiding, laid a pathway of lemon across the weed-infested surface of the ornamental lake. He saw a shadow move in the room from which the light filtered.

When he got closer he saw Hettche standing by the fire, his slim figure neat and lithe. He went up towards the door, and as he did so the moon was swept into a cloud and the night grew black.

He swung open the big oak door and went into the great, broad hall. A solitary light burned at one end of it. The deep niches and recesses lay in shadow and as he passed them he caught the dull glint of armour, for these were the repository of furnishings of an earlier age. He passed them and reached the library door and two hard eyes watched him go.

It opened and closed. The house was very silent.

Tommy Gavillan's hand came out of the depth of his pocket. Very slowly he began to move forward towards the broad stairway. He reached it, made his way upwards, keeping well in the shadow. On the first floor he halted to take stock of his position. There were two lights gleaming faintly, one at either end of the long hall, and these were sufficient to give him his position.

He made his way along cautiously to the right. When he came to a broad oaken door, he turned the handle and went inside. For a second or two he stood there in silence, then turned the key in the lock. He crossed to the window and drew it open. There was a small balcony here. When he stepped on to this he was able to see the blackness of the lawn twenty feet below. In an emergency this would be his line of retreat. A nimble man might manage to drop from the parapet to the lawn. If he did, the woods were sufficiently close at hand to give shelter. He looked over to the wood wryly, then turned to the room itself.

It was large and square, furnished as a sitting-room. By the side of the old-fashioned desk stood two suitcases. He looked at these curiously, felt them. They were light in weight, but were packed. For a moment he pondered their implication. Was Dale Hettche about to go on a journey?

He walked past them and crossed towards the door, which opened into a smaller room. Here there was a single bed, and the furniture which one might normally expect in a bedroom. He crossed to a wardrobe, opened it and drew out a brown jacket which hung at his hand. He ran his fingers through the pockets of it, but apart from a key-ring and a paper book of matches, these were empty.

He turned his torch on the book of matches. It was rather

longer in size than the average, and when he examined it, he
saw it was a bright orange in colour. On the outside of it was
printed:

CLARION CLUB

CHICAGO'S RESTAURANT DE LUXE

He dropped it back into the pocket in which he had found
it, restored the jacket to its position then continued with a
thorough examination of the room. From it, another door led
to a bathroom. He passed into this, drew open the door of the
white enamelled cabinet and stared at the contents.

There was a tin of tooth powder, two toothbrushes, a
bottle of brilliantine, with a French label on it, two small
combs, a bottle of Bay Rum. He searched for what he knew he
would not find, and he did not find it. He closed the door of
the cabinet and stepped out into the room. As he did so, his
eyes were hard and icy, and the line of his mouth bitter.

Cautiously, he turned the key in the lock of the door. It
slid back silently. He looked back into the room, and oddly
enough, there was no elation in his heart. Hettche might have
been brilliant, might have been many things, but his secret
was no longer a secret!

CHAPTER XXVIII

THERE was a glint of coldness in Mandell's eyes as he closed
the door behind his back and stepped into the library.

Hettche had moved away from the fire. He turned now at
the big man's entrance. For a moment or so he watched him,
then:

"You've been over at the Close?"

Mandell nodded irritably.

"Yes. I wanted to see Pat."

Hettche considered him for a moment.

"I've given you my opinion about that business before.
Women have been your downfall, Lee. You can't keep away

from them. The Gavillans are dangerous! I warned you about that. If you'd been a wise man you'd have listened to me. Bill Mandell could have gone a long way in this country. Lee Cutten is a different proposition. This man MacNeill's no fool."

Lee Cutten sat down heavily.

"I know that. He's got me worried." He groped for a cigarette, lit it and stared moodily into the fire. "Gavillan was safe enough. Gavillan never saw me in all his life—never—till he saw me here. There wasn't any danger there, Dale."

The smaller man's eyes were hard.

"Gavillan knew who you were. He knew Mary Lou Slatter." There was something venomous in his voice. "Lee, I made you, I brought you here and I set you up. I warned you to keep back from entanglements."

The younger man scowled. There was a decanter on the cabinet which stood at his hand. He filled out a glass.

"Don't worry, Dale." His voice was peevish.

Hettche watched him coldly.

"I'm leaving for the north tonight," he said and Lee Cutten stared.

"Tonight!"

"Within the hour," Hettche said calmly. "I can see the writing on the wall. The biggest thing we had in England was anonymity, Cutten. Once we lost that, our immunity was gone for ever." There was no anger in his voice, only a calm, deadly coolness. "I warned you about that. We could have lived here for years if you had been careful."

Cutten laid down his glass.

"I didn't bring Mary Lou here."

The smaller man shook his head.

"You didn't. Spain brought her here. But you knew the danger was there. You knew she might talk."

"She won't talk now," Cutten said.

"No. You killed her."

Lee Cutten raised his eyes. For a second he was silent, then:

"I killed her. I figured you knew that."

Hettche laughed coldly.

"It wasn't hard to know. I heard you come in that night. You took a big chance, Lee."

Cutten scowled.

"I had to do it. Mary Lou came here to pick my b
don't know her. I did. I lived with her for a year."

"And left her? There was another girl in it—in M
The big man shrugged.

"What's it to you, Dale? We've all got our wea
don't deny mine, I've never tried to cover up. I've
of a lot of women. I was a fool to marry Mary Lou
never have happened. Anyway, it did. I married
lived to regret it. She followed me here. I don't kno
traced me; but she found me."

"Spain did that for her!"

"Damn Spain!" said the big man. "I should have
down when we began to suspect him."

Hettche shook his head.

"That wouldn't have done any good. If you have
kill. If it isn't necessary—keep clear of it. Spain co
have done anything by himself—not even with M
You blundered badly there. You should have told
her."

Cutten nodded.

"I knew that afterwards. But you're a queer fis
can't figure you out. You've got your own priva
Gavillan. You tried to put him away—when that did
you tried to put him down. I helped you there!"

There was a spot of colour in Hettche's cheeks.

"Well?"

Cutten shrugged his broad shoulders.

"Gavillan is your private hate. Mary Lou was
handled it my own way. I went after her and got h
road. I took her out on to the Mere and dropped
twenty feet of water with a rock as big as my body
legs to hold her." He scowled again. "How was I to
rope would open up and let her rise? I figured she'
for good." He took another drink. "Be reasonable,
was the best way out of it all. If it had come off nobo
have seen her again."

"But it didn't come off?"

"It didn't—but that was bad luck. You tried
Gavillan. That didn't come off either. That was
luck."

There was a little silence.

Hettche took a cigarette from a silver, flat case,
184

a cigarette. He struck a match, puffed, then tossed the spent match into the fireplace. For a moment or two he smoked without speaking, then:

"This place is finished. That means Bill Mandell is finished."

Cutten bit his lip.

"That's more than I bargained for."

"There's another place in Yorkshire," the little man said absently. "I'm making for there. You'll have about a week left. After that, the police will be here."

Cutten considered.

"Damn MacNeill," he said vindictively. "I figured there would be something in that report. He was an hour in his room, writing it. Bolton told me as much." He lit a fresh cigarette. "When I think of the risk I ran to get it too—that damned fellow might have stuck a gun in my belly."

Hettche laughed coldly.

"You had a gun of your own, Lee. If it came to shooting it out, the odds would have been on you. You always had a getaway. And on the motor-cycle you could have lost them, if they suspected you. You'd plenty of cover round about here. No—it wasn't such a risk. It was a good plan, but it didn't come off. MacNeill is too long in the tooth."

"He saw me in the inn," Cutten said. "I told you he was suspicious. He's a foxy old devil."

"Probably so," Hettche said. His eyes went to the fireplace. At the back of it fluttered a blackish web of burned paper, all that was tangible of the report that had been handed over by Inspector Till.

"Yes, MacNeill's pretty shrewd."

Cutten nodded grimly.

"My guess is that Gavillan gave him a lot of his information."

"Gavillan didn't know enough to do that. You've already admitted as much. All Gavillan knew he picked up after the trial. Anyway, I'll give Gavillan his due. He wasn't a squeaker!"

Lee Cutten rose and paced the room.

"I'm not so sure about that. Where is he now? That worries me, Hettche. I can't figure him out. Gavillan isn't the kind to lie down to it. You made a mess of things there. Why the hell did you have to start a feud with a man like that?"

There was an ugly note in his voice. "Mary Lou was different. She could have put the finger on me! She had to die. Gavillan was different. That was a grudge feud! What have you got against Gavillan?"

Hettche's cold eyes looked through him.

"Gavillan? I have an account to balance. One day, I'll do it."

The big man scowled.

"Forget it. A hate is a nasty thing to carry along with you." He looked at the smaller man in exasperation. "You're a queer sort of fellow, Dale. In the three years I've known you I've never got to understand you. You're as big a stranger to me today as you were the day you walked in on me in Liverpool. If you hadn't known about Sheldon and me——"

Dale Hettche rose.

"Forget Sheldon," he said. "Sheldon is dead!"

Lee Cutten laughed softly.

"Is he?"

There was a little silence. The very temperature of the room seemed to drop, and Cutten, not for the first time, felt the menace of this icy, hard-eyed man. He licked his thick lips.

"All right, Dale. We don't want to quarrel, do we? I've been a good man for your purposes and you've paid me well. In return I've done all you asked me to do."

Hettche nodded imperceptibly.

"And even one or two things I haven't asked you to do."

Cutten sighed.

"Mary Lou? I've told you about that. It was bad luck. We won't go into it now, Dale. Some day I'll convince you."

Of a sudden Hettche smiled. There was little humour in his smile, but it lent a new character to his thin features.

"All right, Lee. We'll forget it. If there has to be a post mortem we'll hold it later." He walked slowly the length of the room, paced it once or twice. "I've thought this business over. As I said before, the biggest thing we ever had here was the fact that the police didn't suspect us. Once they started to think about us, the game couldn't last much longer. I've always known that."

"You think we couldn't face it out?"

"We couldn't. MacNeill is bound to be checking up on you. Once he finds out that you are Lee Cutten, you're finished."

Cutten said slowly:

"Once he proves it, you mean."

"Once he suspects it, he'll prove it. So long as you're free from police interference in this country, you can do anything. Once they suspect you, you've got to clear out. England isn't like the States. You could move around there because you've got room to do it. If you were pushed you could always hop down to Mexico or head north to Canada. Here it's different. London is only eight hours from Edinburgh." He came back to the fire, stared into it.

"I told you I'm going north—there's a house in Yorkshire —near Dalewood. It belongs to a London man—Simon Abbott. I am Simon Abbott."

Cutten was interested.

"You've decided to go then?"

"Yes. And at once. You can drive me to Newbury."

Hettche looked down at his watch. "Collis will pick me up there in the morning." For a second he was silent. "Your own time here is limited. I would give you three days at the most. If you're wise you won't stretch it beyond tomorrow."

Cutten considered. A plan of campaign had been long agreed upon. Now he produced the details of it.

"Tomorrow, you say. Right, Dale, I'll leave tomorrow night. I'll put up at Romsey with Fowler for a week, then I'll make for Bristol. I'll be in the north within a week. I'll join Lewis in Sunderland within a fortnight. You can get in touch with me there."

Hettche nodded.

The big man looked at him pensively.

"What about the Fabian Bank job?"

"It goes through," Hettche said.

"If I'm not on the job?"

"Mowder can take over." Hettche went across to the door. "Get the car out. I've got a couple of cases packed. I'll be ready for you when you come down." He made his way up to the floor above. There was a light tweed overcoat hanging in the wardrobe. He pulled this on, removed his heavily rimmed spectacles and replaced them with gold pince-nez. He lifted both cases, tried their weight then walked downstairs.

Cutten had gone out. He could hear the soft crunch of gravel under the wheels of the car. He walked through the door, laid down his cases, closed it and crossed to the car.

Cutten was drawing on his driving gloves. He took one case from the smaller man, tossed it into the rear of the car. The smaller one he laid flat on the floor between them.

"There isn't much room. I'm glad of that. We're liable to get rain before the morning. That's all to the good. Keep people off the roads."

He drew up the collar of his coat as he sank back.

"I'm going to get some sleep, Cutten. Wake me in an hour. I'll drive for a spell after that."

The big man grunted. He drove out along the road which led to Malden Mere, by-passed Meredale, and he was running through open hilly country when his prophecy came true. Rain misted the windscreen and unaccountably his wiper refused to function. He drove on for a mile, but vision was blurred and indistinct. He drew up, got out of the car and wiped the front of the thick glass with a duster, manipulated the wiring. Then, to his relief, there was a little "whirr" and the wiper started.

He was about to get into the car when he heard the sound of a car in the vicinity. It was running at low speed, but when he looked around there was no sign of any light. He got back into the car, warily.

Who was following behind? Was it possible that the car he had heard had pursued him from Marks Malden? There was an odd significance in the fact that it was running without lights. Hettche was still asleep. He did not waken the little man, but drove on for a further seven or eight miles.

They were in wooded countryside now. The road ran through land which was fringed with dark, tall trees, and he was easing the big car down a hill when he heard Hettche stir beside him.

The little man sat up. As he did so he saw a motor-cycle slide past.

"Where are we now?" He peered through the blurred glass ahead of him. "Raining? You expected that."

"I did," Lee Cutten said. "We're about five miles from Collingbourne Ducis. The road ahead takes us through it. After that we'll get on the Hungerford Road. That fellow on the bike has a dirty night for it."

Hettche nodded. He looked at his watch.

"All right, Lee, we'll pull in here for half an hour and keep an eye on the road. It isn't likely we've been followed, but if we have been it would be handy to know about it."

There was a little lane ahead of them. It showed up in the headlamps of the car. Cutten swung to it. It flanked a stretch of wood, and to the left of him he could see only the blackness of a planting. He pulled up, cut the motor and switched off the lights.

Hettche looked at the dashboard clock.

"It's after two o'clock. We can afford half an hour." He opened the case, took a flask from it and screwed off the cap. He raised it to his lips and took a single pull of it, and as he did so Cutten smelled the pungent odour of brandy. He laughed gently and edged round in his seat.

"I thought you didn't drink spirits, Dale?"

Hettche shrugged.

"There's a time and place for everything," he said, and handed the flask across.

Cutten gripped it.

"That's right," he said. He raised the silver lip of the flask to his own, opened his mouth wide.

As he did so, Dale Hettche moved towards him so casually that he did not see his hand come up. There was a revolver in it and the long barrel slid between the big man's teeth.

Cutten gasped once!

Hettche pressed the trigger, and Lee Cutten shivered where he sat. The flask slid from his hand, then the night was still but for the gentle, insistent patter of the rain.

CHAPTER XXIX

FOR a moment the little man sat perfectly still. Then, very gently he relaxed his grip on the revolver. It did not move!

He lifted the flask from the floor. A little of the spirit had run down along the floorboards, but this would soon evaporate and disappear in the night air. He opened the door and stepped cautiously into the darkness. For a moment he stood there, his ears alert for any sound, but there was only the steady hiss of the rain on the grass and the trees. Cautiously he opened the rear door of the car and lifted out the two cases he had brought with him.

Cutten sat as he had died. In the wan light of the dash-board light, he could see the blue-black barrel of the revolver. The dead man's teeth had tightened over it now, held it firmly n position.

For a long moment Hettche stared. This was the end as he had planned it from the hour he had known Cutten had to die. Tomorrow the police would be here! Billy Mandell of Malden Court would be found in his own car, a bullet in his brain, the muzzle of the gun that had killed him still in his mouth. The gun was Mandell's own. If there were fingerprints on it, they could only be the fingerprints of Lee Cutten! There could be no doubts now in the minds of the police.

Suicide!

And if they searched for a motive, Superintendent MacNeill would not be long in supplying one. How much MacNeill knew he could not be certain, but he was satisfied that the Scotsman knew Cutten for what he was.

He closed the door gently. This was the end of another chapter. Cutten had been useful, but his use was gone for ever. Another Lee Cutten might be found. He smiled wryly and began to walk along the lane. For a hundred yards he walked then he found himself in a small clearing. There was a house here. He had visited it no longer ago than yesterday, when he had made his final plans. It was a small house, had been for-merly used by a gamekeeper who had been a family man and had had to move to a house which was closer to a school. For two years Hettche had kept it against just such a situation and moment as this.

He laid down his cases at the door, produced a key and fitted it into the lock. It turned easily. He left the key in the lock and went round to the gable. There was a shed here which had once held a cow. Now a small Austin occupied the space. He opened the doors wide, then returned to the house.

There was a change of clothing in the cases he had brought. Within half an hour, he would be on his way again, and not even Superintendent MacNeill would be likely to penetrate his disguise. By noon he would be in London. There was a flat near Hyde Park which had been rented in his name yet which knew not Dale Hettche. That episode was past.

He lifted the cases, stepped into the darkness of the cottage, and laid them down. He had left a paraffin lamp on the table on his last visit. Now he struck a match and lit the wick of it. The flame climbed upwards smokily as he replaced the funnel. He saw the shadow of his own hand, large and ominous on the cream-coloured wall. Something broad and blurred obscured it. He swung round suddenly and as he did so a hand with the strength of steel in it grasped him by the throat.

"Don't move, Hettche!"

He could not. An arm like a bar of iron held him rigidly. He felt nimble fingers go over him rapidly. There was an automatic in his pocket. He heard a little laugh as it was removed, then, of a sudden, he was free. He looked up into two hard eyes.

"Spain!"

Peter Spain nodded.

"Spain is right. Stand still, Corporal Violet!"

Hettche seemed to shrink as he spoke.

"You—know that?"

Spain went back to the door and leaned against it.

"Sit down, Hettche." He watched the man comply, then:

"Yes, I figured it out. Corporal Violet! I reckon I've done myself a fair bit of good tonight. What do you think?"

Hettche did not speak. For the moment it seemed the whole world had collapsed about him. Then his eyes went to the case at his feet.

"How much?" he asked simply.

Spain shook his head.

"I'm not in the market."

"Twenty thousand?"

The younger man smiled.

"Fifty? Seventy?" Hettche said.

"Double it?"

Hettche smiled coldly.

"I'll double it and add to it. A hundred and fifty thousand, Spain. It's a lot of money."

"Sterling or dollars?"

"Sterling."

"It's a lot, indeed," Spain said. "But you can afford it. You've cleaned up over a million and a half. That's big money in any language, Hettche. I'm glad to have the honour of taking you in."

Hettche froze.

"You mean that?"

"Every word of it," Spain said. He patted the automatic he had taken from the man and dropped it into his pocket. "I'm in the business. Maybe you didn't know that."

"I guessed it," Hettche said.

Spain nodded largely.

"Spainfield, Braddock and Gold. There's no Gold now. Old Johnny Gold got his out in Denver in 1936. Somebody shot him and left him in a ditch. I always thought it was Ike Donlevy. You won't know him. One day I'll find out."

Hettche said slowly:

"Private detectives?"

The young man nodded.

"You could call us that. We call ourselves Security Agents. We only do bank work. My father started the firm—it's pretty small. Not many folks have heard of us. We don't advertise ourselves much, though we're well enough known in the profession. The banking profession."

"And what brought you here—to England?"

Spain looked at him shrewdly.

"You remember the Dexter City Bank robbery in 1933?"

"Yes."

"I thought you would," Spain said pleasantly. "My Dad worked on that. So did Mother. She was the brains of the business. A remarkable head. I wish I could think things out as clearly as she can. You ought to meet her. She's followed this case very keenly—directed it in fact."

"You mean she's here in England?"

"She is. At Blandfort. You may know here as Mrs. Klein."

Hettche had heard of Mrs. Klein. He stared at the younger man.

"So she came over here?"

Spain nodded.

"Yes, it was her idea. It all goes back to the Dexter Bank job. Cutten was in town that night. My father figured he was on that job—so did Mother. She knew him as one of the Sheldon crowd. The case had to be closed. The depression was on the States at the time and the bank couldn't stand the expense of a prolonged investigation—but it put the finger on Lee Cutten."

"I see," Hettche said softly.

Spain smiled.

"I wonder if you do. When my father died, Mother ran

the business. She was beginning to be troubled even then by rheumatism. Later on it became arthritis—but it didn't keep her from using her head. She was always interested in Cutten, and when he was divorced from Mary Lou Slatter, she was interested in that too."

He smiled softly. "Queer? Don't you think it was? Cutten had drifted out of sight. Later on we heard he was in France —that he'd got to England. He came back to the States after that—and we always kept an eye on him—until he disappeared."

"That was when he came to England?"

"Yes. We'd lost him! When we did get to hear of him again it was Mary Lou Slatter who brought us the news."

Hettche stared at him woodenly.

"Mary Lou Slatter?"

"Yes. She had a friend in a show that was in London. Cutten came to London a lot and Kay Stemler saw him once or twice. He didn't call himslf Lee Cutten, he was Bill Mandell and he had a big house in Hampshire, but it was Lee Cutten all right. Kay Stemler wrote and told Mary Lou to come and collect. Mary Lou came to us. That's all there was to it."

Dale Hettche lifted his eyes to meet the brown, insolent ones.

"You had a lot of luck," he said quietly.

"That's true—but we deserved it. We never forgot Cutten. We sank a lot of money into this business, a lot of money and a lot of work. Ada was sure Cutten was working for Corporal Violet. She had a theory about Corporal Violet."

"Had she?"

Spain took a step forward.

"She did. She thought that Corporal Violet was one of the old Sheldon gang. She never thought Corporal Violet was Drew Sheldon."

"Drew Sheldon?"

Spain nodded gently.

"Does that make you think?"

"It makes me think," Hettche said, and there was ice in his voice.

"It should," Spain said. "I'm taking you, Sheldon!" He put out his hand.

Hettche did not evade it, but he looked up.

"I'm not Drew Sheldon!"

"You're not?" There was a smile of cold disbelief in Spain's dark eyes. "Don't tell me that, Sheldon."

Something hard touched him in the small of his back. He did not move at all, but a voice said in his ear:

"No, Spain. He's not Drew Sheldon."

The voice of Tommy Gavillan was harsh indeed.

CHAPTER XXX

HETTCHE did not move. He sat still as though turned to stone, but his cold, deadly eyes were fixed on the gun in the Irishman's hand. It was very steady. Gavillan was like a rock.

"Stand still, Spain," he said. He ran his hand over the younger man, lifted the automatic he had taken from Hettche. He dropped this into his own pocket. From a shoulder-holster he drew a long-barrelled Luger. He held this in his left hand.

"All right, Spain. Turn round."

The young man came round, slowly. There was hate in his eyes, a queer uncomprehending sort of hate.

"Damn you, Gavillan! I didn't figure you were——!"

Gavillan lifted the gun.

"Don't rile me, Spain. Not just yet." There was a warning note in his voice. "I'll do the talking and I'll ask the questions." He let his eyes circle the room. There was a large steel engraving above the fireplace. It hung by a heavy brown cord. He eyed this thoughtfully, then: "All right, Hettche. Get that picture down."

When the little man had laid it on the table, he produced a knife, tossed it to him.

"Cut it off in one length. I want his wrists tied."

Hettche made a businesslike job of it. When he had finished, Gavillan inspected it.

"That's first rate. I couldn't have done better myself." He put away the gun but patted the pocket which contained it. "Don't forget it's there, Spain. I'd hate to have to use it on you."

Spain's eyes were ugly.

"I didn't figure you were in on this, Gavillan. My heavens, what a fool I've been!"

Hettche was staring at them from one to the other, then: "How did you get here?"

Gavillan shrugged.

"I followed you and Cutten. I was in your room tonight at Malden Court. Doing a bit of checking-up. I knew it had to be you, but I couldn't be certain. I couldn't prove it—but I did what was almost as good." He laughed harshly. "Anyway, I was sure you were going to pull out. You had your cases packed and ready. I was in the hall when you were talking about it. It was Newbury you spoke about. I sat on your tail till you drew into the road. I couldn't figure that out—not until I heard the shot!"

Spain looked up sharply.

"What shot? I didn't hear it!"

"It was fired in the car," Gavillan said. "Cutten's dead!"

"Dead!"

"As dead as Caesar. It looks like suicide. There's a gun in his mouth, and the shot came through the top of his head."

Spain stared at Hettche.

"Cutten isn't the type to do a Dutch. I wouldn't believe it. You can't get away with that sort of thing—in England!"

Hettche smiled almost wearily.

"It was suicide. I heard the shot myself. I was a hundred yards away at the time. There was no one else near him."

Gavillan nodded bleakly.

"Unless it was me!" His eyes came round to Spain. "Now it's your turn. How did you get here?"

Spain shrugged.

"Braddock had been watching Hettche for weeks. She followed him here yesterday. She went over the place and found the car—the supply of petrol and oil—she found a gun." He smiled grimly. "I watched Cutten—she took Hettche. I reckon she made the best job of it. We were at the Court tonight when Cutten left. It wasn't very hard for me to figure where you were making for—especially when I saw the cases. I came here straight—passed you on the road."

"By car?"

"By motor-cycle."

Hettche had a recollection of a motor-cyle streaking past them into the night. He nodded thoughtfully.

"I remember that."

"I got here twenty minutes ahead of you," Spain said. "I

ran the bike into the wood. I knew there wasn't a chance you'd see it, you wouldn't want to show a light if you could help it. Not in a place like this. After that I just waited."

Hettche sighed.

"You're cleverer than I gave you credit for, Spain. Where's Braddock?"

Spain smiled his insolent smile.

"Braddock went along to get MacNeill. To the best of my knowledge they'll be on their way by now." He heard the man draw in his breath, saw the colour ebb from the pale cheeks.

Gavillan was looking at him.

"The police! You expect them here?"

"That's right," Spain said. There was triumph in his eyes. "You can do what you please, Gavillan—but they'll get you. Damn you for a dirty double-crossing dog. I didn't——"

Gavillan looked at him wearily.

"Shut up, Spain!"

The younger man's face was twisted.

"I'll say what I please. I figured you were honest! I didn't think you were in this up to your neck. You fooled me, Gavillan. I thought we were hiding you at Blandfort! I thought I was helping you. Instead of that, you were playing me like a fish. You fooled me, Gavillan. Was the girl in it too? Did she——!!"

Crack!

Gavillan's big fist crashed against his jaw! Spain went backwards and down. He lay on the floor and the Irishman drew him up again.

"I'm sorry about that, Spain. I shouldn't have done that. You got me on the raw edge, boy! Pat wouldn't——!"

"Save it," Spain said. He spat blood from his bruised lips. "You've got some nice habits, Gavillan." He laughed harshly, viciously. "You learned your trade in good company. Cutten—Gavillan—Drew Sheldon! I used to be sorry for you, Gavillan. Sheldon took your wife, didn't he? That was what caused the split. She left you for him. She was wise too. He wasn't a yellow, double-crossing dog!"

The Irishman's face was white.

"Spain, I wouldn't say that again! If you do, I'll strangle you with my own two hands." He held them up, took one step forward. For a moment he stood like that, then dropped them.

"All right, you've said enough!" He swung round savagely to Hettche. "Are you ready?"

Hettche was staring at him.

"You're going to let me go?" His voice sounded oddly hollow.

Gavillan nodded.

"I'm going to let you go. I'm going to go with you to see that you do get away." He bent down towards the cases, lifted one of them in his hand. "Are these yours?"

"They are," Hettche said. He lifted the other.

Gavillan looked at his watch.

"It's three-ten! You've got four hours of darkness to help you. It's not a lot." He took one step towards the door. "What's wrong?"

Hettche was looking at Peter Spain.

"What about Spain?"

"What about him then?"

Hettche said slowly:

"He would be better dead."

There was a little silence. Gavillan looked at the gun in his hand.

"So would you," he said thoughtfully. He threw open the door. "All right. This way. I've got my own car at the end of the road. We'll walk to it, and if you're wise you won't try any nonsense. Your best chance is to do what I say."

Hettche walked along at his side. The road was dark and the rain was driving down on them now. The wind had risen, and the bite of it was cold and raw. Together they blundered through the darkness, and finally the outline of a car loomed up ahead.

Gavillan nodded to it in passing.

"Cutten's hearse," he said flippantly. "He deserves all he got. He murdered the girl. I knew that after I'd seen him, although I couldn't figure things out at all."

"Spain told you?"

"He did. What he didn't tell me, the old lady did. She's a remarkable woman. She was right nearly all along the line—about ninety-five per cent, I'd say." He laughed mirthfully. "I didn't figure on this. Queer how life turns out for a feller. I could cut my own throat."

They had all but reached the main road now. Drawn up at the edge of the lane was a car, and Gavillan nodded towards it.

"What were your plans?"

Hettche hesitated, then:

"I was making for London."

Gavillan sniffed contemptuously.

"That's out. The roads will be blocked and patrolled. MacNeill is no slouch. I admire that man more than any I know. All the cops in Christendom will be out. There won't be many folk who'll make London by road tonight."

Hettche licked his lips.

"How long do you think we've got?"

Gavillan sighed wearily.

"I don't know. Maybe an hour; maybe less. If Braddock does what Spain says she went to do, it won't be long. MacNeill is a fast worker. We'll need every minute we've got." He opened the door as he spoke, threw the case into the rear of the car.

"Get in beside me. Put the case in the back!"

Hettche got in and closed the door. He watched Gavillan get in, reach for the starter and switch on the lights.

"Why are you doing this for me?"

The Irishman looked round.

"I'm not doing it for you. I'm doing it for myself. I'm the most selfish feller you know. Always thinking of Number One. Anyway, Pat comes into it too. I guess we can't have everything we want in this life. I've been lucky in a lot of ways. I got rid of all my bad luck at once."

They drove out of the roadway slowly, gathered speed and swung round a bend. Gavillan settled down to drive, his eyes on the road.

"You can't make London. Where else can you hide out?"

"Bristol. I've got a flat there."

Gavillan considered.

"We've just got four hours of darkness. After that there's folk on the roads—traffic gets heavy. We'll have to take the back roads and detour a bit. I'm not too sure of them myself. I'll do my damnedest, but I'm promising nothing. We'll go to Hungerford, by-pass the town and strike west. After that we'll have to take our chance."

He trod down on the accelerator, and the big car leapt forward. The rain was driving in from the west, and it rattled viciously on the glass at his cheek. The windscreen-wiper hummed busily, but for all its assistance the road ahead was blurred and smeared to the vision.

For half an hour they drove onwards through the storm, then Hettche said suddenly:

"There's a car behind us."

Gavillan did not answer for a moment. When he did his voice was strained and harsh.

"I've seen it for a quarter of an hour now. He's sticking close."

"Is it the police?"

"Who knows?" he said. He leaned forward and cut the lights. The road ahead was black—an abyss of steaming darkness. He eased up on the accelerator and their speed fell away. For the space of five minutes he drove like that, and the lights behind them drew closer.

Hettche had turned in his seat.

"They can't be far away," he said. "Half a mile maybe."

Gavillan stood heavily on the accelerator, released it, then:

"We're coming to a side road. Hold hard!" He swung the big car round. The rear of it scraped recklessly along the hedge which flanked the lane. He straightened her up and drove on.

"We're driving into it now," he growled.

This was true. They were heading due west, and the full violence of the wind crashed at them head-on. His face was very close to the windscreen now as he peered into the darkness.

"Where is he now?"

Hettche swung round on his knees and peered through the window at the rear. There was only blackness, then, through the smeared surface of the side window he saw a blurred streak of light on the main road behind them. He watched it for a moment.

"He's gone past."

"Good," said Gavillan. He eased up a trifle. "It's as black as pitch, but we daren't show a light. With a little bit of luck we ought to get out of this. I've got a fair amount of petrol. Enough to take us as far as Warminster, perhaps. The snag is that MacNeill knows the number of this car. Every policeman in the west will have a description of it by the morning."

Hettche swung round.

"Why didn't you let me take the Austin?"

Gavillan sighed.

"You had to have speed. MacNeill would have ridden down your baby Austin within half an hour." He cut his speed a little as something showed up grey-white on his left. "Farmhouse. They built 'em right on the edge of the road in the old days." He drove on for a moment or two, then, "This road's swinging back to the right."

There was an ominous note in his voice and Hettche heard it.

"What do you mean?"

"It's only a loop road," Gavillan said. "We're coming back to the main road—and there's his lights. They're behind us still." He swore softly as he swung the car back on to the main road. "The loop road was shorter than the main road—probably it was the old highway, and the new one has made a wider circuit." He jabbed viciously on the accelerator. "We can't go back. He's seen us now!"

This was true! The car behind was drawing closer, the distance between them narrowing a trifle every minute. Gavillan switched on his lights and they cut two white patches through the driving rain.

"It's a straight race now!" he said thickly. "If the luck holds, we've a chance yet, but——"

As he spoke he saw the road sweep round to the right. He swung round on two wheels and the brewers' lorry which loomed up out of the night was on top of him. He swerved to the left, went into a skid! The big car swung round and the near end of it side-swiped the heavy cabin of the commercial vehicle! There was a rending crash and the wheel was torn from Tommy Gavillan's grip. The car left the road, turned over twice, then righted itself.

It was two minutes later that the police car drew up with screaming brakes. Superintendent MacNeill was out of it before it had pulled up, was running across towards the wreck.

A stammering lorry-driver was struggling to open the door of the car. He succeeded as the Scotsman came up.

"It wasn't my fault, sir," he gasped. "He came round there like a bullet. I couldn't have got out of his way. Nothing could!"

Tommy Gavillan stepped out of the car very groggily. He put his hands up to his head.

"Hello, Mac. What did I tell you? The luck of the Irish." He sagged at the knees as he spoke and Inspector Till gripped him by the shoulders.

"Steady up, Gavillan!"

MacNeill was staring through the shattered glass at the man who lay there. Hettche was very white and still. His body was twisted, and his slim neck lolled horribly.

The lorry-driver shivered.

"Broke his neck! Quick as that it was, mister. A second did it."

MacNeill looked down impassively.

"Corporal Violet," he said slowly. "Well, maybe it was best that way. That's exactly what would have happened to him anyway." He turned round to where Gavillan stood, and his voice was low.

"Why did you do it, Gavillan?"

Tommy Gavillan shrugged.

"That was the way it had to be, Mac."

"You helped him to escape," MacNeill said quietly. "A man that every policeman in Britain was after. Spain had him— and you turned him loose. You'll have to answer for that, Gavillan. You were mad to do it. What did Hettche mean to you? A man you can't have known for——"

Gavillan shook his head.

"I've known him for a long time, Mac." His voice was low, but there was something in it that made the Scotsman stiffen.

"Hettche?"

Gavillan nodded. He leaned over and brushed the dark, thick hair from the dead brow.

"Not Hettche," he said quietly. "Not a man at all, but my wife—Maya Swenson! Maya Gavillan! It's a queer, queer thing that she should go out like this—with me so near!"

He turned round and walked back to the waiting car.

CHAPTER XXXI

"THE Sheldon gang," said Superintendent MacNeill, "broke up in Peel City. Drew Sheldon had gone off with Gavillan's wife. They had been in love for some time though Gavillan had never suspected it. When it did happen, he lost trace of them for several months. When he did get word of them they were in Peel City, living at a big hotel, where they called themselves Mr. and Mrs. Manson.

"Gavillan went there at once and there was a fight. Sheldon took such a beating it affected his mind, and a month later he went into a mental home. He never came out again. He died there about a year ago. His disappearance always puzzled me, for I was never able to trace him. He was committed to this home in the name of Wilbur Manson; had lived and died under that name."

The Commissioner looked over at him.

"And was it the injuries he received in this fight with Gavillan which had this effect on his reason?'

MacNeill shook his head.

"No. Gavillan denies that. He says that Sheldon always was a queer, emotional sort of fellow. He was brilliantly clever, but was always prone to fits of rage and depression. We can check up on that, for the mental home will have his history on record."

"And Gavillan never saw his wife again?"

"No. She had left him for good. Gavillan himself knocked around a bit. He was in the States for a spell, in Canada, then down in Panama. After that he came to England. We know pretty well what happened after he came here. He was pretty fortunate in his investments and he made enough money to live on in comfort. He settled down to live the life of a country gentleman, and to bring up his daughter as well as he could."

Colonel Cameron puffed thoughtfully.

"He was unaware then that Maya Gavillan had come to England?"

"Quite unaware of it. He tells me he had never heard from her or of her from the time he left Peel City. That, I think, would be true. Gavillan isn't the sort of man to keep up with a woman of that type. His pride was probably too great to allow him to think of her much—and his peculiar private circumstances meant that a divorce would have been hard to get. In any event, I don't suppose the problem even came up. She was a closed chapter and since he was finished with the book for good, he didn't propose to open it again."

"And she came over to this country to carry on her operations here?"

"She did. Maya Gavillan was a woman of great capacity.

Gavillan tells me she was a first-class organizer—always had been. She had worked with him and Sheldon in the old days. In any event, her love was for Sheldon. Gavillan, she hated. You very often find when one person has let another person down badly, a hatred of that sort arises. The fact that Sheldon was in an asylum helped to strengthen her hatred against Gavillan who had put him there.

"In any event, Maya Gavillan worked with one or two of the old Sheldon gang after Drew Sheldon went away. As I say, she was a first-class organizer, and she had the cool detachment that was necessary for the job. Cutten, she knew by reputation, although I don't think she had ever met him. That, however, is another point on which we lack exact information. What decided her to come to England is hard to say. Probably she had been in the country and had seen the possibilities. In any event she came to England and summed up her chances. She brought Lee Cutten over—to handle one end of the business. She was Corporal Violet—the brains behind it all. Cutten was the contact man, and a very useful man he proved to be."

"And she ran into Gavillan at Marks Malden?"

"Yes. That, I think, was a pure coincidence. Cutten had set up his headquarters here—and when she came through as Dale Hettche, it must have given her a shock to find that Gavillan and their daughter were living here. Cutten couldn't have known she was Maya Gavillan—it is impossible that he would have allowed a situation like that to develop if he had known. Gavillan, naturally, never dreamed that his wife was in the vicinity."

"But he did think the Sheldon gang or some of them were mixed up in the business?"

"He did. Tommy was pretty astute. Anyway, he'd been in the game long enough to know most of the big fellows who worked it—and the lesser men too. He tells me he compared a lot of the Corporal Violet robberies with the old Sheldon jobs and saw a great similarity. One of the Corporal Violet gang was Lew Friedsohn who was found dead some time ago. Gavillan remembered that Friedsohn had been mixed up in a job with Cutten and Drew Sheldon out in Seattle. There were a number of little things that made him think. I spoke to him about Corporal Violet myself and he admitted he had a theory, but he would never talk about it."

The Commissioner sighed.

"He might have saved everyone a lot of trouble if he had."

"That's true," MacNeill said. "But Gavillan was no squeaker. He didn't intend to tell the police anything. If the old Sheldon crowd were involved that was interesting." He smiled grimly. "And then came his own arrest in connection with that Belgian forgery business. That made him stiffen up."

"That was his wife?"

"Yes. She worked that on her own. I'm positive Cutten had no hand in that. That was the vindictive streak in her—that little bit of hatred. If it had come off, Gavillan would have got a long term. It was pure luck that he escaped. When that didn't work, she carried the grudge a bit farther and Solus and Lavery were put on the job."

Colonel Cameron closed his eyes.

" 'The female of the species is more deadly than the male!' That was Kipling, MacNeill."

"Very likely," said Superintendent MacNeill. His eyes were on the clock. He had a train journey to make, for there was to be a little dinner at Tommy Gavillan's that evening, to which he had been invited and was expected to attend.

"What then?"

The big man rose.

"Gavillan was on the alert," he said softly. "Tommy knew that someone was gunning for him. As I say, he figured it was the Sheldon crowd. At that moment he began to suspect his wife—and I, I am afraid first put the idea into his head."

Cameron was interested.

"How was that?"

"I told him what Inspector Bryde had told me—that he had been tipped off by a woman. I let that slip to Gavillan, and I saw that I'd touched something off. Tommy didn't know many women at all. His experience of them had made him want to keep pretty far away from them. He only knew one woman who bore him that kind of grudge. When they tried to ambush him, he knew that she was behind it."

"But he wouldn't talk about her?"

"No. Gavillan wasn't that sort."

"Extraordinary," said the Colonel.

MacNeill nodded.

"It's a pity he didn't come to me—but he didn't. Instead he went to call on young Spain. He thought Spain was one of the crowd. Spain wasn't too sure of Gavillan himself. He was on the prowl for Lee Cutten—and he knew that Cutten was involved with Corporal Violet. Gavillan came in to find a settlement. Tommy had seen Mary Lou Slatter at the Moorings. When she turned up as a corpse, Gavillan wanted to know what was behind it all. He put a gun in his pocket and went over to Spain to find out.'' He laughed shortly.

"Tommy got nasty and they had to subdue him. More than that, they had to do it in a hurry for I turned up at the precise moment they were handling him. Anyway, after I had gone, they got him over to Blandfort where Mrs. Klein and Braddock had a chance to talk to him. They were able to straighten things up amongst themselves, and they prevailed on Tommy to stay there for a day or two till things came to a head.''

"He should have come to you," said Colonel Cameron bluntly. "What's the police for if people won't come to them?''

MacNeill nodded.

"That's what I thought too, sir. But he didn't. He told them everything except that he suspected his wife was mixed up in it. That was more than he would tell." He glanced at his watch again. "I've got twenty minutes to catch my train, sir.''

The Commissioner sighed.

"I'll read it all in your report, MacNeill. An interesting business. Tell Gavillan to give me a call next time he's in the City.''

"I will," MacNeill said. "Anyway, it's all in the report. Inspector Till writes a very good report. That's the benefit of having gone to Oxford and Cambridge and Hendon and all the best colleges. It makes you very handy when reports have to be written."

"True," said Cameron, and watched his subordinate take his leave.

There was a car waiting in the courtyard, and this deposited Superintendent MacNeill at Waterloo in time to catch his train. It was a comfortable train and almost completely empty, so that he slept well until Winchester was reached.

He walked along the platform here, and when he had handed over his ticket, saw the cheerful countenance of Tommy Gavillan beaming at him from the archway of the platform.

"Hello, Mac. You're up to time." He shook hands. "We'll

get on our way. We've got to pick up Peter Spainfield. I can never get used with calling him that."

"Where is he?"

Gavillan coughed.

"We've run out of whisky," he said.

MacNeill was aghast.

"That's terrible, Tommy."

"Shocking. It's the Government's fault for not giving barley to the distillers instead of making it into sausages. Anyway, Peter knows a feller here who has a bottle or two. He's gone round to have a word with him. A remarkable young feller. Him an' me are just like that!" He laid two thick and stumpy fingers along the edge of the steering-wheel.

MacNeill chuckled.

"Last time he was talking to me about you, it didn't sound like that at all."

Gavillan was suddenly grave.

"I've explained all that to him," he said slowly. "He didn't know—about Maya. I couldn't tell him the truth. He'd have turned me over to you. You know what that would have meant! I had to help her all I could."

MacNeill laid his big hand on the Irishman's shoulder.

"I know, Tommy."

They drove away, slowly. For a few moments neither of them spoke, then MacNeill said:

"When was it that you found out that Hettche was your wife, Tommy? You've never told me that."

Gavillan looked round at him.

"It's hard to say, Mac. That frame-up shook me pretty badly. When you told me a woman was behind it—it just jumped to my mind at once. I couldn't think of anyone other than Maya. I knew she was capable of it—she hated me. I can't tell you how much she hated me.

"Anyway, I tried to pin her down. I figured that it had to be someone who'd been at the Close. I didn't know Mrs. Klein, but I knew she was too old. When I started to think about the Court folk—Hettche came into my mind. He always kept to himself—but he had been at the Close that one night. He had the build. I tried to see him twice at the Court, but both times they told me he was out."

"They told me that too when I called," MacNeill said.

Gavillan nodded.

"That night I went over to the Court and got inside. I'd made up my mind to get into his room and have a look round. I did—but there wasn't a clue until I got into the bathroom of Hettche's suite. Maya was clever, but she'd forgotten one thing—and that decided me."

MacNeill was interested.

"What was that?"

"No razor—no shaving soap—no brush. That was all the proof I wanted—and I searched well for it."

They had turned the corner now and as they did so, MacNeill saw the tweed-clad figure of Peter Spainfield awaiting them. There was a pipe in his mouth and under his arm a parcel of pleasing proportions and symmetry.

Gavillan drew up.

"You got it?" he asked anxiously.

The young man smiled.

"I did. Two bottles, Tommy."

Tommy Gavillan let out the clutch with an alacrity which would have made a driving instructor shudder.

"Grand," he said. "You're a great feller, Spain."

"Spainfield."

Gavillan swore gently.

"Spainfield! Hark at me calling you Spain again! I can't get it out of my mind. Is it Scotch or Irish?"

"Scotch."

MacNeill looked pleased.

"A fine, fine drink. It's a while since I've seen it." He looked at the younger man. "How is the detective business these days? The private side of it?"

Spainfield laughed aloud.

"Booming. We've got a new case in hand—Manfield and Lessing, the Wall Street brokers, want us to handle their work on this side. We're thinking about opening up a London office. Ada suggests I stay here. She's going back to the States for a spell with Braddock."

Gavillan looked round with annoyance.

"Ada's his mother! Hark at the way the rising generation talk about their elders."

"It wasn't like that in my young day," MacNeill said.

Gavillan shook his head.

"Nor in mine. It's the American influence. It won't get far in my home. If Pat was to call me Tommy, I'd put her across my knee an' paddle the seat of her pants. It's all in the bringing up. What you need, young feller, is a father to keep you in order."

Peter Spainfield knocked out his pipe.

"You know," he said suddenly, "you've got something there, Gavillan. I've been thinking along those lines myself for a long while now. We'll need to talk it over."

The Irishman turned.

"Eh? Talk it over? Who?"

"Pat and me," said Peter Spainfield thoughtfully. "Give us time, Gavillan. Give us time!"

THE END